SIXKILLER, U.S. MARSHAL:
BLOOD FOR BLOOD

SIXKILLER, U.S. MARSHAL:
BLOOD
FOR BLOOD

William W. Johnstone
with J. A. Johnstone

PINNACLE BOOKS
Kensington Publishing Corp.
www.kensingtonbooks.com

PINNACLE BOOKS are published by

Kensington Publishing Corp.
119 West 40th Street
New York, NY 10018

PUBLISHER'S NOTE
Following the death of William W. Johnstone, the Johnstone
family is working with a carefully selected writer to organize
and complete Mr. Johnstone's outlines and many unfin-
ished manuscripts to create additional novels in all of his
series like The Last Gunfighter, Mountain Man, and Eagles,
among others. This novel was inspired by Mr. Johnstone's
superb storytelling.

All Kensington titles, imprints, and distributed lines are
available at special quantity discounts for bulk purchases for
sales promotions, premiums, fund-raising, educational, or
institutional use. Special book excerpts or customized print-
ings can also be created to fit specific needs. For details,
write or phone the office of the Kensington special sales
manager: Kensington Publishing Corp., 119 West 40th
Street, New York, NY 10018, attn: Special Sales Department;
phone 1-800-221-2647.

ISBN-13: 978-0-7860-3126-9
ISBN-10: 0-7860-3126-3

First printing: September 2013

10 9 8 7 6 5 4 3 2 1

Printed in the United States of America

Chapter One

As the sun rose, the shadow of the gallows extended over the prison yard and fell across the faces of those assembled in the grim dawn. Some of them raised a hand to shade their eyes from the glare.

They wanted to be able to see the man who was about to be marched to his death.

Reporters, prison officials, and others were relatives of the condemned man's victims. The lawman who had captured Henry Garrett, Sheriff Mike Rasmussen of Kiowa City, Kansas, was there, too.

Despite the early hour, the air was already hot and still inside the prison walls. Rasmussen took off his hat and used it to fan his face, but it didn't do much good.

A phalanx of guards appeared to escort Garrett from the death house. The squat, stone building was small, with room for just the one cell. It had been ringed by armed men ever since Garrett had been locked into it the previous evening. The prisoner had eaten his last meal there.

Rasmussen put his hat on again.

Henry Garrett was in the middle of that group of guards, shuffling forward slowly, his ankles locked into leg irons. He wouldn't be in any hurry to get where he was going, even if he didn't have the leg irons on.

With the guards in the way, Rasmussen couldn't see the prisoner very well. Garrett wasn't big to start with, a slender man of medium height with a lean face and a shock of sandy hair. He didn't look like much, didn't look very frightening.

At least half a dozen people had had good cause to be afraid of him, though, as they stared at him in horror over the barrel of a gun just before he killed them. And there was no telling how many other folks he had murdered that the law didn't even know about. His gang had been responsible for dozens of robberies and shootings while running wild across Kansas, Nebraska, Missouri, and Indian Territory. They hadn't hesitated to gun down anybody who was unlucky enough to get in their way.

Followed by the sober-faced prison warden and a black-suited preacher, the guards drew even with the group of spectators. Rasmussen peered between them and got his first good look at the condemned man.

Several months in prison hadn't changed Henry Garrett much. He was a little leaner, his piercing blue eyes set a little deeper in his gaunt face.

Those eyes were as cold and merciless as ever, though, Rasmussen discovered when they swung to the side and locked on him. The outlaw's gaze still held plenty of power.

Garrett smiled.

Rasmussen's nostrils flared as he drew in a deep breath. He blew it out as Garrett looked away.

The group reached the bottom of the thirteen steps. Still moving slowly, Garrett began to climb them.

That climb seemed to take forever. Some of the spectators shuffled their feet nervously. They had come this morning to watch a man die, but now they weren't so sure they wanted to do that.

Every road had its end, Rasmussen thought. Henry Garrett had come to his. A tall man in a black suit like the preacher's and a broad-brimmed black hat waited on the platform for him. The hangman stood with his hand on the trapdoor's lever as the guards maneuvered Garrett into position.

The warden said in a quiet, gentle voice, "Do you have any last words, son?"

"There ain't much left to say," Garrett responded. "No, wait a minute. There is something." He looked down at the crowd. "Sheriff Rasmussen?"

The lawman swallowed hard and asked, "What is it, Garrett?"

"I just want you to know you never would've caught me, you useless sack o' guts, if my horse hadn't stepped in that damn prairie dog hole."

One of the guards glared and stepped closer to the prisoner, raising the rifle he held as he did so.

The warden lifted a hand to stop Garrett from talking.

"Let him go on," Rasmussen said. "Man's got a right to have his say, especially now."

"That's right. I don't want to leave this world with you thinkin' you're somethin' special, Sheriff, 'cause you ain't. You're just a fella who got lucky." Garrett paused to draw in a breath. "When you get back to Kiowa City, you tell Judge Doolittle and the men who were on that jury I ain't forgot about them, neither. Tell 'em that I went out thinkin' about what they got comin' to them . . . and that I'll see 'em in hell."

"That's enough," the warden said. "This isn't the time or place for threats."

"You're right about that. That's why I'm not makin' threats." Garrett smiled at Rasmussen again. "I'm makin' promises."

The warden signaled to the executioner, who placed a black hood over Garrett's head. The sky pilot opened his Bible and started praying in a soft, rapid voice. The warden let that go on for a minute, then motioned for the preacher to step back.

"In accordance with the laws of Kansas and the sentence handed down by a jury of your peers, Henry Garrett, you are hereby hanged by the neck until dead." The warden gave the executioner a curt nod.

Rasmussen looked away. He heard the clatter of

the trapdoor, the sudden sharp snap of bone, the swift intake of breath from the spectators.

When he turned his head back toward the gallows, the body clad in its gray prison uniform swung slightly back and forth as it hung from the rope.

The shadow it cast stretched out across the prison yard, just like the gallows from which it dangled.

In a cell in another part of the prison, Simon Garrett sat on his bunk and watched the slanted rectangle of gray light that came through the small, barred window. It faced east, and he could have stood up, turned around, stepped up onto the bunk, and looked out directly at the dawn.

Instead, he waited, tracking the time by the way the light grew brighter and brighter. Another wing of the prison blocked the sun, so it didn't shine directly into Simon's cell until half an hour after it had risen.

When that gray light turned red and gold, Simon knew his younger brother Henry was dead and had been for a while. He closed his eyes and took a deep breath.

A few minutes later a guard wearing a blue uniform and a black-billed cap came along the aisle between the rows of cells and paused on the other side of the bars from Simon. "Reckon it's all over. That no-good, murderin' brother of yours is nothin' but worm food now, Garrett."

Simon rested his hands on his thighs and

breathed deeply as he fought to keep the emotions raging inside him under control. He didn't want to give this man—or any of the others inside the prison—the satisfaction of seeing how his brother's death affected him.

"Yeah, one of the guards who was there told me all about it. He told me how your little brother screamed and fought and begged for his life while they forced him up the steps to meet the hangman."

That was a lie, Simon thought. Henry never would have begged. Never.

"Pissed his pants, too," the guard went on. "Did a little jig in midair while he was chokin' to death. I'll bet it was a right entertainin' show. Too bad they're not gonna do the same thing to you."

Simon Garrett was serving a five-year sentence for armed robbery. He had done four years of the allotted time, with one to go. Before he had been caught, convicted, and sent away, the Garrett gang had been his. Henry hadn't been much more than a kid in those days.

He had grown up in a hurry, though, taking over the gang when Simon went to prison. He had led them on bigger and better jobs than Simon ever had, until his luck ran out and his horse broke a leg while he was fleeing from a posse.

"I don't guess it really matters," the guard said. "You'll be back here sooner or later, and we'll get another crack at you. You'll wind up dancing on air, just like your brother."

Simon kept his eyes down and acted like he didn't hear the guard. The man let out a bored,

frustrated snort a
shoes smacking agai
echoes that cascaded aro

Simon didn't stand up un
died away. Then he turned
clenched his left hand into a fist, a
against the stone. His lips pulled bac
teeth in a grimace as he drove his fist aga
wall again and again until his hand was a blo
broken hulk.

It didn't matter. It wasn't his gun hand.

d walked away, his thick-soled
st the floor and setting up
nd the big cell block.
til those echoes had
oward the wall,
nd slammed it
k from his
nst the
ody,

7

One year later

Kiowa City, Kansas, was quiet. Except for the three saloons and the parlor house on the edge of town, all the businesses were closed.

Most of the residences were dark, as most folks had already turned in for the night. Here and there, the yellow glow of lamplight could be seen in a window. In those homes, somebody was sick or just couldn't sleep.

Off to the west, skeletal fingers of lightning clawed through the night sky, followed by a distant rumble of thunder. A summer storm lurked out there along the railroad tracks. It might move in later, or it might break up before it ever reached the settlement.

Sheriff Mike Rasmussen wouldn't mind if it rained. Even a brief shower might break the stifling blanket of heat that had laid over the plains for the past couple weeks.

His office was on the first floor of the brick courthouse in the square at the center of town. Despite the late hour, he sat at his desk, laboring by lamplight over an expense report for the county commissioners.

He wrote a word or two, made a face like he had just bitten into a piece of sour fruit, chewed on the black mustache that drooped over his mouth, and wrote a little more. Not a breath of air stirred in the room despite the open windows.

It was easy for him to hear the gunshots that suddenly shattered the peaceful silence.

Rasmussen's head snapped up. He dropped the pen, splattering a few splotches of ink across the paper.

The gunshots continued as he leaped to his feet. They seemed to be coming from one of the town's residential areas a couple blocks away.

The sheriff had taken off his gun belt and hung it on a peg near the door when he had come into the office. Now he grabbed the belt and slung it around his hips as he hurried into the hallway.

The night-duty deputy sat behind a desk at the end of the corridor. He had a look of alarm on his face.

Rasmussen fumbled with the gun belt's buckle as he trotted toward the deputy. "Grab a shotgun, Carl," he ordered. "We need to find out what's goin' on out there."

"Yes, sir!"

Kiowa City had a town marshal, Emory Bannister, who broke up saloon fights and threw drunks in jail, but that was all he did. He had made it clear to the town council that he wasn't getting mixed up in any gunplay.

So the council contracted with the sheriff's office to handle any serious problems. Like all politicians, the county commissioners were always responsive to anything that generated extra revenue they could spend, so they were in favor of the deal.

Hatless, Rasmussen charged out of the courthouse and across the lawn. With the gun belt finally fastened, he drew the holstered Colt revolver.

The shooting stopped, but a swift rataplan of hoofbeats followed it. Rasmussen could tell by the sound that several horsebackers were galloping away into the darkness.

That knowledge disturbed him almost as much as the gunshots. Neither boded well for any peace and quiet the rest of the night.

The screams he heard as the hoofbeats faded away just made it worse.

"Come on, Baird!" he flung over his shoulder at the deputy as he ran along the street.

Carl Baird, whose wife had a reputation for baking the best pies and cakes in the county, had a belly to prove it. He was already huffing and puffing as he hurried to keep up with the sheriff.

The screams led them to a white, two-story frame house with a couple cottonwoods in a yard surrounded by a picket fence. Kiowa City had a lot of houses like that. It was a pleasant, prosperous place, a far cry from the wild, hell-on-wheels cow town it had been ten years earlier when the railhead reached it.

Rasmussen remembered those days and wouldn't have gone back to them for anything.

Other people on the street had heard the screams. Several men came out of their houses wearing nightshirts to find out what was happening. A few carried guns. One wild-eyed hombre gripped an axe in his hands.

"Sheriff, what was all that shooting?" somebody called to the lawman as he hurried by. "Who's that screaming?

"I don't know," Rasmussen replied, "but I'm damn sure gonna find out!"

Nobody had been killed in Kiowa City for more than a year, not even in a saloon shooting. It had been a remarkable run of peace—shattered now.

Rasmussen flung open the fence gate and charged up the flagstone walk. Charles Houston and his wife Agnes lived here. Houston was a partner in the hardware store and one of the settlement's leading citizens.

He wasn't exactly a rich man, though, not the sort likely to have his house broken into by outlaws bent on robbing him.

The front door stood wide open. The screams from inside had died away, replaced by wracking sobs.

Rasmussen went up the steps to the porch in a couple bounds. Behind him, Deputy Baird called, "Be careful, Sheriff! Some of the varmints could still be in there!"

The lawman bit back a curse. Baird was a halfway decent deputy who could follow orders, but he wasn't the smartest fella to ever come down the pike.

"That was them we heard riding away, Carl. You can stay out here, though, just in case they come back."

Baird gulped and said with obvious reluctance, "All right, Sheriff."

Despite what he'd told the deputy about the gunmen being gone, Rasmussen was careful as he stepped into the foyer of the Houston house. He stopped right there, his jaw tightening at the scene in front of him.

A man lay crumpled at the bottom of a staircase leading to the second floor. Next to him knelt a woman, sobbing as she shook him. Her hair was in disarray, and both of them wore nightclothes.

"Charlie!" she said between gasping, choking sobs. "Oh, Charlie, please wake up."

Rasmussen muttered a curse under his breath. He knew both folks, considered them friends. He slid his Colt back in its holster as he took a reluctant step toward them. "Agnes. It's Mike Rasmussen. You better let me take a look at him."

Not that it would do any good. Rasmussen knew that from the pool of blood spreading out around Charles Houston's body. The edge of that crimson tide was already touching the foyer rug.

"Agnes," Rasmussen said again. He reached down and took her arm.

She pulled away from him. "He'll be all right. I know he'll be all right. He just needs to wake up."

"Sure, sure. Why don't you go in the parlor now and let me take a look?"

Agnes Houston finally let him help her to her feet. He steered her toward the parlor and called, "Carl!"

Baird appeared in the doorway. He licked his lips and said, "Yeah, Sheriff?"

"Go get some of the neighbor ladies and bring 'em over here." Rasmussen added in a whisper, "And do it right damned now!"

Agnes was still too shocked and confused to answer any questions. He didn't really need her to tell him what had happened. He had noticed several splotches of blood on the stairs, and that was enough to tell him the story.

Somebody had kicked the door open, and hearing the racket, Charles Houston had come to investigate. The intruders had shot him as he stood at the top of the stairs, causing him to tumble down the flight.

That hadn't been enough to satisfy their blood-lust, though. Judging by the shots Rasmussen had heard and the amount of blood soaking Houston's nightshirt, the killers must have stood over the body and continued to pour bullets into him until he was shot to pieces.

Agnes Houston could plead all she wanted to, but her husband was never going to wake up.

The sheriff settled her into an armchair.

Several of the women who lived on the street bustled into the house a minute later, casting horrified glances at Houston's body as they passed through the foyer to the parlor. Rasmussen turned the grieving widow over to their care and went back to the body.

He stopped counting bullet holes when he reached eight. Oddly enough, none of the shots had struck Houston in the face. His features were untouched except for a scrape on one cheek that must have happened while he was falling down the stairs. His eyes were wide open and staring in shock and disbelief.

Rasmussen grimaced and turned away. As he did, a stocky figure hurried across the porch and into the house.

"Is it true?" Judge Ephraim Doolittle asked. "Charlie Houston is dead?"

Rasmussen sighed heavily and pointed at the body with his thumb. "You can see for yourself, Judge. Nobody survives getting shot that many times."

"Dear Lord, dear Lord," Doolittle muttered. He was a plump man with the round, pleasantly ugly face of a bulldog and white hair parted in the middle and a little askew at the moment. He had been roused from sleep.

Rasmussen could tell that the judge had dressed

hastily; not everything was lined up and buttoned right.

"Who would do such a thing?" Doolittle went on.

"I don't know," Rasmussen said. "Everybody liked Charlie. I don't think he had an enemy in this town."

"He owned a business. Surely there were disputes from time to time with the public. . . ."

"Bad enough to cause something like this?" Rasmussen shook his head. "I doubt it. I'll talk to his partner, Jeremy Stone, but I don't think he'll have any idea, either."

"How many men did this?"

Rasmussen frowned. "Judging by the hoofbeats I heard when they rode out of town, I'd say three or four, at least. Maybe half a dozen. Mrs. Houston might be able to tell us more once she calms down some."

"Then they had a reason. If one man was responsible, he might be just a . . . a lunatic. But if a whole group of men burst in here and did something this terrible, they had a reason, Sheriff."

"I think you're right, Judge. We'll figure it out."

"This is terrible," Doolittle said again. "Just terrible."

Rasmussen couldn't argue with that.

Several hours later, the sheriff was tossing and turning in his bed in the rooming house, trying to banish the gruesome images from his mind and go to sleep. The storm was still prowling and rumbling in the distance, when a possible explanation for Charles Houston's killing occurred to him.

He sat up in bed, stared wildly into the darkness of his room for several seconds, and then lifted a slightly shaking hand to wipe away the beads of sweat that had just popped out on his face.

Chapter Three

Deputy U.S. Marshal John Henry Sixkiller paused on the steps of the redbrick federal courthouse in Fort Smith, Arkansas, as someone behind him called his name. His right hand moved a little closer to the butt of the revolver holstered on his hip. He hadn't recognized the voice, and during his career as a deputy marshal and before that as a member of the Cherokee Lighthorse, he had made enemies—plenty who wouldn't mind putting him six feet under the ground.

So it just made good sense to be ready for trouble, even in front of the building where his current boss, Judge Isaac Parker, held court.

John Henry turned and spotted a man hurrying up the steps after him. The fellow didn't look particularly threatening . . . unless, of course, he were to take off that derby hat he wore and start slapping people with it.

"Something I can do for you, friend?" John Henry asked in a mild voice.

The stranger was huffing and puffing, a little out of breath. "My, you're awfully tall for an Indian, aren't you, Mr. Sixkiller? I had a hard time catching up to you."

"I'm only half Cherokee," John Henry said, "and some of them are pretty tall, anyway. Despite what some white folks might think, all Indians aren't short and squatty."

"No, no, of course not. I didn't mean that. I just mean it's a hot day to be chasing someone."

"I don't recall asking you to chase me," John Henry drawled.

The man ignored that and stuck out a hand. "I'm Calvin Ettinger." Then he added, "From *Harper's Illustrated Weekly*," as if John Henry ought to already be aware of this fact.

"Oh," John Henry said. "That explains it, then."

"Explains what?"

"In a checkered suit like that, I didn't much think you were from around these parts. Now that I know you come from back east, it all makes sense."

Anger flashed in Calvin Ettinger's eyes. He was half a foot shorter than John Henry, but he didn't appear to be afraid of the bigger man.

"I've been sent here to Arkansas to do a story about you, Marshal. The famous Indian lawman. I hope I can count on your cooperation."

"I never figured on being famous, and like I said, I'm only half Cherokee. Maybe I'll half cooperate."

"You don't like me, do you?" the journalist asked.

"I don't know you, Mr. Ettinger," John Henry said. "But I do know my boss, and I know he won't like it if I keep him waiting. So I'll say good day to you."

"Wait a minute," Ettinger said as John Henry turned away. "Do you think you could find a few minutes to talk to me later?"

"That all depends on what Judge Parker has to say," John Henry told the man over his shoulder.

Once he was inside, John Henry took off his broad-brimmed, cream-colored felt hat. He wore a faded blue work shirt with the sleeves rolled up over muscular forearms, denim trousers, and comfortable boots.

He wasn't an exceptionally big man, but he was more powerful than he looked and moved with catlike grace. His thick dark hair came from his Cherokee father, his startlingly blue eyes from his white mother.

Some people looked down on half-breeds, but he had never felt the least bit inferior to anybody. He had been raised to have a quiet confidence in himself, to not look for a fight . . . but to take no guff from any man. He was good with his fists and good with his gun, but never drew the weapon unless he intended to kill somebody with it.

Somebody who needed killing . . .

Parker's clerk told him to go right in and see the judge. John Henry hung his hat on a hat tree and went on in.

The goateed, solemn-looking federal jurist was at his desk, signing a stack of papers. He glanced up at his visitor and without saying anything used his eyebrows to signal that the deputy marshal should sit down.

"Is that a stack of arrest warrants, Judge?" John Henry asked as he sat in the Morocco leather chair in front of the desk and cocked his right ankle on his left knee.

"As a matter of fact, it is," Parker said as the pen continued to scratch on paper. He set one of the documents aside, dipped the pen in the inkwell, and signed the next paper in the stack. "Some days it seems like I sign these from the time I get here in the morning until I go home at night."

"There's lots of crime in the territory," John Henry observed. "Lots of lawbreakers to bring to justice."

"Indeed."

"I reckon I'm going after some of 'em?"

"Not this time." Parker replaced the pen in its holder and flexed his fingers to work a cramp out of them. "I'm sending you to Kansas."

That was a little unusual but not unheard of.

Parker and the deputy marshals who worked for him were sometimes referred to as the law west of Fort Smith, and Kansas was definitely west of Fort Smith. So Kansas fell under Judge Parker's jurisdiction.

"Trouble up there?"

"I wouldn't be sending you if there wasn't," the judge said. "A gang of outlaws has been busy holding up trains in the vicinity of Kiowa City. They've stolen the mailbags from the express cars, along with other things, of course."

"Messing with the mailbags makes it Uncle Sam's business," John Henry guessed.

"That's right." Parker clasped his hands together in front of him on the desk and leaned forward slightly. "However, while the train robberies are the official reason I'm assigning you to this case, Deputy Sixkiller, that's not the only reason."

"There's more to it than that, eh?" John Henry nodded. "Can't say as I'm surprised. If I can speak freely, Judge, you look a mite worried."

"I am worried," Parker said. "Very worried. I received a letter from an old friend of mine, a Kansas state court judge named Ephraim Doolittle. He lives in Kiowa City, and he claims there's more to what's going on up there than a simple gang of train robbers. The holdups are just to keep them in funds. They're really after something else."

"What might that be?"

"Vengeance. Blood for blood."

John Henry sat up at that statement and leaned forward. He had chased down train robbers before, and while he would again if that was necessary, this job was starting to sound a little more interesting. "I'm listening, Judge."

"In the past three weeks, two men from Kiowa City have been murdered. In the first attack, five armed, masked raiders broke into the man's house and gunned him down in front of his wife. He was shot twenty-seven times."

John Henry let out a low whistle. "It takes a powerful hate to do something like that. Who was this fella, and what did he do to make somebody that mad at him?"

"His name was Charles Houston. He and a partner owned the local hardware store."

"Business dispute?" John Henry guessed. "The partner hired some hardcases to do him in?"

"No. They were best friends."

John Henry shrugged. "Sometimes friends fall out."

"Yes, but that wouldn't explain the second killing. A man named Lucas Winslow lived in town but owned some acreage out in the country that he farmed. He drove out there every day in his wagon to work in those fields. One evening last week he didn't come home for supper. His wife sent their son out to the farm on a mule to look for him."

"And he'd been shot, too?"

Parker shook his head. "No, someone sank a

post into the ground, tied Winslow to it, and worked him over with a knife until he bled to death. He was still alive while they were doing it to him. Most of it, anyway."

John Henry's casual attitude was gone now. "That's even worse than shooting a man all those times while he's already unconscious or dead."

"Yes, and it makes you wonder what the killers are going to do next. Wonder . . . and worry."

"Any connection between Houston and Winslow?"

"Winslow was an occasional customer at the hardware store. So they were acquainted. But according to both men's wives, they weren't close friends. They didn't go to the same church. Winslow was a Baptist, Houston a Methodist."

"Yeah, there's a real denominational gulf there," John Henry said dryly.

Parker wasn't amused. "There was only one real connection between the two men, and after Winslow's body was found that connection was brought to Judge Doolittle's attention by the local sheriff, a man named Rasmussen."

The judge paused and John Henry waited, knowing from experience that he had to let Parker get around to these things in his own way.

"A little more than a year ago, Houston and Winslow both served on the jury for a trial in Kiowa City," Parker said after a moment. "An outlaw named Henry Garrett was charged with murder, convicted, and sentenced to hang. The sentence was carried out a few weeks later."

"Henry Garrett," John Henry repeated. "I think I remember the name. He had a gang working with him. If some of them are out to settle the score for him, why would they have waited a year to get started?"

"There's more to the situation. Henry Garrett's older brother Simon was also an outlaw. In fact, he was the one who put the gang together when Henry was just a boy. Several years ago, Simon was arrested and sent to prison for armed robbery. He was behind bars when his brother was hanged."

"But he's not now," John Henry guessed.

"That's right. He served his sentence and was released a month ago."

John Henry leaned back in his chair and propped his right ankle on his left knee again. "Well, there you go. Simon Garrett got out of prison, rounded up his old gang, and now he's going after the members of the jury that sent his brother to the gallows."

"As well as Judge Doolittle. According to Sheriff Rasmussen, who was there for the hanging, Henry Garrett threatened all of them on the day he was executed. His last words were that he would see them in hell."

"So now you want me to head up to Kiowa City and put a stop to it?"

"That's exactly what I want you to do, Marshal Sixkiller, hopefully before another innocent man is killed."

John Henry got to his feet and nodded. "I'll be starting today, Judge."

Considering the possibility that that nosy reporter from back east might be hanging around waiting for him, he slipped out the courthouse's back door.

Chapter Four

The quickest way to Kiowa City was by making railroad connections. Sixkiller loaded his big gray horse Iron Heart into a boxcar and rode the rails, studying the reports on the case and the background about Kiowa City that Judge Parker had given him.

The town was located on the Union Pacific Railroad. In fact, Kiowa City owed its very existence to the railroad. It had sprung into being as a crude tent city during the line's construction, the sort of "hell on wheels" settlement that was common on the frontier in those days.

At first, it was nothing but a squalid conglomeration of saloons, dance halls, brothels, gambling dens, and hash houses where a man was equally likely to die from bad whiskey, the pox, or a knife between the ribs.

Then the herds of longhorns began to arrive from Texas, filling a vast swath of cattle pens that appeared seemingly overnight. For months the sounds of hammering and sawing could be heard around the clock as men labored under the merciless sun to build a town, and then more men took their place and worked by lantern light to continue the task.

After a time, the railhead moved on, and with it went the herds. But by then the roots of a real town had been put down, so Kiowa City—named after the Indians who'd been fought off several times during the dangerous first few months of the settlement's life—survived.

Farmers and ranchers moved in, drawn by seemingly endless stretches of open, fertile land. Businesses thrived. The Indian trouble faded away.

From time to time, savage marauders still plagued the area, in the form of white outlaws instead of Kiowa war parties. Trains were stopped and held up, banks were robbed, and occasionally a family traveling alone by wagon would be set upon and killed, all their belongings looted.

The area wasn't as dangerous as it once had been, not all that long ago, but it wasn't exactly civilized, either.

When the train reached the last station before his destination, John Henry got off, put his saddle on Iron Heart, and led the horse down the ramp from the boxcar.

He was ready to ride now.

Unlike some lawmen who liked to strut around with a star pinned to their vest, when John Henry started a new assignment and rode into a new place, he preferred have his badge and bona fides tucked away where nobody could see them.

A lot of time, he was able to pick up important information about the case before anybody found out that he was actually a star packer for Uncle Sam. It had worked before and he hoped it would work again.

After leaving the train, he swung wide and approached Kiowa City from the south. The terrain was flat for the most part, broken only by low, rolling hills, so he was able to spot the line of telegraph poles that followed the railroad quite a while before he reached them.

A plume of smoke to the west marked the approach of an eastbound train. By the time he reached the town, the train had pulled in at the depot, a big gray and brown stone building located at the south end of Main Street.

As he circled the station and rode across the tracks, he looked along the street and saw the squat courthouse sitting in the middle of the town square a few blocks away. A few cottonwood trees dotted the lawn around the building.

Kiowa City had more trees and was just greener in general than most of the countryside because of the presence of Kiowa Creek. It ran just north of the settlement, roughly paralleling the railroad tracks before turning south to flow into the Smoky Hill River a few miles away.

A nice-looking town with three broad avenues running north and south and a dozen cross streets, it was home to several thousand people.

Some of those people had to be living in fear because of the brutal killings that had taken place. John Henry was going to do his best to put a stop to that and allow Kiowa City to go back to its peaceful, sleepy ways.

His first move in that campaign was to angle Iron Heart to the right and head for a large building on that side of Main Street. PARADISE SALOON was painted in bright blue letters on its whitewashed false front.

The saloon was big enough to have four hitch racks lined up in front of it, and although the racks weren't full, several saddle horses were tied at each of them, indicating that the establishment was doing a brisk business even in the middle of the afternoon.

John Henry swung down from the saddle and looped the big gray's reins around an empty spot. He took off his hat, sleeved sweat off his forehead, and settled the hat back on his head at a jaunty angle.

He stepped up onto the boardwalk in front of the saloon and pushed through the batwings, the spurs that he never used on Iron Heart jingling a little.

Logically, he knew that not every saloon west of the Mississippi looked and smelled the same, but sometimes that seemed to be the case. The differences between this one and all the others were minor. The lushly endowed naked lady in the big painting behind the bar was a redhead instead of a blonde or brunette. The brass rail at the bottom of the bar and the spittoons were polished a little brighter than some.

The clientele was the same, though—a mixture of cowboys, sodbusters, bullwhackers, and townsmen. John Henry didn't spot any cavalry uniforms, which meant there wasn't a military post within a day's ride.

Girls in short, brightly colored, spangled dresses made their way between the bar and the tables, delivering drinks, laughing at risqué comments made by the customers, and not shying away too much from wandering hands that got too bold.

On one side of the room, a roulette wheel and a faro layout went unused at the moment, but three poker games were going on at the tables. The slap and shuffle of cards and the clicking of chips provided an almost musical accompaniment to the constant talk and laughter.

Men were lined up from one end of the long hardwood bar to the other, keeping two aprons busy pouring drinks.

John Henry sidled toward a gap in the line of drinkers.

Nobody paid much attention to him, other than a few quick, incurious glances when he'd come in. That was fine for the moment, since he was just after information and didn't want anybody noticing him too much.

Sooner or later, he would have to make a splash in order for the plan he had developed on the train to work. He was counting on his instincts to tell him when the right moment for that would be.

Resting his left hand on the hardwood, he nodded to the bald, mustachioed drink juggler who came along the bar to take his order. "Is the beer cold?"

The bartender chuckled. "Mister, at this time of year nothin's cold in these parts. But it's about as cool as you'll find this side of Denver."

"That'll do just fine, then," John Henry said with a grin.

The bartender filled a mug from a tap and slid it in front of John Henry, saying, "Four bits."

John Henry dropped a coin on the bar, picked up the mug, and took a healthy swallow as if he'd been riding for a long time and had plenty of trail dust in his throat to wash away.

The beer was cool, so the bartender had been right about that, and not too sour. John Henry nodded in satisfaction.

Nobody was demanding his attention at the moment, so the bartender lingered, picking up a glass and polishing it with the rag he carried. "Don't think I've seen you around here before."

Strangers were always of interest in a frontier town, John Henry knew. Anything to break the monotony. "I just rode in," John Henry replied. "This looks like a nice place."

"Kiowa City or this saloon?"

"Both."

"Yeah, it's a good place to live," the man said. "Most of the time, anyway."

John Henry frowned slightly, as most men would

under the circumstances. "What do you mean by that?"

"Nothin', nothin'," the bartender said, shaking his head. "Are you looking for work?"

"Could be. I had in mind maybe trying to find a riding job. Any of the spreads around here hiring?"

"The Anvil might be. That's the biggest ranch in these parts. A man named J.C. Carson owns it. His foreman is Dell Bartlett. If you can make a hand, they can probably use you." The bartender's muddy gaze dropped briefly to the walnut grips of the Colt on John Henry's hip.

"If you can use that," he went on, "they'd be more likely to find a place for you, I'd say."

"Carson likes to hire men who are gun handy?" John Henry asked. He hadn't been sent there to look into the activities of some local cattle baron. Such men sometimes had the habit of trying to run roughshod over their neighbors. They often believed they were a law unto themselves, especially the old-timers who had been some of the first settlers in a region.

But John Henry was curious by nature and believed in indulging that curiosity whenever he could. You never could tell when a seemingly useless bit of information would pay off.

The bartender suddenly looked worried that he might have said too much. He answered curtly, "I never said anything against the Anvil." He turned away, adding, "I got business to tend to," even though no one along the bar had summoned him as far as John Henry could tell.

An empty mug thumped rather violently onto the hardwood next to John Henry. The man who had put it there wiped the back of his hand across his mouth. "Yeah, the Anvil is a good spread to ride for . . . if you don't mind working for a damn range hog."

John Henry turned his head and looked the man up and down. The hombre was stocky and dressed in dusty range clothes. His battered hat was pushed back to let a tangle of rust-colored curls spill out.

"You have something against that fella Carson?" John Henry asked mildly.

"I've never even spoken to the man. But Bartlett and the rest of his crew are mighty touchy when it comes to any cattle straying over the line, either comin' or goin'. Carson's plenty protective of his range. More than one cowboy from a smaller spread has crossed the line to go after some strays and wound up either shot at or jumped and beaten up."

"That doesn't sound like a very good neighbor."

"He's not. But he's always right there, Johnny-on-the-spot, when somebody decides to sell out, offering a heap less than the place is worth."

"Nobody has to take his money," John Henry said. "They can always wait for a better offer."

"Sure, but once word gets around that Carson has his eye on a place, there won't *be* a better offer. People don't want to get on his bad side."

It was the sort of story John Henry had heard

before. Some of the biggest ranches in the West had been put together in such high-handed fashion.

Unfortunately, intimidation like that wasn't really illegal. It certainly wasn't the sort of federal crime that fell under his jurisdiction. He shrugged. "Thanks for the information, friend. I haven't made up my mind what I'll do yet."

The redheaded cowboy looked in the mirror behind the bar and grunted. "If you want to get a better idea about the Anvil, talk to these hombres just coming in. They ride for Carson."

John Henry half turned to look at the three men who pushed through the batwings, one after the other, and came into the saloon. They were decked out in range garb, too, and there was nothing unusual about them except for the revolvers they carried, which were relatively new and obviously well cared for.

The three men headed for the bar, and John Henry got a good look at the last of the trio. A shock of recognition jolted him. The third man was Jimmy Deverill.

John Henry had arrested him less than a year earlier for running whiskey in the Nations.

Deverill looked right back at him and stopped short. His eyes widened, and any hope John Henry had that the ex-con wouldn't recognize him disappeared as the man exclaimed, "You peckerwood!"

He punctuated the curse by clawing at the gun on his hip.

Chapter Five

There was no time to think. Delaying long enough to do that would just get him a bullet in the brisket. John Henry let his instincts take over.

His Colt came out of its holster in a smooth draw so swift it was hard for the eye to follow. Deverill had cleared leather, too, but John Henry's gun barrel tipped up just a shade faster.

People near the line of fire piled out of the way, yelling and tripping in their haste. The roar of the two guns sounded so close together it was almost like one blast.

John Henry's bullet was first by a hair, and that was all the advantage he needed.

The slug smashed into Deverill's chest and knocked him back a step so that when his finger jerked the trigger the gun wasn't quite high enough. The bullet chewed into the floor a yard in front of John Henry's boots.

Deverill didn't fall right away. He stood there

swaying as he struggled to raise his gun and fire again.

The Colt was rock steady in John Henry's hand. His thumb rested on the hammer, ready to let it fall for a second shot. If Deverill's gun came up a little more, he intended to put a bullet in his brain.

Deverill opened his mouth. He got out, "You damned—" before a gush of crimson choked off the curse. His revolver slipped from his fingers and thudded to the floor. He followed a heartbeat later, smashing his face into the sawdust as he fell. He probably didn't feel it since death spasms were already rippling through his body.

One of the men who had come into the Paradise Saloon with Deverill looked at John Henry. "What the hell?" he said into the shocked silence.

John Henry didn't lower his gun. Deverill's compadres might decide to join the ball, although they showed no signs of it at the moment.

"Jimmy Deverill, right?" John Henry said with a curt nod toward the dead man.

"Yeah, that's right," replied the one who had spoken. "You know him?"

"Used to run whiskey with him down in the Nations." Since he didn't know either of the other men, John Henry thought it was a pretty safe bet they hadn't been mixed up in Deverill's liquor smuggling operation in Indian Territory.

Instinct had done its job and allowed him to beat Deverill to the draw. He quickly turned his mind to figuring out how to use the unexpected trouble to his advantage. Thoughts flashed through his brain. Deverill had a reputation as a man who was hard to get along with. Deverill had been known to double-cross his partners.

John Henry went on. "That is, I ran whiskey with him until he lit a shuck with my share of the profits. I swore I'd kill him for that, and he knew it. I reckon that's why he slapped leather as soon as he recognized me."

John Henry paused and then added coolly, "If you fellas are thinking about settling the score for him, you probably ought to be thanking me instead. Whatever you're partnered in, he would have double-crossed you sooner or later."

"We're not partners in anything," the third man said. "We just ride for the same brand right now. There's nothing crooked about it."

"Hard to believe where Deverill's concerned. He was crookeder than a dog's hind leg."

"You can put that gun away, mister. Deverill drew first. It's his own damned fault he wasn't quite fast enough to take advantage of it."

John Henry lowered the Colt's hammer and pouched the iron. "Well, since Jimmy can't do it anymore, I reckon the least I can do is buy you boys a drink."

Both men smiled.

"We'll take you up on that," one of them said.

Clearly, Deverill hadn't been that well-liked by his companions. John Henry was glad of that. He didn't want to have to fight a pitched battle only a few minutes after coming into Kiowa City.

The sharp tang of burned powder smoke still

hung in the air as John Henry and the other two men turned toward the bar. Deverill's corpse remained facedown on the floor, all but forgotten now that the shooting was over.

John Henry signaled to the bartender for another beer and indicated with a gesture that the man should draw a couple for the other two hombres.

The rusty-haired cowboy he'd been talking to earlier frowned, shook his head, and walked out of the saloon, evidently disgusted with what he had just witnessed. The other customers slowly began drifting back to the things they'd been doing before the shooting started.

John Henry said, "I hope me killing that varmint won't put your boss in a bind or get the rest of the crew too upset."

"Not likely," one of the Carson men replied. "Deverill never had a good word for anybody, and he wasn't much of a hand, either. He was only good for one thing."

"Gun work?" John Henry guessed.

The man shrugged.

The bald-headed bartender put three mugs of beer on the bar. John Henry paid for the drinks, and as he picked up his mug, he said to his new companions, "I'm glad you fellas are being reasonable about this."

The second man laughed. "After seeing that draw of yours, it ain't likely we'd be anything but reasonable. It was mighty fast and slick."

"It's kept me alive this long," John Henry said dryly.

They sipped their beers, but before they had a chance to continue the conversation, heavy footsteps thudded on the boardwalk outside. Someone slapped the batwings aside and came into the saloon in a hurry.

Watching in the mirror, John Henry saw that the newcomer carried a shotgun. The man was medium height, packed a little extra weight around the middle, and had a rough-hewn face dominated by a large nose and a thick black mustache.

A star was pinned to his brown leather vest.

"What in blazes happened here?" the man demanded in a loud, angry voice.

"That's Mike Rasmussen," the man standing next to John Henry said under his breath. "The local sheriff."

Rasmussen went on, "Who shot this man?"

John Henry took another long drink of his beer, then set the mug on the bar and turned toward the lawman in a casual, unhurried motion. "That would be me," he drawled.

"And who the hell are you?" Rasmussen wanted to know.

John Henry had considered that very question during his trip to Kiowa City. He didn't want to use his real name. Most of his activities as a deputy U.S. marshal had been carried out in Indian Territory, but some of his jobs had taken him to Kansas.

He didn't think his name would be that well-known, but he didn't want to risk it being recognized.

The chances of running into somebody who knew his face were bad enough already, as the previous few minutes had proven beyond a shadow of a doubt.

"Saxon," he said, using the name he had decided on. "John Saxon."

"New in town, aren't you, Saxon?" Rasmussen snapped.

"Just rode in a little while ago." John Henry paused, then added, "And I can't say as the place strikes me as being all that friendly so far, under the circumstances."

"What happened here?" Rasmussen jerked the Greener's twin barrels toward the corpse. "Coy, is that Deverill?"

"Yeah," replied the man who had done most of the talking to John Henry. "And I won't lie to you, Sheriff. He drew first. Saxon here was just defending himself."

"Was there some sort of argument between them?"

John Henry said, "No, he grabbed iron as soon as he came in and got a good look at me. The trouble between us goes back a ways, Sheriff."

"Maybe you were justified in shooting him, but that's not my decision to make. I'll be taking you in until there's an inquest, Saxon."

John Henry's eyes narrowed, as if this development wasn't exactly what he wanted. "You're arresting me?" he said as if he couldn't believe it. "On what charge?"

"Suspicion of murder will do."

"It was self-defense," John Henry said, making his tone sound angry and amazed. "Anybody in here can tell you that."

"They'll have to convince the coroner's jury. Like I said, it's not my job to judge." Rasmussen made a curt gesture with the shotgun again. "Let's go."

This was actually working out pretty well for John Henry, but he put a stubborn, angry expression on his face anyway. "You can't do that. It's not right."

"I'm tired of people thinking they can get away with anything around here. Come on, Saxon."

John Henry understood now. Sheriff Rasmussen was frustrated by the recent murders and the possibility that the rest of the jury and Judge Doolittle were marked for death, too. The sheriff hadn't been able to do anything about it so far, and the judge had appealed for outside help. That was likely to rub any conscientious lawman the wrong way.

Even though John Henry understood, he wasn't going to waste the opportunity. He squared himself up to Rasmussen and said, "I don't intend to get locked up when I didn't do anything wrong."

Once again, people in the saloon began scurrying to get out of harm's way. They cleared an even wider swath, since the loads of buckshot would spread out more.

Rasmussen glared at John Henry for a long

moment. "Before you get too big for your britches, mister, you'd better take a look over your shoulder."

"So you can cut loose your wolf with that Greener?" John Henry said. "I don't think so."

The unmistakable metallic ratcheting of a gun being cocked came from behind him, followed by a man's voice saying, "You better think again."

John Henry tensed. Rasmussen must have sent a deputy around the saloon to come in the back way. That was actually a pretty smart move.

The second man's voice was nervous, and John Henry knew there were few things in this world more dangerous than a nervous man with a cocked gun in his hand. "Sheriff, tell your deputy to take it easy and not get trigger-happy. If you're that bound and determined, I reckon I'll come with you."

"Now you're making sense," Rasmussen growled. "Take your gun out, careful-like, and put it on the bar, then step away from it. Use your left hand."

John Henry could shoot just about as well with his left hand as he could with his right, but the sheriff didn't know that. Slowly, he followed Rasmussen's orders.

Rasmussen motioned again with the shotgun, moving John Henry away from the bar, out of reach of the Colt. The lawman moved in then. He lowered the shotgun and pulled a pair of handcuffs from his pocket.

"Turn around and put your hands behind your back."

John Henry started to do as he was told, but as Rasmussen came closer, he made a fast turn and lunged for the shotgun.

The grab missed. Rasmussen grunted, twisted, and brought the weapon up in a stroke that ended with the stock slamming into the side of John Henry's head. The blow caused John Henry to fall to his knees.

Rasmussen didn't stop there. He hit him again.

John Henry stretched out on the floor only a few feet from the body of the man he had killed a short time earlier. A black wave shot through with red streaks washed over his brain.

Things weren't going exactly like he had anticipated, he thought, but it took care of the first step in his plan, anyway.

Chapter Six

John Henry stirred on the bunk, opened his eyes, lifted his head a little, and let it fall back on the thin mattress. Pain set up a crescendo inside his skull. A groan escaped from his lips as he closed his eyes again.

"Don't bother pretending you're not awake. I heard you and saw you move."

John Henry cracked one eye. Sheriff Rasmussen sat on a three-legged stool outside the cell, puffing on a black briar pipe that wreathed a cloud of tobacco smoke around his head.

Rasmussen took the pipe stem out of his mouth and went on. "You're a damned fool, you know that?"

Slowly, John Henry forced himself to sit up and swing his legs off the bunk. He ran the fingers of both hands through the thick tangle of his dark hair and sighed as he leaned forward and tried not to be sick. "So I've been told, Sheriff. What are you referring to, specifically?"

"I talked to everybody who was in the saloon when you killed Jimmy Deverill. Every single one of them swears up and down that Deverill drew first and that you shot him in self-defense. All you had to do was spend one lousy night in jail, and the inquest would have cleared you."

"I don't like being behind bars. It give me the fantods. I can't stand it."

Rasmussen snorted. "You'd better get used to it. You resisted arrest and assaulted a peace officer. That's going to land you at least a six-month sentence, more than likely."

John Henry lifted a hand, rubbed the lump on his head, and smiled ruefully. "I think you're the only one who landed a blow, Sheriff. Seems to me that you're the one who did the assaulting."

"The law doesn't see it that way." Rasmussen stood up. "You'll go up before Judge Doolittle tomorrow, after the inquest into Deverill's death. One of my deputies will bring you some supper after a while."

"I'm in no hurry. I'm not hungry."

"Law says I got to provide a meal. Whether you eat it or not is up to you." Rasmussen walked out of the cell block. The heavy wooden door closed with a solid thump behind him.

John Henry took a look at his surroundings. He was in a good-sized cell block with half a dozen barred enclosures on each side of a center aisle. The floors and outer walls were stone.

Each cell had a single small, barred window set high in the outside wall. Because of that, John

Henry had a hunch the jail was located in the basement of the county courthouse he had seen earlier.

"Say, mister, I heard about what you did. The sheriff's right. You *are* a damned fool."

Evidently, John Henry wasn't the only prisoner. He looked to his right. An empty cell was next to his, but in the cell beyond that, a man stood leaning against the bars with a grin on his face.

He was about thirty, a medium-sized gent with brown hair and a cocky grin on his handsome face. His suit was a little threadbare but had once been of good quality.

"I don't recall asking your opinion," John Henry replied in a sullen tone.

"No, but I'll offer it to you anyway," the man said brightly. "My name's Nick, by the way. Nick Mallette. With an *e* on the end."

John Henry didn't say anything.

"You don't have to tell me who you are," the other prisoner went on after a moment. "Carl told me all about you while you were still out cold. That's Carl Baird, one of the sheriff's deputies. The one who helped Rasmussen bring you in, in fact. He's a talkative sort."

"Like you," John Henry said.

Mallette chuckled. "Oh, he talks even more than I do, Saxon. He told me how you outdrew Jimmy Deverill and gunned him down. That's pretty good. Deverill was fast."

"He had to be. A man with as many enemies as he had would have been dead in a hurry if he wasn't fast."

"Sort of like you, eh?"

Despite the ache in his head, that comment made John Henry smile. "Yeah, sort of like me, I guess." He paused, then asked, "Why are you locked up in here, Mallette? You don't exactly look like a desperado."

"Well, looks can be deceiving. Actually, though, despite my current circumstances, I'm not an outlaw. I'm a gambler. Slick fingers and the gift of gab, you know."

"You've got the last part, all right. It can't be illegal to gamble in Kiowa City, though. I saw several poker games going on in the Paradise."

"Gambling's not illegal. Killing people is."

"You killed somebody?"

"Oh, not here. Don't get me wrong. It was back in Kansas City. And the fellow didn't give me any choice. It was supposed to be a friendly game, but he thought I had a fifth ace up my sleeve and took offense at the idea. What I really had up my sleeve was a derringer, and he was a little too slow getting his gun out."

Mallette shook his head. "First and only time I've ever had to resort to violence to get myself out of a fix. And I had to go and kill a state senator's brother."

"So justified or not, you had to light out," John Henry said.

"That's right. I made it this far before a lawman recognized me from the wanted posters the Kansas City authorities sent out to all the surrounding states. A lot of people around here seem to think that Sheriff Rasmussen isn't too bright, but the man's got a good eye. I'll give him credit for that."

The fugitive gambler sighed. "I suppose I shouldn't have stayed around here as long as I did. I should have spent the night, played a game or two and fattened my poke, picked up a few supplies, and headed for the Silver Skull."

John Henry frowned. "What's that, a saloon? I never heard of it."

"Really? An hombre like you? I figured you'd know about it since according to Carl, you're some sort of badman."

"I haven't spent much time in these parts," John Henry said quickly to cover up any possible mistake on his part. "Most of my hell-raising has been down in Texas and the Nations."

"I'm new to the area myself," Mallette said. "But a fellow told me about the place over a card table one night, a couple towns back. He said that if I ever found myself riding some lonely trails and listening to the owl hoot, I should head for a place called the Silver Skull. It's an old ranch that's supposed to be somewhere northwest of here, and the fellow who was telling about it said men who ride on the wrong side of the law are welcome there."

That was just the sort of information John Henry had been looking for. Such outlaw sanctuaries were common down in Indian Territory, and it stood to reason they would exist in Kansas, too. He would have led his fellow prisoner around to the subject if he'd had to, but Mallette's natural garrulousness had saved him the trouble. "Sounds like just the sort of place I might like to stop over. You wouldn't happen to have directions to it, would you?"

"No, but the man who told me about it said that if I was in the right area, I'd know it. I found that rather puzzling, but he didn't offer any other explanation." Mallette laughed. "If you plan to search for it like some sort of El Dorado, my friend, you're going to have to wait a while. At least six months, I believe the sheriff said."

"I can't wait that long," John Henry said. "I'd go loco if I had to sit in here for that long."

"Considering what I have waiting for me back in Kansas City, I'd gladly stay here for as long as they want to keep me," Mallette said. "It won't take that long for some Missouri deputy sheriffs to show up and fetch me back there, though."

"For shooting a man when he drew on you first?" John Henry asked with a frown.

"Yes, the situation does rather resemble yours, doesn't it? They seem to take a more lenient attitude toward self-defense out here, and like I said, the dead man *was* the brother of an influential politician."

"Still, it doesn't seem right."

"Not to me, either, but what can a person do?"

"I don't know about you," John Henry said, "but I'm going to get out of here."

Mallette straightened from his casual pose leaning against the bars between cells. "You're talking about escaping?"

"Like I said, I can't stay in here. I'll go loco if I do."

"Could you . . . if you do get away . . . is there a chance you might take me with you?"

John Henry didn't answer right away. Having a fugitive like Mallette with him might come in handy with his plan, making his pose as an outlaw more believable, but it would mean helping the man escape from justice. John Henry had only Mallette's word for what had happened back in Kansas City. The gambler might actually be guilty of cold-blooded murder.

There was no question about the guilt of whoever was responsible for the deaths of Charles Houston and Lucas Winslow, whether it was Simon Garrett or someone else. That was the case that had brought John Henry to Kiowa City, not some killing over a poker table back in Kansas City. "I'll think about it. You and I don't know each other. I'll have to decide if I can trust you. You should be thinking about the same thing."

"Considering the alternative, Saxon, not trusting you would probably be the death of me!"

Chapter Seven

The deputy who brought supper for the prisoners was the same one who had thrown down on John Henry from behind in the Paradise Saloon. "Step back away from the bars," Carl Baird warned as he approached the door of John Henry's cell with a tray. "The sheriff warned me not to get too close or take any chances with you, Saxon. He said you're a fast gun."

"I'm pretty harmless in here, I'd say," John Henry told him with a smile.

"Yeah, but only as long as those bars are between us."

Baird slid the tray through the slot in the door designed for that purpose. John Henry took it and didn't try anything. He was actually a little hungry now that his headache had faded.

"Here you go, Nick," Baird said when he gave Mallette his supper.

"Thanks, Carl. Any word on when those deputies from Missouri are supposed to be here?"

"Not that I know of. But you'd have to ask the sheriff about that."

"All right. Thanks anyway."

Baird hesitated. "I'm sorry you're in such a terrible fix, Nick. You don't seem like such a bad hombre."

"Well, I appreciate that," Mallette replied with a smile. "I've had a lot of good luck in my life. Maybe the bad luck just finally caught up to me."

"Yeah, it'll do that," Baird said. "I'll be back for those trays later." He left the cell block.

John Henry sat on his bunk and asked quietly, "Is he as dumb as he sounds and acts like?"

"Good-hearted is more like it, rather than dumb. Carl doesn't want to believe the worst of anybody, even prisoners. He'd rather believe the best."

"That's not a very good quality for a lawman to have."

"You sound like you're speaking from experience," Mallette said with a speculative frown on his face.

"I've dealt with plenty of them." John Henry left it at that for Mallette to draw his own conclusions.

The meal consisted of a chunk of roast beef between two slabs of bread, plus a cup of watery stew and another cup filled with coffee. None of it required any utensils, so there was nothing for a prisoner to squirrel away and use as a weapon later on.

The food was surprisingly good for jailhouse grub. The beef was tender, the bread freshly baked, and the stew savory. Now that the pounding in his head had eased up considerably, John Henry was hungry, so he enjoyed the meal.

As he sipped his coffee, he said through the empty cell to Mallette, "I've got another reason I can't afford to be stuck here for the next six months."

"A pretty girl waiting for you somewhere?" the fugitive gambler asked with a smile.

"That would be nice, but no. It's more a matter of not wanting trouble to catch up to me the way it did to you."

"Ah. You've got reward dodgers out on you, just like me."

John Henry nodded. "From Texas. I'm not sure if they've made it all the way up here to Kansas yet, but I don't want to take the chance. There's a hangrope waiting for me, too, if I get sent back to Fort Worth. I just wish it was that pretty girl you mentioned, instead."

"Both can be the death of a man if he's not careful," Mallette said.

"Now you're the one talking like a man with experience."

Mallette laughed. "Well, I haven't experienced a hangrope directly, but I have known my share of pretty girls. I'm beginning to think that you and I are kindred spirits, Saxon." The gambler lowered his voice, although it was unlikely that anybody else was listening. "All the more reason for us to work this escape together.

"What did you have in mind?" John Henry asked, pretending to be wary.

"Like I told you, Deputy Baird is a good-hearted soul. If I call out to him and tell him that you're choking, he'll rush in here to help you. All he has to do is get within reach. You can grab him through the bars, yank him against them, and either knock him out or get his gun."

John Henry considered the plan. It sounded like it might work, and he had been figuring all along that he would try something like that. Having Mallette involved would make the ploy even more believable.

He had a backup plan, too, which involved revealing his true identity to Rasmussen and convincing the sheriff to cooperate, but he preferred to make his escape seem as real as possible. "All right. We'll give it a try. When?"

"Carl will be back in a little while to get the trays. We'll make our move then."

John Henry nodded.

Twenty minutes went by, and then they heard the sound of heavy footsteps descending the staircase from the first floor. Deputy Baird appeared at the end of the hallway and ambled toward the cells.

John Henry slumped forward, choking and gagging as the deputy stumbled toward the bars.

"Carl!" Mallette cried. "Saxon's choking on something! You've got to help him!"

Baird's eyes widened. He started to rush down the corridor toward John Henry's cell, but then he stopped short and frowned, obviously leery of a trick. "What happened to him?"

"I don't know!" Mallette said. "He just started making that godawful sound, and then his face got all red. I think he must be dying!"

John Henry had his head down so Baird couldn't see his face and realize Mallette was lying about it being flushed. The deputy still hesitated, so John Henry dropped to his knees, groaned and hunched over, and then pitched forward to lie twitching and writhing on the stone floor.

"I'll go get help," Baird said.

"The poor bastard will be dead by the time you get back, Carl!" Mallette argued.

Muttering under his breath, the deputy started toward John Henry's cell again, pausing on the other side of the bars with his hand on his gun butt. "Saxon! Saxon, can you hear me? What's wrong with you?"

John Henry made a horrible gasping noise, as if he were struggling to draw in one last breath and failing.

"Damn it." Baird bent down to reach through the bars, stretching out his left hand in an effort to snag John Henry's collar and pull him closer.

John Henry's hands shot up without warning and grabbed the deputy's arm. He hauled the deputy toward the bars.

Baird barely had time to yelp and try to draw his gun before his head smacked into the iron bars with a solid thump. His eyes rolled up in their sockets and he went limp.

Careful to gauge the impact so it would stun Baird without doing any permanent damage, John Henry held the deputy against the bars with his right hand. He reached through with his left, plucked Baird's gun from the holster, and pressed the barrel into the hollow under Baird's jaw.

The deputy blinked rapidly and tried to regain his senses. After a moment, his eyes focused again.

"Keep quiet and you live, Deputy," John Henry told him. "Let out a yell and I won't have one damned reason not to go ahead and pull the trigger."

"Wha . . . what do you want?" Baird asked, struggling to get the words out. The gun muzzle was prodding painfully against his throat.

"What do you think I want? Get your keys out and unlock this door!"

"I . . . I can't reach it."

"You'd better try," John Henry said in an ominous tone. "You're no good to me if you can't."

Baird tried to swallow and couldn't. He fumbled a ring of keys from his pocket and reached over to fit one of them into the cell door. It was almost out of his reach, but not quite, and after a few seconds, his awkward effort was rewarded. The key went into the lock and he turned it.

John Henry stood up, raising the deputy with him. They shuffled over to the door, which John Henry kicked open. He came out in a hurry and looped an arm around Baird's neck from behind as he shifted the gun barrel from the deputy's throat to his side.

"Now me." Mallette's voice shook a little, indicating that he was nervous. He probably wondered if his fellow prisoner was going to keep his word.

"Unlock Mallette's cell," John Henry ordered Baird.

Baird did so. "You can't get away. There are half a dozen deputies right upstairs—"

"No, there's not," Mallette interrupted him. "Rasmussen doesn't even have half a dozen deputies. More like three or four, and there are usually only two on duty at a time. Right now, since it's after supper but the evening rush hasn't started yet in the saloons, Carl may be holding down the fort for the whole town."

"Is that right, Deputy Baird?" John Henry pressed harder with the gun barrel. "Don't even think about lying to me. I don't have a damned thing to lose by killing you."

"If . . . if you kill me, you'll hang for sure!"

John Henry grinned. "Maybe, but they can only hang me once, and that's just what'll wind up happening if I stay around here long enough for those Texas wanted posters to catch up to me. Now, tell me what we're liable to run into up there, and tell me the truth."

Baird sighed. "Nick's right. Sheriff Rasmussen has gone to supper. None of the other deputies have come on duty yet. The sheriff and one of the other men will start on evening rounds later."

John Henry's instincts told him that Baird was

telling the truth. The man wasn't really cut out to be a deputy. He wasn't tough enough, mentally or physically, for the job.

Mallette had come out of the cell. "If you want your things back, Saxon, I can show you where to find them. I'd like to get my derringer and a few other items as well. They'll be locked up in a cabinet in the sheriff's office."

"And I'll bet one of Carl's keys will unlock that cabinet," John Henry said. "Come on."

The next few minutes in the sheriff's office were tense ones. Rasmussen or someone else could come in at any time. John Henry knew he could always fall back on producing his badge and identity papers from his saddlebags, but he didn't want to have to do that unless it was absolutely necessary.

Baird unlocked the cabinet, allowing John Henry to reclaim his gun belt and holstered Colt. He drew his own gun, then tucked behind his belt the revolver he had taken from Baird.

Mallette took a small, spring-loaded holster with a derringer in it from the cabinet and fastened it onto his right forearm, under his shirtsleeve. The cabinet also contained a sheathed dagger that he strapped onto his left forearm.

"You really didn't have room up your sleeves for that fifth ace, did you?" John Henry asked.

"I don't need to cheat to win," Mallette said with complete confidence. He picked up a couple decks of cards on a shelf inside the cabinet and stuck them into inside pockets of his coat.

"Ready to get out of here?" John Henry asked.

Mallette took a black, flat-crowned hat from the cabinet and settled it on his head. "Now I am."

"Give me that dagger of yours," John Henry growled. "Unless you'd rather cut the deputy's throat yourself."

Baird made a little squeaking sound.

Mallette stared at John Henry. "We didn't say anything about killing him!"

"Can't leave him alive to sound the alarm." John Henry made his voice as hard and grim as possible. It was all an act, of course, but neither of the other men knew that.

"Can't we just tie him up and gag him? The sheriff won't be back for a while. We'll have time to get a good lead before anybody finds out we're gone."

John Henry pretended to think about it. The gambler's reaction to his threat to kill Baird told him a lot about the man. He had a hunch Mallette wasn't a cold-blooded killer and there was at least a good chance the shooting back in Kansas City had been self-defense as he had claimed. That meant helping him escape from the Kiowa City jail wasn't as bad as it might have been.

John Henry expected to hear a few choice words about the subject from Judge Parker anyway . . . providing the rest of his plan worked and he made it back to Fort Smith alive.

After a couple of heartbeats, John Henry snapped, "Make it fast."

Mallette did so, finding some cord in the desk

and using it to bind the deputy's hands behind him. He used Baird's own bandanna to gag him.

John Henry marched Baird back downstairs to the cell block and shoved him into the cell Mallette had occupied. Baird stumbled and fell onto the bunk.

"That'll hold him," John Henry said. "Let's get out of here."

"I'll need a horse."

"We ought to be able to do something about that." Adding horse thief to the list of his bendings of the law wouldn't make things too much worse, John Henry thought.

They left the courthouse through a side door. The streets of Kiowa City weren't busy at the moment. As Baird had said, it was the lull between supper and the rowdiness that would begin later in the saloons.

John Henry and Mallette stuck to the shadows as much as possible anyway, but they had to come out into the open when they reached the Paradise Saloon. Iron Heart was still tied to one of the hitch racks in front of the saloon.

John Henry picked another likely looking mount and pointed it out to Mallette. "Ever stolen a horse before?" he asked dryly.

"No, but I think I'm about to," Mallette said.

Without hurrying, they moved to the rack and untied the reins. No one paid much attention to them. John Henry swung up into the saddle with the ease and athletic grace of a born horseman. Mallette mounted a little more awkwardly.

He had just settled into the saddle when a man came out of the saloon, stopped short, and yelled, "Hey! What the hell? That's my horse!"

John Henry whipped out his Colt and put a bullet into the boardwalk at the man's feet, causing him to let out an alarmed yelp and dive back through the batwings.

"Come on, Nick!" John Henry wheeled Iron Heart around, making sure he headed northwest.

It would be better if Mallette could keep up, but it wasn't absolutely necessary.

The gambler managed to hang on and gallop out of Kiowa City as people shouted behind them. "Now what?" Mallette called to John Henry over the pounding hoofbeats.

"Now we see if we can find that Silver Skull of yours!"

Chapter Eight

John Henry had all the confidence in the world in Iron Heart's speed and stamina, and he had tried to pick a horse for Mallette with those things in mind, too, but he couldn't always tell from looking at an animal how it would hold up.

He thought they had a good chance of outdistancing any posse in pursuit. He knew Sheriff Rasmussen wouldn't allow two prisoners—one of them a wanted murderer—to escape from his jail without going after them. The darkness would help, too. The moon was only a thin sliver in the sky. Even an Indian couldn't have tracked them by its meager light.

John Henry kept them moving at a fast pace for the first few miles, then hauled back on Iron Heart's reins. "We'd better walk the horses for a ways and let them have a breather."

"That's all right with me," Mallette said as he slowed his mount, too. He groaned. "I'm used to riding in stagecoaches, or buggies belonging to pretty women. A saddle really hands out a pounding to one's, ah, nether regions, doesn't it?"

John Henry laughed. "You'll get used to it. A good horse is better than a stagecoach any day of the week."

"I guess I'll find out," Mallette said ruefully. "I'm on the dodge now more than ever before, since I've got jailbreaking and horse stealing to add to my list of crimes."

"I could have left you back there," John Henry pointed out.

"And I'm glad you didn't," the gambler said. "Don't get me wrong, Saxon. I couldn't afford to stay locked up any more than you could. In the long run, it would have been the death of me, just like it would for you."

Of course, there weren't any wanted posters out there for John Saxon, since that alleged killer and badman didn't exist, but Nick Mallette didn't know that and it was best to keep him in the dark.

While they were walking the animals, John Henry checked their back trail frequently, even stopping completely a few times so he could listen for the sound of distant hoofbeats. He hadn't seen or heard anything.

He thought it was likely that Rasmussen was back there somewhere, but with luck, the sheriff would give up the pursuit by morning.

After a quarter hour, John Henry said, "That's enough walking. Let's get some speed up again."

They heeled their horses into a run.

The hours and the miles rolled past. The moon

and stars wheeled in their courses through the night sky.

John Henry and Mallette alternated running and walking their horses until John Henry finally called a halt. "Might as well get down. We need to let them blow for a while, or we won't be going anywhere."

"I'll defer to your judgment in such matters," Mallette said as he dismounted. "I've probably ridden more tonight than I have in the entire rest of my life."

He was unsteady and had to grab one of the stirrups to keep from falling when his feet hit the ground. He got his legs back under him in only a few moments.

John Henry took down one of the canteens slung from his saddle, unscrewed the cap, and swallowed a long drink of water before offering the canteen to Mallette.

The gambler grunted his thanks and took it. "You wouldn't happen to have a good cigar in there, too, would you?"

"Afraid not," John Henry said. "Not even the makin's. I don't use the stuff."

"Just as well. We probably shouldn't be striking matches. Someone might see the light."

John Henry grinned. "That's right. We'll make an owlhoot out of you yet, Nick."

"Yeah, I'll be a regular desperado in no time." He took another sip of the water and handed the canteen back. "How are we going to find that ranch? Neither of us know where it is."

"We've been headed the right direction, if what that fella told you was true. How trustworthy do you think he was?"

"I'm sure no one *ever* lied over a poker table before."

John Henry laughed again. "Well, for now we're going to assume that he was telling the truth. It'll be light in another hour. We'll scout around then and see what we can see. The important thing is that we're miles from Kiowa City and the sheriff isn't right on our tail."

"Yes, and I'm thankful for that."

When John Henry judged that the horses had rested long enough, they mounted up again and rode on, continuing in a generally northwestward direction.

Like nearly all of Kansas, the terrain was considered flat, although it had a gentle roll to it. Here and there, ridges or rocky knobs stuck up to break the monotony.

As the sky began to lighten to gray behind them, John Henry spotted a dark line along the horizon up ahead. Some sort of escarpment or similar formation jutted up from the plains.

Dawn broke in a hurry. The sun seemed to leap into the sky, flooding the prairie with light. The illumination washed over the two fugitives and rolled on like a tide until it hit the ridge John Henry had noticed earlier.

Both riders reined in abruptly, and Mallette let out an awed exclamation. "I'll be damned."

Perched on the edge of that escarpment, glowing silver in the dawn light, was a gigantic skull.

After a couple of seconds, John Henry laughed. "I've seen some odd rock formations in my life, but I reckon maybe that one is the most eye-catching."

"That's what it is? Just a rock formation?"

"Unless you think a hundred-foot-tall giant died and somebody stuck his skull up there. You can see the way the elements have rounded it off and bored holes in it that look like eyes. It probably only looks like a skull from a distance like this. Up close, you'd be able to see all the other irregularities."

"Well, it certainly made a chill go up my spine for a minute. Why is it silver like that? It's almost like it's . . . glowing."

"Something in the mineral composition, I suppose. I doubt if there's any actual silver ore. We're not in the right part of the country for that. But some other mineral that resembles it could be mixed in with the rock."

Mallette frowned. "You sound sort of educated for an outlaw, John."

John Henry's mother had been a schoolteacher, but of course he couldn't explain that. Instead he said, "No rule says that a man can't read, even when he's on the dodge."

"I suppose that's right."

"That's got to mark the location of the Silver Skull Ranch," John Henry went on. "You can sure enough see how the place got its name."

"How far are we from Kiowa City?"

"At least twenty miles."

"I guess that's far enough out in the middle of nowhere for a place like I heard about. A place where . . . men like us . . . would be welcome."

"Let's go find out," John Henry suggested.

The skull-like rock formation gave them something to steer by as they rode toward the ridge. They didn't know if the outlaw ranch lay below that height or on top of it, but John Henry figured they could locate it without much trouble.

In the brightening light, he suddenly noticed a plume of dust rising in the air ahead of them. He hauled back on Iron Heart's reins and pointed to the telltale dust. "Hold on, Nick. Somebody's coming."

"But if they're ahead of us, they can't be a posse from Kiowa City, can they?" Mallette asked.

"No, but we still don't want to run right into them without knowing who they are. That's never a good idea." John Henry turned the gray to the left. "Let's see if we can find a place to hole up for a few minutes."

Mallette had been following his lead ever since they left the settlement, and that didn't change now. The two men quickly rode south.

It was hard to find hiding places out on the open prairie, but after a few minutes John Henry spotted a dry, shallow creek bed. He led Mallette down into it.

They dismounted, and John Henry got both horses to lie down. He handed their reins to Mallette. "Hold them. Hang on tight. Iron Heart won't give you any trouble, but I don't know about that other horse."

"What are you going to do?" Mallette asked as he took the reins.

"Have a look at whoever that is."

John Henry took a pair of field glasses from one of his saddlebags and stretched out at the edge of the creekbed. A long, gentle slope rose in front of him. The riders came into view near the top of it. He put the glasses to his eyes and focused on the horsebackers.

There were half a dozen of them, and they were too far away for him to make out many details. All but one of the men wore range clothes.

The one who rode in the lead was better dressed. His profile was hawk-like under an expensive, broad-brimmed hat. He had the look of a successful cattleman, but of course John Henry had no way of knowing whether that was true. He had never seen any of the men before.

He would recognize that hombre in the lead if he ever saw him again, though.

The riders passed on without noticing the two fugitives. When they were out of sight, John Henry took the reins back from Mallette and let the horses get up again.

"Who do you think they were?" the gambler asked.

"I don't have any idea. But they can't tell anybody they saw us out here, can they?"

"No, I suppose not. Is that what life as an outlaw is like, always hiding and dodging trouble?"

"You were on the run before you got to Kiowa City. You ought to know what it's like."

Mallette sighed. "Yes, but I was doing my hiding out in towns, not in the middle of nowhere."

"That didn't work out very well for you, did it?"

"No," Mallette replied with a wry chuckle. "No, it did not."

They mounted up and rode on toward the ridge. John Henry's prediction proved accurate—the closer they got to the big knob of rock, the less it looked like a human skull. All the odd lumps and extra holes were visible now.

John Henry saw a few cattle grazing here and there, but didn't get close enough to read their brands. There was no ranch house below the ridge, which meant it had to be up above somewhere.

He studied the face of the escarpment, looking for a trail, and finally picked out a line that zig-zagged back and forth up the ridge, which rose about a hundred feet from the surrounding plain. "There's the trail." He pointed it out to Mallette.

"Whoever owns the ranch can't bring cattle down something like that, can he?"

"Why would he want to do that? He can make a living taking a cut from the loot gathered up by the men who come looking for a hideout."

"Is that how that works?" Mallette shrugged. "That makes sense, I suppose. But you'd think he would at least try to give the appearance of operating a working ranch."

"There could be another trail down somewhere else along the ridge that's easier." John Henry looked over at the gambler. "You're a curious hombre, aren't you?"

"No reason a man who's on the dodge can't be curious about things," Mallette said with a smile, paraphrasing what John Henry had said to him earlier.

"No, I reckon not," the lawman replied. "When we start up, keep your eyes open. Do you know how to use a rifle?"

"I'm afraid I've never fired one in my life."

John Henry grunted and pulled Deputy Baird's pistol from behind his belt. He held it out to Mallette. "Take this, then. But don't use it unless you have to."

"You think we'll run into trouble?"

"I don't know what we'll run into, but whatever it is, I want to be ready for it."

They had reached the bottom of the ridge. The skull-like protuberance loomed above them. John Henry started up the trail, keeping Iron Heart to a steady walk.

Behind him, Mallette started to say something. John Henry held out a hand, motioning sharply for his companion to be quiet. The hoofbeats of their horses sounded loud enough without adding any talking to them.

The early morning air was already getting hot. It was going to be another scorcher.

Even with the trail meandering back and forth, it didn't take long for the two riders to reach the top. John Henry reined in and let Mallette come up alongside him. They saw several buildings about half a mile off.

Unless John Henry missed his guess, they had found the Silver Skull Ranch.

Someone had found them, too. A handful of riders suddenly burst out from behind the nearby rock. John Henry could have reached for his gun and put up a fight, but instead he sat motionless in the saddle and waited.

"Saxon!" Mallette said in alarm.

"Just wait," John Henry told him. "This is what I figured would happen."

"Well, I sure as hell hope you figured right," Mallette said as the hard-faced riders surrounded them and leveled guns at them.

Chapter Nine

One of the riders edged his horse ahead of the others. He wore a brown hat, brown vest, butternut shirt, and denim trousers. The hat brim shaded a rough-hewn but handsome face. Tight blond curls showed under the hat. The gun he held was rock-steady.

Oddly, he wore a glove of what looked like soft buckskin on his left hand, although his right hand—his gun hand—was bare. "Who are you gents," he demanded, "and what are you doing here?"

John Henry kept his own hands in plain sight, not wanting to give any of the men an excuse to get trigger-happy. He drawled, "We could ask the same thing of you, amigo."

"Yeah, but there are more of us than there are of you. And we've got the drop on you. So that gives us the right to ask the questions."

"Can't argue with that," John Henry admitted. "My name's Saxon. This is Nick Mallette."

"Wait a minute," Mallette protested. "Maybe I wanted to use an alias."

"It's a little late for that," John Henry said. "If these fellas are who I think they are, we've got to trust them, anyway."

That comment drew an amused chuckle from the blond man, but the others remained grim and menacing.

"Just who do you think we are, Saxon?"

"I think you're from the Silver Skull Ranch . . . which makes you outlaws, same as us."

"So you're on the run, are you?"

"We broke out of the jail in Kiowa City last night."

The leader's smile disappeared and his face hardened at John Henry's words. "You didn't happen to kill that damned sheriff on your way out of town, did you?" he asked harshly.

"Rasmussen?" John Henry shook his head. "No, we didn't have to kill anybody . . . in Kiowa City. But I've got a murder charge hanging over me down in Texas, and Nick here has a date with a hangrope in Missouri."

Under his breath, Mallette said, "I sure hope these fellows aren't bounty hunters."

The blond man smiled again. "Not hardly, Mallette. Your friend's hunch was right. The law wants us, too . . . but we don't have to worry about that as long as we're here, and as long as the boss goes along with it, neither do you."

John Henry said, "You're not the boss?"

The man didn't answer directly. "Come on.

We'll take you to the ranch house. Just keep your hands away from your guns. You don't want to make anybody nervous."

The gunmen fanned out on both flanks as John Henry and Mallette rode toward the ranch buildings. As they got closer, John Henry saw that the barn, corrals, and bunkhouse appeared to be well cared for. So was the low, sprawling main house. Out on the mostly treeless plains, it must have cost a pretty penny to freight in enough lumber to construct all those buildings.

Maybe that was why the ranch's original owner had gone broke and abandoned it. He might have spent all his money on the buildings and neglected his stock.

John Henry saw at least a dozen horses in one of the corrals. Quite a few men were staying at the Silver Skull.

That supported the theory that Simon Garrett and his gang had made their headquarters there while carrying out their campaign of terror against the men he held responsible for his brother's death.

A figure came out onto the ranch house's porch to watch their arrival. Long, thick waves of auburn hair fell around the woman's shoulders, leaving no doubt about her gender despite the fact that she wore denim trousers and a man's shirt. The way she filled out those clothes made it pretty plain, too.

A thin rawhide thong, laced through a piece of leather with studs of silver and turquoise, was fastened around her neck as a bit of colorful decoration.

She had a gunbelt strapped around her sleekly curved hips, as well, something you didn't see on many women, even out on the frontier.

Hooking her thumbs in the gun belt, the woman spread her feet a little and stood in a mannish stance, waiting for them. As the group of riders came up to the porch and reined in, she called, "Who are these men, Simon?"

John Henry managed not to react, even though his first impulse was to glance over at the blond gunman beside him. He had come looking for Simon Garrett, but maybe Garrett had found him instead.

Of course, the man might be somebody else named Simon . . . but John Henry had a hunch that wasn't the case.

"They say their names are Saxon and Mallette," the man replied. "They came riding up the trail, bold as brass."

"That's because someone told us that if we were in trouble and needed a place to go to ground, we ought to look for the Silver Skull," John Henry said.

"Is that right?" the auburn-haired woman said. "Who told you that?"

Mallette said, "I didn't catch his name. We were playing cards together over in Salina, I believe it was. He wore an eyepatch, if that helps. And he only had three fingers on his left hand."

John Henry's first impression had been that the woman was handsome, but not really pretty. He changed his mind when she smiled at the description

Mallette gave her. It transformed her face into something beautiful.

"Three-Finger Pete," she said. "An old friend. If he trusted you enough to tell you about this place, I suppose you must be all right. Before you get down from those horses, though . . . what are you on the run from?"

"Killings in Texas and Missouri," John Henry said.

"They claim to have busted out of the Kiowa City jail last night," Simon put in.

Without hesitation, the woman asked the same question as Simon. "Did you kill Sheriff Rasmussen?"

"No. Didn't kill anybody in Kiowa City." John Henry shrugged. "Well, that's not exactly true. I had to gun an old enemy of mine in the Paradise Saloon. That's what landed me in jail to start with, even though that shooting was self-defense."

"Who did you kill?"

"Jimmy Deverill."

John Henry saw the reaction on the woman's face and heard the breath that Simon drew in sharply beside him. They knew who Deverill was, all right.

"He double-crossed me in a whiskey running deal down in Indian Territory," John Henry went on. "He knew I'd be gunning for him if our trails ever crossed again, so as soon as he saw me and realized who I was, he slapped leather."

"Deverill was supposed to be fast," Simon said.

"He was. Just not fast enough."

The woman smiled again. "You may have the rest of the crew from the Anvil gunning for you now."

"Actually, a couple of them were there in the saloon when I killed Deverill." John Henry added dryly, "To tell you the truth, they didn't seem all that broken up about it. They even let me buy them a drink afterward."

That brought a hearty laugh from the woman. "All right. You can light and stay a while, I suppose. And I'm glad you didn't kill Sheriff Rasmussen. He's on our list to take care of, isn't he, Simon?"

The blond gunman just grunted.

John Henry had no further doubt that the gunman was Simon Garrett. "You must have a powerful hate for that lawman."

"Among others."

With that, the woman turned and disappeared back into the house.

With Garrett and several of the other gunmen accompanying them, John Henry and Mallette led their horses into the corral and unsaddled them. The other men put away their horses, too. Iron Heart made it clear with a few nips of his teeth that the other animals would be wise to leave him alone.

John Henry carried his saddle into the barn that adjoined the corral and placed it on an empty sawhorse. As the others came in, he asked Garrett, "What's the lady's name?"

"Her name is Lottie, but don't get any fancy ideas about her, Saxon."

"Your personal property, is she?"

That drew a genuine-sounding laugh from Garrett. "Lottie Dalmas isn't anybody's property, mister. The reason I told you not to get any ideas about her is because she's liable to nail your co-jones to a post if you try anything. That gun she carries isn't for show. She's damned good with it. And did you notice that rawhide necklace she wears?"

"I did," John Henry admitted.

"It's attached to a sheath with a bowie knife in it that hangs down her back. You can't see the handle because of her hair, but she can get it out in a hurry. She's good with it, too."

John Henry remembered the condition of Lucas Winslow's body when it was found. "I'll remember that."

"You'd be wise to." Garrett stuck out his hand and shook with John Henry and Mallette. "I'm Simon Garrett, by the way. This is Roy Currier, Billy Stoppard, and Lance Hillman." Garrett nodded to each of the other three outlaws in turn.

Mallette said, "Howdy, fellas."

"I'll introduce you to everybody else later on," Garrett continued. "Come on, I'll show you where you can bunk."

As the men walked toward the long, low bunkhouse, John Henry said, "So this place belongs to Lottie?"

"That's right. Me and the boys who ride with me

have been staying here for a while, but she has other hombres passing through from time to time, like the two of you. The price is fair. It's based on a percentage of the loot from any jobs you pull while you're here, or you can pay for your room and board like regular renters if you want."

Mallette said, "What if you're, ah, low on funds when you get here?"

"Lottie will front you your keep for a while," Garrett said with a shrug. "But you'll have to do some jobs to pay her back."

"I don't know about Nick here, but I could use some work," John Henry said. "How about it, Garrett? Could you find a place for a couple good men in your bunch?"

"If you really gunned Jimmy Deverill, I might be able to use you."

"I can give you my word on that." John Henry's tone made it clear he wouldn't take kindly to having that word questioned.

Garrett jerked his chin toward Mallette. "I don't know about Slick here, though. He doesn't look like the sort of hombre who usually rides with us."

"It's Nick . . . and I'll do whatever you want, Mr. Garrett," Mallette said. "I really need a place to lie low for a while."

"I'll think about it," Garrett said. They had reached the bunkhouse. He opened the door and nodded them into the shadowy interior.

John Henry placed his saddlebags and Winchester on the empty bunk he picked out. Mallette didn't really have anything other than the clothes on his back and the gun John Henry had given him, so he dropped his hat on the thin, blanket-covered mattress of another empty bunk.

Half a dozen men were already in the bunk-house. One of them who was stretched out on a bunk swung his legs to the floor and stood up. He kept rising for what seemed like a long time. When he was upright, he towered a good six and a half feet above the rough planks of the floor. His lined and pitted face looked like it had been hacked out of a tree trunk. It was topped by a shock of hair the color and consistency of straw.

The tall man's body was lean but corded with muscle. He frowned as he stared at Mallette, and after a moment he rumbled in a gravelly voice, "Don't I know you?"

Mallette licked his lips nervously and shook his head.

"I, ah, don't think we've met, friend. I believe I'd remember you if we had."

The giant's frown deepened. "Are you sayin' I'm too ugly to forget?" he demanded.

"No, not at all, not at all," Mallette replied hastily. "You're very impressive-looking. Distinctive. Memorable."

"Ugly! I know it." The man took a step toward Mallette. "Everybody here knows it. You might as well say it."

"Take it easy, Sven," Garrett said. He added, "This is Sven Gunderson."

John Henry had heard a hint of a Scandanavian accent in the big man's voice, although it was faint enough to indicate that Gunderson had spent most, if not all, of his life in America. Probably out on the frontier, where a lot of immigrants from Sweden and Norway had found new homes.

Gunderson stepped closer to Mallette and lifted a hand to poke the gambler in the chest with a long, blunt forefinger. Mallette took a step back.

"Maybe I don't know you," Gunderson rumbled, "but I've run into plenty of men like you. You wear your fancy suits and think you're better than everybody else."

"I don't think I'm better than anybody, I swear," Mallette said as he lifted his hands and held the palms out toward Gunderson.

The giant suddenly seized Mallette's wrists, moving with unexpected speed for such a big man. "Soft hands!" he roared. "I knew it. You're a gambler. A damned tinhorn gambler, always goin' around cheatin' people like me and takin' our hard-earned money!"

"No, no, I swear—"

John Henry glanced around at the other men in the bunkhouse, including Simon Garrett. They were all watching with interest, but none of them made a move to interfere.

It was possible Gunderson did this every time a new man showed up at the Silver Skull, just to establish his dominance right away, John Henry thought. Every group had its pecking order.

John Henry didn't want to be at the bottom of that order. That was what would happen if Gunderson prodded Mallette into a fight and then beat the hell out of him. Since John Henry and Mallette had come in together, such humiliation would reflect badly on John Henry, too.

Besides, he just didn't like bullies.

He stepped up behind Gunderson and tapped the giant on the shoulder. "Hey."

Gunderson let go of Mallette's wrists, swung around ponderously, and glared at John Henry with an expression as dark and ominous as a storm cloud about to break. "What the hell do you want?"

"If you've got a problem with my partner there, you've got a problem with me," John Henry said.

"Oh? Is that right?" A broad grin creased Gunderson's face, and even though John Henry would have doubted that it was possible, the expression made the man even uglier. "What do you figure on doin' about it?"

"This." John Henry launched a punch at Gunderson's head.

Chapter Ten

John Henry put a lot of power behind the punch. The blow landed solidly on the big man's jaw. It should have put Gunderson on the floor.

But he just stood there. His head had barely moved, and the grin on his face wasn't the least bit shaken.

John Henry uttered a heartfelt, "Ahhh, hell!"

The giant let out a bellow as his hands shot out and grabbed John Henry by the shoulders. The grip felt like a pair of bear traps snapping shut.

His feet came off the floor, and before he knew what was happening he found himself flying through the air. He came down hard on one of the bunks and bounced off to land on the floor. The bunk was probably all that saved him from at least one broken bone. The impact was still enough to drive the air from his lungs and leave him gasping.

The sound of Gunderson's feet stomping across the floor toward him was like a buffalo stampede.

That warning penetrated John Henry's stunned mind and galvanized him into action.

He rolled desperately to the side as one of the huge man's massive, booted feet crashed down on the space where John Henry's head had been an instant earlier. It would have crushed his skull like an eggshell if he hadn't gotten out of the way.

He reached up, grabbed Gunderson's leg, and heaved. That trick had always upended an opponent.

Gunderson just stood there for a moment, unmoving as a mountain, leering down at him. Then he lifted his foot to kick John Henry in the face.

Once again, John Henry rolled out of the way of that massive boot just in time. He came up on hands and knees and scrambled a couple yards before climbing to his feet.

He could have drawn his gun and blown a hole through his hulking opponent, but at that moment he wasn't sure if a bullet would even slow down the runaway freight train that was Sven Gunderson, let alone stop him. Besides, he had started this bareknuckles brawl, and he had to finish it the same way if the men in the bunkhouse were ever going to respect him.

Gunderson charged, swinging wild punches with the hammer-like fists at the end of his tree trunk arms. He was surprisingly fast, but had no technique whatsoever.

Probably he had never needed any boxing ability to win a fight. His size, reach, and strength would have been enough.

John Henry ducked under the looping swings and shot a pair of punches, left and right, into Gunderson's belly.

His fists just bounced futilely off the layered, rock-hard slabs of muscle.

While John Henry was close, Gunderson tried to envelop him in a bear hug that would lead to broken ribs and possibly death. John Henry twisted away from the deadly embrace and shot an uppercut to Gunderson's chin.

Once again, it was like punching rock.

So, the big man didn't have a glass jaw, and hitting him on the button didn't do the job, either. John Henry moved back, breathing hard.

His hands ached. He knew he was going to wind up breaking his knuckles if he kept on pounding away at the seemingly invulnerable Gunderson.

Everybody had a weak spot, though. It was just a matter of finding it. John Henry didn't like to fight dirty, but sometimes a man didn't have any choice.

As Gunderson charged again, John Henry kicked him in the groin.

Gunderson laughed and flicked out a punch that clipped John Henry on the jaw.

Even that glancing blow was like a stick of dynamite exploding in his face. He flew backward and rammed up against one of the thick beams that supported the bunkhouse roof. His vision blurred and he would have fallen if not for the beam at his back.

His sight cleared in time to see a fist that looked like it would have filled a bucket rocketing at his face. John Henry's legs were unsteady to start with, so he let them fold up and dropped out of the way. Gunderson's fist slammed into the beam.

That brought an actual grunt of pain from the giant and caused the grin to disappear from his face. He bellowed again and tried to kick John Henry. The lawman flung himself out of the way and rolled across the floor.

As he came up to one knee, he saw something unexpected. Nick Mallette leaped at Gunderson from behind and landed on the big man's back. He wrapped his legs around Gunderson's waist and started flailing punches at his head.

Gunderson brought up his left arm and drove his elbow back at Mallette's head. It was as casual and effective as swatting away a bug. Mallette sailed through the air and came crashing down on one of the bunks.

The gambler deserved some credit for trying. And his attack served one purpose. It had distracted Gunderson long enough for John Henry to get his feet under him and set himself for another punch. There was one spot he hadn't tried yet. . . .

As Gunderson turned back toward him, John Henry darted forward and snapped a sharp right to the big man's nose.

The punch landed perfectly, and hot blood spurted under John Henry's knuckles as Gunderson howled in pain. As he took an involuntary step back, the first time he had been rocked in this fight, John Henry bored in and shot a left hook to the same place.

Another right followed it with blinding speed. Crimson welled from Gunderson's nose and coated the lower half of his face as tears of pain trickled down his cheeks.

Gunderson brought up his ham-like hands, but instead of striking out at John Henry, he pressed them over his face to protect his bleeding nose. As he stumbled backward, his legs bumped against one of the bunks and he folded up on it, rolling awkwardly onto his side and drawing his knees up as he curled into a ball. He whimpered pathetically.

John Henry almost felt sorry for him.

Almost.

Some of the other outlaws had called out encouragement to Gunderson during the battle, not that he had appeared to need any. Now they stood around, looking on in stunned silence . . . as if they were seeing something they had never witnessed before.

That was entirely possible. It might have been the first time Gunderson had ever lost a fight, maybe in his entire life.

A female voice confirmed that, saying coolly, "You just chopped down a tree with your bare hands, Saxon. How does that feel?"

John Henry looked over at the door and saw

Lottie Dalmas standing there, one shoulder propped against the jamb. He summoned up a smile, flexed his fingers, and answered her question. "Sore as hell."

"Your hands will hurt worse come morning," Lottie said as she straightened. "You ought to soak them in some brine. Simon, why don't you see about that?"

"Sure, Lottie," Garrett replied.

"A man as fast on the draw as Saxon is supposed to be, we don't want his hands so stiff they won't work." Lottie turned to leave, but paused. "Bring the two new men to supper in the main house tonight."

"Sure," Garrett said again, but he didn't sound quite so happy about it.

The blond gunman took John Henry to the cook shack. Mallette tagged along, still holding his chin and working his jaw back and forth to make sure nothing was broken.

"It felt like he walloped me with a two-by-four," Mallette explained.

Garrett ignored that and told John Henry, "Nobody ever put Sven down before. Probably because nobody ever got close enough to hit him in the nose like that. He's got arms like an ape. If he'd ever gotten hold of you, Saxon . . ."

"I know," John Henry said. "I was lucky."

"Or smart. How'd you know to hit him in the nose?"

"It was the only place I *hadn't* hit him so far."

At the cook shack, Garrett introduced John Henry and Mallette to the cook, a gnarled, whiskery old-timer named Cribbins.

"Fix up a pot of brine so Saxon can soak his hands," Garrett told the old man. "He just knocked Sven Gunderson down and had him bawling like a baby."

Cribbins peered owlishly at Garrett. "You been guzzlin' quarts of bust-head? I thought it sounded like you said this fella just whipped that big ol' Swede."

"That's what happened," Garrett assured him. "You're not any more surprised than the rest of us."

Cribbins looked John Henry up and down. "I been rustlin' grub for bad hombres for nigh on to thirty years, and I never seen a varmint like the Swede before. He's half-horse, half-bear, and half-gator. And a scrawny little fella like you whipped him?"

Mallette said, "You can't always judge by appearances."

"No, but sometimes you can . . . tinhorn." Cribbins snorted. "Sit down on that barrel over yonder, Saxon. I'll fix up a bucket of brine for you."

Garrett said, "I'll come back to get you later. Don't let Lottie asking you to supper go to your head, Saxon. She's just being polite."

"Sure," John Henry said. "I understand."

When Garrett was gone, Cribbins said, "You're eatin' supper with the Flame tonight?"

"You mean Miss Dalmas?"

"Some folks call her the Flame of the Prairie on

account of that hair of hers. Sometimes it looks like it's brown, but other times it looks like it's on fire. All depends on the light."

"She doesn't invite all the new men to supper?"

Cribbins just looked scornfully at him.

That was all the answer John Henry needed.

When he and Mallette left the cook shack an hour later, his hands weren't as stiff and sore as they had been before he soaked them in the brine. They might still be a little painful to use, but John Henry didn't think his draw would be slowed down any. That was the important thing.

Quietly, Mallette said, "I think our new friend Mr. Garrett is a bit jealous of the attention our hostess is paying you."

"You were invited to supper, too, you know," John Henry pointed out.

"Yeah, but that's only because I rode in with you. I don't mind saying that I've always been pretty lucky with the ladies, but I know when one of them is interested in me and when she isn't. You're the one Miss Dalmas has her eye on, John."

"I didn't come here for romance. All I want is to lie low for a while, let the hue and cry over our escape die down, and then move on. I had thought about seeing if I could get a job at the Anvil, even after shooting Deverill, but I reckon that's out of the question now."

"You wanted to ride for J.C. Carson?"

John Henry looked over at Mallette. "You know the man?"

"Only by reputation," the gambler said. "I always

keep my ears open when I'm in a new town, and I heard quite a bit about Carson before Sheriff Rasmussen realized I was wanted and clapped me in jail."

"What do they say about him?"

Under the circumstances, John Henry wasn't sure why he was interested in the rancher unless it was just habit. A wise man asked questions and learned as much as he could about everything that went on around him.

"That he's pretty ruthless about getting whatever he wants. His foreman, Dell Bartlett, has a reputation as a gunman, and so do most of the other men who work for him. He's been feuding with the other big cattleman in the area, Jed Montayne, for years."

"Sounds like a range war in the making," John Henry commented.

"Yeah. A setup like that would be a good opportunity for a man like you to make some money if you weren't already running from the law."

"There's always somebody else who needs a hired gun," John Henry said offhandedly. "If it's not this range war, there'll be another one coming along before you know it."

He was wary as he and Mallette went into the bunkhouse. It was possible that Sven Gunderson might be lying in wait for him and want to get even.

Gunderson just sat on his bunk, though, and glared at John Henry and Mallette as they came in. His nose had stopped bleeding, but it was swollen and somebody had fastened a plaster on it, the white color standing out in stark contrast against Gunderson's deeply tanned face.

John Henry got a clean shirt from his gear and washed up at the pump behind the bunkhouse, dousing his head and shaking it to make the water fly away from his hair.

Mallette didn't have any extra clothes, but he stuck his head under the water, too, to get rid of the trail dust. The two of them looked slightly more presentable when Simon Garrett came to get them and escort them to the main house for their supper with Lottie Dalmas, the so-called Flame of the Prairie.

Chapter Eleven

"You two be on your best behavior," Garrett warned them as they went in.

"I always am around a beautiful woman," Mallette said. That comment drew a frown from the outlaw, which the gambler blithely ignored.

The house was furnished like most ranch headquarters, with heavy chairs and divans, a long dining table, thick rugs on the floor, an assortment of rifles and shotguns hanging on pegs, and a massive fireplace that would provide heat in the winter but was cold at that time of year. Oil lamps in wagon wheel chandeliers that hung from the ceiling cast a smoky yellow glow over the room.

The stuffed and mounted heads of several antelope were displayed on the wall above the fireplace. They looked a little moth-eaten, like they had been there a while—probably trophies belonging to the ranch's original owner. The other furnishings appeared to be relatively new.

Lottie Dalmas was waiting for them in front of

the fireplace. She wore a dark blue dress with a low, square-cut, white-trimmed neckline that revealed the creamy, freckle-dusted upper swells of her breasts.

The dress meant she wasn't wearing a holstered revolver anymore, and John Henry didn't think she could hide a sheathed bowie knife in the outfit, either.

The fact she was unarmed didn't mean she was any less dangerous, though. Any woman who could run an outlaw sanctuary and apparently rule it with an iron hand had to be respected at all times.

"Good evening, gentlemen," she greeted John Henry and Mallette. "Thank you for joining me. How are your hands, Mr. Saxon?"

"They'll be all right," John Henry said. "I might think twice about picking another fight with your friend Gunderson, though. Punching him was sort of like punching a stone wall."

Garrett grunted, but didn't say anything.

"Not exactly," Lottie said. "Show them, Simon."

Garrett hedged. "I don't think—"

"I said show them." The sharp tone of her voice removed any lingering doubt about who was the boss.

Garrett hesitated, but only for a moment. Then he lifted his left hand and used his right to tug the buckskin glove off.

"Good Lord," Mallette said under his breath.

John Henry didn't say anything and managed

to keep his face impassive, but what he saw was shocking.

Simon Garrett's left hand was twisted and misshapen and covered with angry scars that looked like they hadn't been there long. It was like someone had taken a hammer and brutally smashed every bone in his hand. The fingers were stiff and immobile, hooked permanently into bent claws. He could hold a horse's reins with them, but that was all they would be good for.

"That's what punching a stone wall is like," Lottie said softly. "And Simon inflicted that punishment on himself."

"Why would anybody do that?" Mallette asked.

"I was in prison," Garrett said. In an impressive display of self-control, his face and voice betrayed no emotion. "I got word that my brother was dead. I didn't think about what I was doing. I was just so full of hate right then that it had to come out somehow."

A ghost of a smile appeared on his lips. "I wasn't completely loco. I didn't use my gun hand. But every time my fist hit the wall, it was like I was dealing out punishment to the men responsible for Henry's death."

"Henry Garrett," John Henry said. "That name's familiar. I think I've heard it. He used to lead a gang of desperadoes up in these parts."

"It was my gang!" Garrett stopped short and drew in a deep breath. When he resumed, he sounded calm and in control again.

"It was my gang starting out, and then I landed behind bars. Henry took over. He wasn't much more than a kid, but he kept the bunch together."

Henry Garrett had done more than that. The information John Henry had gotten from Judge Parker made it clear that Henry had led the gang on more daring and successful raids than his older brother ever had. That must have bothered Simon if he had heard about it while he was in prison.

Any resentment he felt hadn't diminished his love for his brother, though, otherwise he wouldn't have smashed his own hand in blind rage when he heard that Henry had been hanged. Judge Ephraim Doolittle's idea that Simon Garrett was behind the murders of Charles Houston and Lucas Winslow had to be right.

But there might be more to it than that. So far it seemed that Lottie Dalmas was pulling Garrett's strings. What was her connection with the Garrett brothers?

And why had she made Simon Garrett reveal his self-mutilated hand to two strangers?

"I owe Henry a lot," Garrett went on. "That's why I swore a vow that I'd settle the score for him. But Lottie's the one who showed me how."

"It's the judge and the jury who are to blame for Henry's death," Lottie said. "Along with the sheriff, of course, but Rasmussen is a fool. It was pure luck that he captured Henry. The judge, though, and the men who sat on that jury, they were the ones who made sure that he died. They're the ones who need to pay. It's not enough just to kill them, though."

She smiled coldly. "They need to suffer first, and nothing makes a man suffer more than being scared. Deep down, lying in his bed at night, soaked in a cold sweat scared. That's why they're dying one by one."

"And that was your idea," John Henry said.

"It was." Lottie's voice held a note of macabre pride.

Nick Mallette said, "That's . . . quite a story. But why are you telling us about it?"

"We can always use another good man," Garrett said. "Saxon's the sort of hombre I'd like to have riding with us. Revenge for Henry isn't all we're after. Before we're through, we're going to strip this whole part of the country. Every bank, every express shipment on the railroads, every herd of cattle on the ranches. It'll be a cleanup like nobody's ever seen before. We'll make all the other outlaw gangs out there look like pikers."

That was certainly an ambitious goal. Whether Garrett and his bunch could pull it off was pretty doubtful, even with Lottie Dalmas masterminding their plans. Eventually the law would catch up to them and smash them.

But before that happened, a lot of innocent people might die. Others might be ruined.

John Henry knew he needed to put a stop to it before Garrett drew in even more thieves and killers and the gang got too big to stop without a lot of bloodshed. "Those are big plans. I wouldn't mind being part of them. But what's to stop a posse from coming in here and wiping out the whole lot of you?"

"Nobody knows we're holed up here. Everybody in these parts thinks this ranch is abandoned and has been for years. Besides, you saw that trail up the bluff. It's the only way for miles around to reach this spot. We keep guards at the head of it all the time. Four men with rifles can hold off a posse from there. Hell, they could hold off an army!"

"What about from the northwest?"

Lottie explained. "There's a deep ravine about two miles from here in that direction. It's too deep and the walls are too sheer for horses to get across, and it runs for miles, just like that rimrock on the other side. We have men patrolling it, just in case anyone tries to sneak up on us. We might as well be in a fortress here."

"But if that's true, then you're bottled up, too," John Henry pointed out. "A posse could keep you from getting out, just like you can keep them from getting in."

Lottie just smiled and didn't say anything. She didn't seem concerned about the possibility John Henry had raised—which meant she had at least one more card to play. But it didn't look like she was going to reveal it.

"The food is ready," she said. "Let's eat."

She led them over to the long table, where Simon Garrett held her chair for her when she sat down at the head of the table. John Henry and Mallette waited until Lottie was seated before they took their chairs. They were to Lottie's left, facing Garrett to her right across the table.

A Mexican woman Lottie called Valencia brought in platters of beefsteak, potatoes, and greens, along with loaves of fresh-baked bread and a bowl of gravy. The steaks probably came from rustled cows, but it was possible the Silver Skull Ranch raised a few head of beef to feed its visitors.

The food and coffee were good. The plump, middle-aged Valencia obviously took care of the house while Cribbins rustled grub for the rest of the outfit. She did a fine job of it.

John Henry and Mallette made small talk. Lottie would get back to the plan she and Simon Garrett were carrying out when she was good and ready. John Henry didn't see any need to rush her and maybe make her suspicious.

That moment came after supper, after Valencia had filled snifters from a cut-crystal decanter of brandy and passed them around the table. Lottie lifted hers. "To revenge."

"To revenge," Garrett echoed.

John Henry and Mallette lifted their glasses, but didn't say anything.

After everyone drank, Lottie looked over at John Henry. "Are you sure you're interested in joining up with us, John? You didn't know Henry. You don't have any personal reason to risk your life avenging him."

"I like the setup you have here, from what I've seen of it so far. Looks like a good deal in the long run for a man like me. I'd say that helping you out now would be a good investment for my future."

Garrett snorted contemptuously. "Most men in our line of work don't think past the next job. Hell, they don't think past the next bottle of whiskey or the next woman."

Lottie took another sip of her brandy. "John's not a common outlaw. You can tell that just by talking to him."

"Oh, I'm on the wrong side of the law, you can be sure of that." John Henry was aware that Garrett was frowning again, probably because of Lottie's flattery of him.

It was like she was trying to stir up trouble . . . which was entirely possible. One way to judge a man was to see how he reacted when things went wrong.

"How about you, Nick?" Lottie asked the gambler. "Are you interested in staying with us for a while?"

"Well, I was sort of planning to move on to California sooner or later," Mallette said. "I've always heard about the Barbary Coast in San Francisco. I think I'd like to see it for myself and try my luck in the saloons and gambling halls there. But I suppose that can wait. I don't mind lending a hand here for the time being, if you think I can be of help."

"You're the sort of man who'd make a good spy. Not in Kiowa City, of course, because you're already known as a fugitive there. But later, when our bigger plans get started. Information is going to be important to us."

Mallette grinned. "Tongues wag over a game of cards. That's a good place to pick up rumors about money shipments and payrolls and the sort of things you'd need to know."

"You're a thinking man, too," Lottie said. "I like that."

"Thinking's fine," Garrett snapped, "but sooner or later this business comes down to fighting."

"From what I saw in the bunkhouse, John can handle that part of it just fine. And if he gunned down Jimmy Deverill, he's good with that part, too."

John Henry just sipped his brandy. His goal in getting himself arrested had been to bust out of jail and then infiltrate the gang responsible for the murders of Charles Houston and Lucas Winslow so he could stop them from wiping out the rest of the jury and Judge Doolittle. So far it seemed to be working, but he still had to be careful.

"Of course we can't let just anyone join up with us, you know," Lottie went on. "You might be planning to double-cross us. You might even be working for the law."

Mallette said, "No offense, ma'am, but you couldn't be more wrong about that. Even before I got that trumped-up murder charge levied against me, I was usually walking on the shady side of the street. And John here, well, from the sound of it, he's been mixed up in even more things than I have, or that fellow Deverill wouldn't have thrown down on him."

"I believe you, Nick. But still, just for my own piece of mind, I'd like to be sure."

She nodded to Garrett, who scraped his chair back and stood up. An unpleasant smile played around the corners of the outlaw's mouth. He walked over to the front door and opened it. "Bring him in."

John Henry's fingers tightened on the brandy snifter. Whatever these two were up to, it couldn't be good.

It was even worse than he expected. Two of the gang came into the room, dragging an unconscious man between them. Two more followed with drawn guns.

John Henry set his drink down and rose to his feet, turning toward the newcomers. He fought to keep his face from revealing the bleak anger that flooded through him.

The two men dropped their unconscious burden on the floor practically at John Henry's feet. The round, bland face of Deputy Carl Baird, now battered and bloody, stared up at him.

Baird was out cold, but he was still alive. John Henry was able to make out the ragged rising and falling of the star packer's chest.

"If you're as far on the wrong side of the law as you claim, John," Lottie said coolly from the head of the table, "then you won't mind putting a bullet through this deputy's brain."

Chapter Twelve

"My God!" Nick Mallette exclaimed as he leaped to his feet. "That's Carl Baird, one of the deputies from Kiowa City."

"I know," Lottie said. "A couple of our men jumped him after he got separated from the posse Sheriff Rasmussen brought out to search for you and John. They thought he might turn out to be useful, so they brought him back here."

John Henry rested his hand on the butt of his Colt. "I don't know. He seemed pretty harmless to me, but if you want him dead—"

"No!" Mallette cried. "Damn it, John. I already had to stop you from cutting his throat—"

"What did you say?" Garrett broke in.

"When we broke out of jail, Carl was the deputy John jumped," Mallette explained. "He wanted to go ahead and kill him then. He was going to . . . to cut his throat."

"Then he shouldn't mind killing him now," Lottie said calmly.

John Henry started again to draw his gun. "I don't mind. It's liable to get your floor a little messy, though."

"Wait, wait!" Mallette said. "Baird always treated me decent. I'd hate to see him killed for no good reason."

"Oh, the hell with this." John Henry's gun came out of leather. He pointed it at Baird's head and eared back the hammer.

Mallette took a quick step toward him and grabbed his wrist. John Henry let the gambler force the gun up, away from Baird, but he turned sharply toward Mallette. "What the hell do you think you're doing?"

"I'm sorry, John. I . . . I just think it would be a mistake to kill the deputy." Mallette licked his lips and went on hurriedly. "We might be able to get more use out of him later on."

"How do you figure that?" Garrett's voice dripped with disdain.

"Well . . . I know you said the law can't get to you here, Miss Dalmas, but what if that happened sometime despite all your precautions? You might need a hostage, and the deputy would be a good one."

"Are you saying we should keep him prisoner here?" Lottie asked.

"That makes sense to me. There's really no point in killing him."

"What about to prove that John really wants to be one of us? Wouldn't that be a good reason?"

"He's already come within a whisker of killing

the deputy twice! That ought to be proof enough, shouldn't it?"

"And you've stopped me twice," John Henry said coldly. "You've laid hands on me, too. I don't cotton to that, and I won't forget it, either."

Mallette let go of John Henry's wrist and stepped back. "I'm sorry. I know it doesn't make sense to you, to any of you. But I just think it would be smarter to keep Deputy Baird alive for the time being."

A tense silence stretched for several seconds. Finally, Lottie said, "I suppose you might have a point, Nick."

Garrett disagreed. "If we keep that damned lawman alive, we'll have to feed him and keep a guard on him all the time. I say it's too much trouble."

"We can afford the provisions, and some of the men could use something to do, to keep them out of trouble," Lottie said. "Put your gun up, John."

"Are you sure?" John Henry asked. "He helped Rasmussen get the drop on me in the saloon. The way I see it, I've got a score to settle with the varmint."

"There might be a better time to settle it."

"Fine," John Henry said grumpily. He lowered the revolver's hammer and pouched the iron. "But when that time comes, I want to be the one who sends him over the divide."

"Third time is the charm," Lottie said with a smile. She flicked a hand at Baird's unconscious form. "Get him out of here. Lock him up in the smokehouse. That'll make a good prison for him."

John Henry continued glaring at Mallette as two outlaws picked Baird up and dragged him out. The other two gunmen went with them.

That had been a close call and had almost ruined everything, John Henry thought. But thanks to Mallette's reaction, John Henry's pose as an outlaw and gun-wolf was still intact. If Mallette hadn't spoken up the way he had, the past few minutes might have gone considerably differently.

Lottie said, "Why don't we all sit down and finish our brandy, gentlemen?"

Garrett held her chair for her again.

"When will you be making another move in your plan?" John Henry asked.

"Are you eager for action, John?"

He shrugged. "I've never been much of one for sitting around and doing nothing."

"Be patient," Lottie advised him. "Some things can't be rushed. Vengeance is one of them. But when the time comes, you'll be part of it."

John Henry nodded. He had to be satisfied with that, at least for the moment. He hoped it wouldn't be too long before there would be new developments, though.

He was used to living on the knife edge of danger, but this one was pretty damned sharp.

Simon Garrett stood on the front porch of the main house smoking a cigar and watching the two new men go back to the bunkhouse. From time to time his jaw clenched and his teeth clamped down hard on the cylinder of tightly rolled tobacco. Without taking off the glove, he used his right hand to massage the left hand.

"Hurting tonight?" Lottie asked from behind him.

He turned his head to look over his shoulder. Most of the lamps in the house had been blown out. Only a faint glow came through the open door to silhouette her sleek body in the thin silk wrapper she wore.

"It's fine," Garrett said. "No worse than it always is."

"Pain can be a helpful reminder of what we have to do."

"I suppose." Garrett paused. "I could have done without having to show it off to those two strangers."

Lottie didn't apologize. The notorious Flame never did. "They're not strangers now. They're allies."

Garrett snorted. "Mallette's a weakling. He'll never be any good to us."

"You never know about things like that. Anyway, he came in with Saxon, and I didn't want to risk losing him."

"It didn't seem to me like they're that close."

"But why take a chance? It doesn't cost us anything to let Mallette live for a while, just like that deputy."

Garrett puffed on the cigar and blew out a cloud of smoke that was silver in the moonlight. "I don't see why you're so bound and determined to bring Saxon into the bunch. Sure, he must be fast on the draw if he downed Deverill, but plenty of men are good with a gun. I'm pretty fast myself."

"He's insurance," Lottie said.

"Insurance? Against what?"

"Deverill was probably the most dangerous man on Carson's payroll," she explained. "That means if Carson decides to double-cross us later on, we'll have a better chance of stopping him."

"Carson's not going to double-cross us. When he was here earlier, he seemed satisfied with the way things are going."

"What about once he's gotten what he wants and doesn't need us anymore?" Lottie asked. "He might be satisfied with the way things work out and still betray us."

"He'd be a damned fool to do that. The whole thing would come back on him as bad or worse than it does on us. Hell, it was all his idea!"

"He thinks it was his idea." Lottie's voice was steely. "I would have gone after Doolittle and the others, anyway. They deserve to die for what they did to Henry." Her words took on a tone of dry amusement. "Getting Carson to pay us for settling the score is just a bonus."

Garrett flicked the cigar butt into the yard in front of the ranch house. "Maybe so," he said, but didn't sound completely convinced.

Lottie put a hand on his arm. "Stop worrying and come on to bed, Simon. I haven't steered you wrong yet, have I? Everything will work out fine.

If you're worried about Saxon, we'll keep an eye on him and take care of him at the first sign of trouble. And when we don't need him anymore . . . we'll get rid of him just like Mallette. Simple as that."

"Can't be soon enough to suit me." Garrett turned and took Lottie into his arms.

Chapter Thirteen

The next few days were tense ones for John Henry. There wasn't much to do on the Silver Skull Ranch. He stood a couple turns on guard duty at the head of the trail, near the giant rock formation that looked so much like a human skull from a distance.

Other than that, he hung around the bunkhouse, getting to know the other members of the gang and subtly pumping them for information about the plan Lottie Dalmas and Simon Garrett had hatched to avenge Henry Garrett.

The problem was that the men didn't know much and cared even less. Lottie and Garrett had promised them a big payoff in the long run, and for the time being they had whiskey and cards to pass the time, along with an occasional train robbery to keep some loot flowing. It was pretty much all they cared about. They just followed orders when the time came.

The mention of a big payoff intrigued John

Henry. He couldn't see how murdering the members of the jury that had convicted Henry Garrett, along with the judge who had presided over the trial, was going to profit the outlaws anything. That question just added to his sense that more was going on than he knew about.

Garrett came to him one morning. "Saddle up your horse, Saxon. You'll be riding out to the ravine today to keep an eye on it."

"All right," John Henry replied with a nod. He had been wanting to take a look at that ravine, so he was fine with the job. "Anybody else going along?"

"Yeah, I'll send a couple of other men, too. Anybody in particular you want to work with?"

John Henry shook his head. "That's up to you. It doesn't really matter to me."

"Fine. Be ready to ride in ten minutes."

John Henry found Mallette in the bunkhouse and told him he was riding out to the ravine.

"I wish I could come with you, John." Mallette looked around the room and lowered his voice. "I get the feeling most of these fellas still don't like me much."

"Go find Garrett and ask him if you can come along," John Henry suggested.

"Yeah, I'll do that." Mallette hurried out.

John Henry went to the barn and saddled Iron Heart. He was leading the big gray outside when Mallette approached and shook his head.

"Garrett said he'd already given the job to a

couple other men and wanted me to stay here at the ranch. I've got a bad feeling about this, John."

"You'll be fine," John Henry said. "Just stay out of everybody's way."

"I'll try." Mallette paused. "I'm glad you haven't held a grudge against me for what happened the other day."

"You mean that business with the deputy?" John Henry shrugged. "You helped me out when it came to escaping from that jail, Nick, and I helped you. That made us pards. I'm not going to forget that. Just don't lay hands on me again."

"I won't," Mallette promised. "Be careful out there at the ravine, John. I don't really trust Garrett."

John Henry smiled. "I've lived this long by not really trusting anybody."

A few minutes later he rode northwest with a couple outlaws named Purcell and Byrne, who had handled the duty before and knew the trail to use. It didn't take long to reach the ravine where three more members of the gang were waiting for them.

The men going off duty waved and rode past them toward the ranch.

Purcell reined in and told John Henry, "We divide the ground into three sections and ride back and forth along the ravine. Since you're new, Saxon, we'll give you the middle section and make it easy for you. Ride a couple miles northeast, then turn around, come back here, and ride a couple miles southwest. Four miles, back and forth, with this rendezvous as the center point. Got it?"

"Sounds simple enough," John Henry said. "What am I looking for?"

"Anybody trying to get across that ravine. If they do, you stop 'em."

"Has anybody ever done that?"

"Not while I've been around here," Purcell admitted. "But it could happen one of these days, and the Flame doesn't like to take any chances."

"The Flame of the Prairie," John Henry mused. "That's what I heard somebody call her the other day."

"Never you mind about that. Just do your job."

John Henry nodded. "Sure. How long do I stay out here?"

"Until we come back and get you."

John Henry nodded again. Purcell and Byrne rode off, vanishing in opposite directions along the giant slash in the earth.

John Henry walked Iron Heart along the rim, studying the ravine to his left. He wasn't sure what had formed it. While he knew something about geology, he was far from an expert on the subject.

The ravine was at least fifty feet deep and maybe half that distance wide. It ran fairly straight, almost as if a giant pair of hands had dug in its thumbs and split the earth open along here, like peeling an orange.

The walls were almost sheer, but they were rugged. A man could probably climb down in there and back out again, although he would be risking a bad fall if he slipped. There was no way a horse could handle those slopes, though.

John Henry supposed that if the ravine were unguarded, a large enough force to take the outlaw stronghold might climb into and out of it and sneak up on the place on foot. For the most part, though, the Silver Skull appeared to be as impregnable as Lottie claimed it was.

The sound of hoofbeats made him rein in and turn to look toward the ranch. He spotted a rider a couple hundred yards away, coming toward him at a trot.

Even at that distance, John Henry could tell how big the man was. His eyes narrowed.

It was Sven Gunderson.

John Henry waited where he was, a few yards from the edge of the ravine. He didn't know what Gunderson was doing out there, but suspected it couldn't be anything good.

Maybe he was jumping to conclusions. All he knew was that he was going to continue to be watchful and careful. He rested his right hand on his thigh near the butt of his gun.

Gunderson reined in when he was about ten feet away. He didn't have the plaster on his nose anymore, but it was still red and swollen. He glared at John Henry. "Garrett told me to come out here and help you, since you're the new man."

"I don't need any help," John Henry said. "You can go back to the ranch and tell him that."

Gunderson snorted. "Tell him I didn't follow orders? I don't think so. Have you seen his hand?"

"I've seen it," John Henry replied curtly.

"That's what he did to himself when he was

mad. What do you think he'd do to somebody else if they riled him?" A hollow laugh came from the big man. "If you'd seen some of the things he's done to the men he hates . . ."

John Henry started to say something about the murders of Charles Houston and Lucas Winslow, but he caught himself in time. The drifting gunman and outlaw he was pretending to be wouldn't know anything about those killings. And "John Saxon" hadn't really been in Kiowa City long enough to have picked up any gossip about them. Instead he said, "If you want to patrol the ravine, go right ahead. Just stay out of my way."

"Garrett said to stay with you."

"Well, he's not here, is he? He won't know where you rode and who you were with unless you tell him. I'm not going to say anything about it."

Gunderson lifted his reins, shrugged, and said grudgingly, "All right, if you—"

He stopped in the middle of his sentence, drove his spurs into his horse's flanks, and sent the animal lunging forward as it screamed in pain. Gunderson's mount was a big bay—a horse had to be big to carry his weight—and the cruel raking of the rowels made it react instantly.

John Henry had suspected some sort of trick, but even though he immediately tried to jerk Iron Heart out of the way, he didn't have quite enough time. Gunderson was on him in the blink of an eye. The bay rammed a shoulder into Iron Heart and staggered the big gray.

John Henry's gun flashed into his hand as

Gunderson kept driving the bay into Iron Heart. Gunderson plucked a coiled lariat from his saddle and slashed at John Henry with it.

The lawman's gun roared, but the heavy lariat struck his arm just as he pulled the trigger and knocked his aim off. The bullet whined harmlessly through empty air.

John Henry realized that Gunderson was trying to force him and Iron Heart over the rim and into the ravine. That had probably been his plan all along. The business about Garrett sending him was just an attempt to catch John Henry off guard.

The gray stood up valiantly to the attack, but the other horse had the advantage in weight and Iron Heart was already off balance from the initial collision.

John Henry kicked his feet out of the stirrups as he felt his mount start to fall. He threw himself out of the saddle as Iron Heart crashed to the ground a few feet short of the edge. Unfortunately, John Henry's momentum carried him toward the brink.

He twisted in midair to slow himself and landed at the very edge of the rim. His free hand clawed at the ground to keep from going over.

Hoofbeats thundered as Gunderson rode at him. John Henry scrambled aside, hoping that Gunderson had cut it too close and would plunge over the edge himself. The big Swede hauled back on his reins and stopped short of the rim.

John Henry had managed to hang on to his gun when he fell. He whipped it up, but before he could fire, the toe of one of Gunderson's boots caught him on the wrist in a vicious kick. The Colt flew out of his fingers and went spinning away.

Gunderson dove out of the saddle and landed on top of him like an avalanche. Gunderson's weight drove the air from his lungs and made his ribs groan.

John Henry snapped a punch at Gunderson's nose, but the man blocked it just in time. Now that he knew his own weak spot, Gunderson would do everything in his power to protect it.

"I'll kill you!" Gunderson growled. "Nobody does what you did to me and gets away with it!" He hammered punches at John Henry's head.

John Henry blocked most of them, but a couple got through and landed with stunning power. His brain was spinning like the wheels of a runaway wagon.

He flung his right leg up and hooked the calf in front of Gunderson's neck. The man was immensely strong, but John Henry had the leverage to push him away for a second—just long enough for the lawman to roll out from under him.

With Gunderson's weight no longer pressing on his chest, John Henry could breathe again. He forced himself to his feet in time to meet Gunderson's charge.

The Swede's sledgehammer fists exploded through the air. John Henry ducked and weaved and even though a few of Gunderson's punches caught him, they were only glancing blows.

Even so, that was more punishment than he could continue to absorb for very long. He had to find some way to reach the big man's nose again if he was going to have any hope of surviving the battle.

Gunderson windmilled a right. John Henry leaned away from the flailing blow and kicked Gunderson in the stomach, hoping that would double the big man over and bring his nose down where he could hit it.

Gunderson grunted and stumbled a little, but that was his only reaction. He brought his right around in a backhand that landed on John Henry's shoulder. John Henry's arm went numb from the force of the blow, and it sent him tumbling off his feet.

Both men were still dangerously close to the edge. As John Henry fell, he scrambled with hands and feet for purchase to keep from rolling off.

He caught himself, raised his head, looked past Gunderson, and saw that the two horses were fighting it out as well. Iron Heart and the bay had reared up on their hind legs and were slashing at each other with their fore hooves.

John Henry would have helped his old friend, but he had his hands full at the moment. Gunderson bull-rushed him again and tried to sweep him into a bear hug.

For a second, the deputy marshal considered letting Gunderson grab him, on the chance that he could then reach the Swede's nose, but it was too risky. Gunderson might crush his ribs before he could do enough damage to the big man's weak spot.

John Henry darted and twisted aside. He clubbed both hands together and smashed them into the small of Gunderson's back. The impact made Gunderson take a stumbling step toward the edge.

John Henry hit him again with both hands. If he could land enough blows like that, he might be able to drive Gunderson over the brink.

Gunderson caught himself and turned with shocking speed. One of his ape-like arms flashed up and his fist landed on John Henry's jaw. The brutal punch sent John Henry to the ground again.

Gunderson pounced like an ape, too. One hand locked around John Henry's upper left arm, the other caught hold of John Henry's thigh. "Now you'll pay for what you did!" Gunderson bellowed as he held John Henry over his head. Dust flew around his feet as he stampeded toward the edge.

To his horror, John Henry realized that Gunderson intended to throw him into the ravine, where he would plummet to almost certain death.

Chapter Fourteen

In the seconds he had left before disaster befell him, John Henry realized that Gunderson had made a mistake. Dangling from the big man's hands, he could finally reach the outlaw's tender nose.

He kicked it as hard as he could, driving a boot heel into the center of Gunderson's face with enough force to rend cartilage and shatter bone.

Gunderson howled and let go of John Henry to clap both hands over his ruined face. The lawman fell awkwardly onto Gunderson's shoulders as the giant leaned forward, stumbling from the blinding agony of the kick. John Henry's weight made him pitch forward, out of control and unable to stop himself.

He went head-first over the ravine's edge.

Gunderson's horrified bellow filled the air as John Henry landed at the very brink. He couldn't stop, and slid over, plummeting down.

He fell for only a fraction of a second before he

crashed into something that stopped his fall. He slapped his hands against the earthen wall of the ravine and dug his fingers into it. He clung there, his heart pounding from the fear of falling.

When his brain was working clearly again, he lifted his head to look around. He had landed on a tiny ledge about ten feet below the rim, barely wide enough to support him and only about four feet long. He'd been lucky to land perfectly. Otherwise, he would have continued falling all the way to the bottom.

For the moment, he was stable. He breathed heavily until his pulse stopped racing. Then he took stock of the situation and tried to figure out his next move.

He couldn't climb up out of the ravine from where he was, that was for sure. The part of the wall right above him was sheer, with no protruding roots or knobs that could serve as handholds.

But he couldn't stay where he was, so if he couldn't climb up, maybe he could climb down. He craned his neck and twisted it so he could look below him.

The first thing he saw was Gunderson's body. The big man lay facedown at the bottom of the ravine, unmoving. For the moment at least, he was no longer a threat.

John Henry spotted a little crevice about six feet below him. If he hung by his hands from the ledge, he could get a boot toe in there. With that to support him, he thought he could reach out to his right and get hold of the wall where it jutted out slightly.

His eyes traced a path of similar handholds and footholds that would be dangerous, but he didn't see any other way to reach the bottom.

Well, short of falling. That thought put a grim smile on his face.

His breathing and pulse back to normal, he got a good grip with his hands and eased his legs off the ledge. Hanging on tightly, he worked his toe into the crevice, then let go with his right hand and reached for that handhold.

It took a good twenty minutes to negotiate the forty feet to the bottom of the ravine, and by the time he dropped the last few feet and landed on solid ground, his nerves were stretched almost to the breaking point and his muscles were trembling from the effort he had made.

But he was down, and he was still alive.

That was more than he could say for Sven Gunderson. His head sat at an odd, unnatural angle on his neck. The Swede was big enough and strong enough to stand up to a lot of punishment, but he couldn't shrug off a broken neck.

John Henry left Gunderson there and started walking along the bottom of the ravine, where patchy grass and a few scrubby bushes grew. As he walked, John Henry scanned the southeast wall for a place where he could climb out.

It wouldn't do him any good to climb out on the northwest side. That would put the ravine between him and his horse, and between him and the ranch, as well.

He hoped Iron Heart was all right. He didn't hear any sounds of the horses fighting anymore.

After the climb down, he wasn't looking forward to making an ascent, but he didn't have any other option except waiting for Purcell and Byrne to come back. He didn't know how they would react when they found out that Gunderson was dead. It would be better to meet them on level ground, with his gun back in its holster.

A clump of brush grew against the base of the wall up ahead. John Henry didn't pay much attention to it at first, but as he came closer he noticed something intriguing. When he reached the brush, he pushed some of it aside to reveal what it concealed.

The dark mouth of a cave lay behind the brush. It was an irregular opening, barely wide enough and tall enough for a man to turn sideways and squeeze through it.

That was interesting—caves weren't that common in this part of the country—but he wasn't curious enough to explore it. He might have walked right on past it, but then he glanced at the wall of the ravine and spotted something else that made him frown.

A number of small ledges jutted out on that wall. They formed a fairly regular pattern that extended all the way up to the rim.

John Henry stiffened as he realized those ledges had been formed by someone hacking away the sod. Positioned like they were, they resembled a ladder going up the side of the ravine. They would make climbing out a lot easier.

He turned back to the cave mouth and fished out the little tin container of matches he carried in his pocket. He took out one of the lucifers and snapped it to life with his thumbnail. When he extended his arm into the cave, the flickering light from the match showed him a narrow passage that twisted away into the darkness under the earth.

The cave was a natural formation; he had no doubt of that. But that wouldn't stop someone from taking advantage of it. Moving sideways, John Henry edged a few feet into the cave and lit another match when the first one had burned down almost to his fingers. He penetrated a little deeper into the underground passage.

He stopped and studied the flame at the end of the match, squinting slightly against its glare as he held it in front of his face. The flame leaned a little toward the opening.

John Henry had thought he could feel air moving, and the match flame confirmed it. There had to be an opening somewhere at the other end of the cave.

Whether it was big enough to allow a person to climb through it or just provided some ventilation, he didn't know. And the only way to find out was to follow the cave all the way to its other end.

He didn't want to do that. There was no telling how far the cave ran or what sort of obstacles he might encounter along the way. He didn't want to risk getting trapped. Besides, he didn't like small, enclosed places to start with.

His nerves were jumping again. He backed toward the opening.

It felt good to step out into the daylight. Before continuing his search for a way out of the ravine, John Henry paused and took stock of his discovery.

Only one explanation really made sense. That cave, either naturally or through the addition of man-made tunnels, ran all the way to the ranch house and served as an escape route that could be used under dire circumstances.

John Henry shuddered at the thought of following that dark, narrow, twisting passage for a couple miles under the earth, but he supposed it would be possible to flee that way if the danger was bad enough. Folks could generally do whatever was necessary to survive.

He wondered if that bolt hole was the work of the Silver Skull's original owner or if Lottie Dalmas was responsible for it. It seemed like something she would have done, a precaution in case the law ever got past her guards.

Of course, if the ranch's original owner had put in the escape route, it was possible Lottie didn't even know about it. John Henry thought that was doubtful, but he couldn't rule it out.

Either way, the cave's existence was another interesting bit of information he filed away in his brain, along with a myriad of other things that might come in handy later on.

He resumed his search, and twenty minutes

later found a place where the southeast rimrock had caved in slightly, creating a slope that could be climbed.

John Henry was glad to see it. He had been starting to worry that he might have to follow the ravine to its end before he could get out . . . and if that had proven impassible, he might have had to turn around and walk all the way to the other end.

When he reached the top, he paused and had a look around before he showed himself. No riders were in sight. He climbed to his feet and started walking quickly back toward the spot where he and Gunderson had battled. He figured he would find Iron Heart somewhere in that area.

The big gray found him first, trotting toward him and tossing his head as if to ask John Henry where the hell he had been. With only an assortment of scrapes and scratches on him from the fight with the other horse, Iron Horse seemed to be in pretty good shape. He butted John Henry lightly with his nose.

John Henry rubbed it as he laughed. "It's good to see you, Iron Heart."

John Henry didn't see Gunderson's bay anywhere. Unlike Iron Heart, who would never abandon John Henry, the Swede's horse had probably returned to the barn when Gunderson didn't climb out of the ravine.

John Henry swung up into the saddle and rode along the rim until he reached the spot where the Swede had jumped him. He dismounted and glanced into the ravine. After seeing that Gunderson had a broken neck, he hadn't expected the giant to get up and walk around again, but the sight of the sprawled body was reassuring, anyway.

John Henry needed only a few moments to locate the gun he had dropped earlier. He brushed the dirt off it, checked the barrel to make sure it wasn't fouled, and then slid the Colt back into leather. The weight of it on his hip felt good.

With that done, he went back to patrolling the stretch of the ravine as he had been ordered. He wondered if Garrett had really sent Gunderson out here, and if he had, had he told the Swede to kill "John Saxon"? Or had that been totally Gunderson's idea?

He might never know, John Henry realized, and to tell the truth, the answer didn't really matter.

The important thing was that he was still alive and Gunderson was dead.

And the mission that had taken John Henry there in the first place could continue.

Chapter Fifteen

Late in the afternoon, John Henry spotted another rider coming toward him along the ravine from the northeast. It was Purcell, and Byrne soon joined them from the southwest.

"Any problems during the day?" Purcell asked John Henry as the three men gathered at the rim.

"Not a one," John Henry lied with a straight face. "I didn't see a soul."

Byrne pointed. "That looks like a fresh bruise on your jaw."

"Must be the light," John Henry said. "Or one still fading from that scrap the other day."

Both outlaws looked suspicious, but they didn't say anything else.

That told John Henry they must not have known about Gunderson coming out to jump him. "What do we do now?"

Purcell pulled a turnip watch from his vest pocket and opened it to check the time. "Our relief ought to be along in a few minutes. We wait for them, and then we go back to the ranch and take it easy until the next job the boss has for us."

"You mean Garrett."

"Yeah, sure," Purcell said. "Who else?"

"I just sort of had the feeling that Miss Dalmas is really calling the shots around here."

Purcell shrugged. "It's true nobody messes with the Flame."

"How did she come to be running a ranch for outlaws, anyway?" John Henry knew owlhoots liked to gossip as much as anybody.

Purcell hesitated about replying, but Byrne said, "She came by it natural-like. Her daddy was Harley Dalmas."

John Henry shook his head. "Don't reckon I know the name."

"He raised hell all over western Kansas and Nebraska back before the war. The Injuns were causing plenty of trouble then, but they never bothered Harley because he ran guns and whiskey to 'em. Somewhere along the way he met Lottie's ma and married her. When the war came along, he rode with Quantrill and Bloody Bill and got a leg blowed off. But that didn't stop him. After the Rebs surrendered, Harley went back to doin' the only thing he knew, bein' an outlaw. He had to stump around on a peg to do it, though, and came a time he had to quit. He took over this ranch, and the Flame was with him. She wasn't much more'n a kid at the time, but she helped him run it and learned everything he could teach her about bein' a ruthless cutthroat. When he crossed the divide, she just kept on runnin' the place."

Purcell said disgustedly, "Do you have any words left in that scrawny carcass of yours, or did you spew 'em all out?"

"Well, hell, the man asked a question, and Lottie never said not to tell anybody about her past, did she?"

"Maybe not, but that doesn't mean you've got to spill your guts, and hers, too."

John Henry said, "I won't mention hearing the story. I appreciate you satisfying my curiosity, though, Byrne."

The outlaw was starting to look a little worried that maybe he had said too much after all. He told John Henry, "Just don't go blabbin' about it, and we'll be fine."

"You've got a deal."

A few minutes later, the three outlaws taking their place on guard duty came into view. As they rode up and reined in, one of the newcomers said, "Have any of you fellas seen Gunderson out here today?"

"The Swede?" Purcell asked with a puzzled frown. "Why would we have seen him?"

"He disappeared sometime during the day, and then later his horse came in looking pretty beat up. The horse came from this direction."

Purcell, Byrne, and John Henry looked at each other. John Henry pretended to be as baffled as the other two.

"I didn't see him," Purcell said. "And it would be hard to miss somebody as big as him."

Byrne added, "I didn't see him, either, but I thought I heard a shot come from somewhere around here, about the middle of the day."

"So did I," John Henry said without hesitation, "but I never saw anything out of the ordinary."

"Let's ride along the rim a ways and have a look," one of the other men suggested.

They were going to see Gunderson's body in the ravine, and it was in the section he'd been patrolling, John Henry thought. His brain worked quickly, trying to come up with an explanation for why he hadn't noticed the corpse.

It didn't take them long to reach the spot where Gunderson had gone over the edge. Byrne reined in, exclaimed, "Hey!" and pointed down into the ravine.

"That's him, all right," one of the other men said as he leaned over to peer at the sprawled body. "Looks like he fell. Maybe he shot a snake and his horse spooked or something, threw him off too close to the edge."

Purcell asked, "How come you didn't notice him down there, Saxon?"

"Well, look how close we are to the edge," John Henry replied. "I was riding a few yards back from the rim so the very thing this other fella just described wouldn't happen to me, Purcell. From that angle, I couldn't see him."

The explanation made sense, although it also made him look less than diligent in his duties as a guard. Better that than having Gunderson's friends know he'd been responsible for the big Swede's death, though.

Of course, he really *wasn't* responsible, he told himself. It had been Gunderson's idea to come out and try to kill him. The big man would still be alive if he hadn't done that.

"All right, somebody's gonna have to go down there and get a rope on him so we can haul his carcass out," Purcell said. "Byrne, you're the lightest. You get the job."

"Me? I'm not very good at climbing," Byrne protested.

"We'll tie a lasso around you and lower you down there. You can tie it around Gunderson and we'll haul him back up."

"Just don't forget to throw the rope back down to me when you get through," Byrne said. "I don't want to have to climb out of that hellhole."

The recovery operation went fairly smoothly. The rope was tied to the saddle horn on one of the horses, and it took the mount backing away from the rim plus the other five men hauling on the rope to lift Gunderson's dead weight.

When they had the body on level ground, Purcell looked at the damage to Gunderson's face. "Must've landed right on that nose of his when he fell, and that broke his neck."

One of the other outlaws added, "The Swede was a pretty touchy son of a gun, but he was a good man to have on your side in a fight."

That was about the highest accolade men such as these could pay to a fallen comrade.

"Hey!" Byrne yelled from down in the ravine. "I said don't forget about me!"

Purcell untied the rope from Gunderson's body and tossed it back down to Byrne. A few minutes later, they had pulled him up on the rim again, without as much effort as had been required for Gunderson.

"Now that we've got Gunderson up here, what do we do with him?" John Henry asked. "He's so damned big, I'm not sure any of our horses can carry him. Even if one of them did, that man would have to walk back to the ranch."

"We can leave him here for now," Purcell said. "We'll ride on back and send some of the boys with a wagon for him. The coyotes won't drag him off before they can get back. That makes the most sense."

It did to John Henry, too. He hoped Garrett wouldn't give him the job of fetching Gunderson's body or even worse, burying it.

He wasn't going to mourn for Sven Gunderson.

He was going to think some, though, about the discovery he had made today.

Nobody really mourned Gunderson. He was laid to rest with a minimum of fuss and ceremony, in a small fenced-in cemetery a few hundred yards from the ranch house. A couple dozen weather-faded wooden crosses marked the location of earlier graves.

There were only two headstones in the cemetery, rounded pieces of granite that were also starting to show the effects of time and the elements. Lottie Dalmas paused in front of them as several of the outlaws shoveled dirt back into the grave containing Gunderson's body.

Her parents were buried here. She remembered very little about her mother. She had gotten her red hair from the woman, and that was her only real legacy to her daughter.

Everything else that made Lottie who she was had come from her father.

Garrett came up behind her. "Do you think Saxon killed him?"

Lottie glanced back over her shoulder at him. "You mean Gunderson? From what Purcell said, Saxon seemed as surprised by the whole thing as any of them."

"That could have been an act," Garrett insisted.

"Of course it could, but you saw Gunderson's body. There's no doubt his neck was broken, and he must have done it falling into the ravine." Lottie smiled coldly. "Do you really think Saxon could have snapped Gunderson's neck like that?"

"No," Garrett said grudgingly. "But he could've pushed him over the edge, I suppose."

"I have my doubts about even that. No, I think Purcell's idea is right. Gunderson was riding too close to the rim and his horse threw him for some reason."

"Why was he out there in the first place? He wasn't on guard duty."

"He might have been looking for Saxon," Lottie said. "I wouldn't rule that out. But I'm pretty sure he didn't find him, or else it would have been Saxon's body they pulled up out of the ravine."

"I guess you're right," Garrett said with a shrug. "And I guess it doesn't really matter why Gunderson's dead. What's important is that we've lost a good man."

"Not that good," Lottie snapped. "Gunderson was hard to control. We both know that. He was always liable to fly off the handle and do something stupid. Recruiting Saxon and Mallette makes up for what we lost in Gunderson."

"I still don't trust those two."

"I know you don't . . . but you don't have to, Simon. I do, and that's all that matters."

Garrett flushed at being put in his place like that, but he didn't say anything else. He might be the leader of the gang, but she was the mistress of the outlaw sanctuary.

Of course, he could take it away from her, but he wouldn't do that. There was too much history between them. Even though Henry had come along and taken his place, his feelings for Lottie were still too strong for him to ever betray her.

She looked at the tombstones for a moment longer, then turned away, toward the buggy that had brought her to the cemetery. "We need to get back to the house and start planning. Dell Bartlett brought a note from Carson this afternoon."

"Why didn't I know about that?" Garrett said with a frown.

"You were sleeping, and I didn't see any need to wake you."

"What does Carson want now?"

"He's getting antsy. He wants us to go ahead and make our move against Montayne."

"I thought the idea was to kill him right in the middle of the bunch, so nobody would suspect it was for any reason other than him being on that jury."

"That *is* the reason Montayne has to die, as far as I'm concerned," Lottie snapped. "But it gets him out of the way so Carson can move in on his range, so it's worth it for him to pay us for our help. Carson gets what he wants without having to go through an outright range war to get it."

"I know the plan," Garrett said sullenly. "You don't have to explain it to me."

"I just don't want you to lose sight of what's really at stake here, Simon." Lottie climbed into the buggy and took hold of the reins leading to the black horse hitched to it. "It's the debt those men owe for what they did to Henry . . . a debt they're all going to pay in blood."

Chapter Sixteen

The next day, Simon Garrett assembled the members of the gang in the bunkhouse and told them, "We're ready for the next move. We're going after Jed Montayne."

"That won't be easy," one of the men said. "He's got a mighty hard-nosed crew working for him on the J Slash M. We may have a hard time getting to him."

"That's why we've got to draw him out," Garrett said. "It'll be a lot easier to lay our hands on him if we get him away from his headquarters."

John Henry recognized Montayne's name from an earlier conversation with Nick Mallette. Montayne was one of the biggest ranchers in the area, the main rival to J.C. Carson's Anvil spread.

However, he hadn't known until now that Montayne was also a member of the jury that had convicted Henry Garrett.

Simon Garrett went on. "If we run off some of Montayne's herd, he'll come after the rustled stock. We'll use it to lead him right into a trap. If some of his men get killed"—Garrett shrugged—"well, that'll just be too bad for them."

He went on to explain that they would raid the J/M herd that night as it grazed along Sweetwater Creek, north of Kiowa City.

"The tracks will be easy enough to follow. We'll run the stock through Packsaddle Gap, and when Montayne and his hands come through there, we'll be waiting for them." Garrett paused. "But here's the most important thing to remember. *Don't kill Montayne.* The Flame has her own plans for him, and she won't be happy if he dies quick and easy from a bullet."

That brought grim chuckles from several of the men. Obviously, they had seen Lottie Dalmas in action before, taking her vengeance for Henry Garrett. John Henry remembered what he had been told about how Lucas Winslow's body had been found, tortured almost beyond recognition.

Purcell asked, "Is everybody going along on tonight's job, Simon?" He glanced at John Henry and Mallette, so it was clear who he was talking about.

"Almost the whole bunch," Garrett replied. "Old Cribbins will stay here, and a couple men to guard the trail. The rest of us will be riding an hour after dark, so be ready."

He named the two men who would remain behind on sentry duty, and John Henry was glad Garrett didn't single him out for that chore. With that done, Garrett stalked out of the bunkhouse, leaving the men to talk about the raid they would carry out that night.

"Looks like I'm going to be a rustler," Mallette said to John Henry as he sat down on his bunk. "That's certainly not the profession I started out to follow."

"Fate always has its own plans for us," John Henry said.

"And a sense of humor as well," Mallette added wryly. "I, uh, sort of hope it's all right if I stick fairly close to you tonight, John. I never did this sort of work before."

"Sure. Just don't get in the way."

"I'll certainly try not to."

John Henry acted like he wasn't worried about the gang's plans, but actually his mind was racing, trying to figure out a way to save Jed Montayne and his men from being bushwhacked.

The obvious method would be to prevent the raid from taking place, but he doubted that would be possible. He might be able to spoil the ambush, though, and give the rancher and his crew a chance to escape being massacred.

If it was a fair fight between the cowboys and the outlaws, men would die, for sure, but that would give John Henry time to get back to the ranch and capture Lottie. Her as his prisoner would break up the vengeance scheme to wipe out the jury and Judge Doolittle . . .

It was something to ponder, anyway, an opportunity to seize if the chance came up.

An air of excitement and anticipation hung over

the ranch that afternoon. While the outlaws all knew that their lives would be at risk during the raid and the subsequent ambush, at least there would be some action again.

Men such as these lived for the ringing blare of six-guns, the tang of powder smoke, the heart-pounding surge of sensation that went hand in hand with the knowledge that their lives could end at any instant.

In that respect, they weren't so much different from many of the lawmen who pursued them, John Henry knew. It wasn't actually a game, but if it had been, the higher the stakes the better.

Tonight there would be no higher.

Nick Mallette licked his lips nervously as he got ready to mount up. He wore range clothes instead of his gambler's outfit; an assortment of clothes had been left at the ranch over the years by fugitives who passed through there, and Lottie had told Mallette to take his pick from them.

"You look like a real cowboy, now," John Henry told him with a smile as they stood outside the barn, holding the reins of their horses. "Or an owlhoot."

Mallette took off his black hat and looked down at the faded blue shirt, the black leather vest, and the denim trousers. Lottie had given him a gun-belt, too, and it was strapped around his waist. "I just hope I won't let anybody down. I've never rustled cattle before. Hell, that jailbreak is really the most illegal thing I've done."

"Other than murder," John Henry pointed out.

"I told you, that killing was self-defense. Just because I was charged with murder doesn't make it so."

"You're right, Nick. Sorry I said that."

Mallette shook his head. "Don't worry about it. I guess to a certain extent, we are what the world thinks we are."

"Now that's profound, amigo. Here comes Garrett. You ready to ride?"

"As ready as I'm going to be," Mallette said.

"All right, everybody get mounted," Garrett called as he strode up to the group. "We want to get to Sweetwater Creek before the moon rises."

The men, more than a dozen of them, swung into their saddles and rode toward the skull-shaped rock and the zigzagging trail that led down the escarpment.

John Henry and Mallette were in the middle of the group. John Henry didn't know if that was coincidence or if Garrett had given orders to keep the two of them surrounded because they were the newcomers and not fully trusted yet.

It didn't matter. John Henry wasn't ready to make his move and wouldn't be until later in the night. For now, he was going to act like a full-fledged member of the gang.

Garrett led the night riders through the darkness toward the J/M ranch. It took more than an hour to get there. When they were close to their destination, Garrett held up a hand and called a soft-voiced command for them to halt.

They were at the top of a slight rise. Spread out before them, visible in the starlight, was a broad valley with a dark line through the center that marked the thicker vegetation along the meandering course of Sweetwater Creek. The dozing cattle were gathered in dark clumps that dotted the rangeland.

"We'll work the gather from right to left," Garrett said quietly. "When we've got two or three hundred head, point them north toward Packsaddle Gap."

One of the men said, "I took up the owlhoot because I was sick of chousin' cows and eatin' trail dust, Simon."

"It won't be a long drive," Garrett said. "You can stand it for tonight."

Another man asked, "What about Montayne's riders?"

"What about them?" Garrett said callously. "I told you, if anybody gets in your way, kill him. We want Montayne to come after us, and if some of his men are dead that'll just make him more angry . . . and less likely to worry about a trap."

John Henry's guts clenched. Innocent men might die tonight, and there wasn't a damned thing he could do about it, not with odds of more than twelve to one against him. He had to hope for the best and take comfort in the knowledge that he was doing his job and trying to prevent more murders later on.

That was pretty skimpy comfort, though.

"All right, let's move out," Garrett ordered. "Spread out and get those cattle moving."

John Henry, Mallette, and two outlaws named Whitt and Palmer headed for a bunch of cattle. As they rode, Mallette said again, "I've never done anything like this before. How do I drive cattle?"

As a young man growing up in Indian Territory, John Henry had hazed many a head of stock from one place to another. "You probably won't have to do anything to get them moving except ride up behind them. If you have to prod them any, take your lasso, leave it coiled up, and swat them on the rump with it."

"All right, if you say so." Mallette didn't sound convinced, but he heeled his horse forward and kept pace with the others as they moved up to the cattle.

As John Henry had predicted, the big, ungainly beasts lurched into motion when the riders pressed them. All across the range along the creek, men called out softly, waved their hats over their heads, and kept their horses moving. They began pushing the bunches together to form a larger herd.

Evidently none of Montayne's riders were in the vicinity, or else they would have showed up, probably with guns blazing. It was possible no J/M hands were close enough to realize the cattle were being rustled. John Henry allowed himself to hope that would be the case.

That hope was dashed almost immediately as a shot suddenly blasted from the direction of the creek. John Henry looked that way and saw a handful of riders splashing across the stream. Colt flame bloomed in the darkness as more guns went off.

There was no longer any need for stealth. Several outlaws let out strident whoops and returned the fire. Muzzle flashes split the night with their orange glare.

"Drive 'em!" John Henry shouted as he sent Iron Heart crashing against the rear end of the nearest steer. He yanked his lasso from the saddle and used it to slash at the rumps of the other cattle close to him. The animals bellowed and broke into a clumsy run.

Whoops and gunshots and the rumble of hooves filled the air. None of the bullets came close to John Henry, Mallette, Whitt, and Palmer as they drove the cattle northward.

John Henry looked over his shoulder toward the creek. Flame still spurted from gun muzzles here and there, but the shooting seemed to be dying away. He thought he heard the swift rataplan of galloping hoofbeats and wondered if the J/M punchers were retreating. If any of them survived, they would light a shuck for the ranch headquarters in search of help.

Then the pursuit would be underway, a pursuit that Garrett intended to end with an ambush at Packsaddle Gap, wherever that was.

The shooting stopped, and the cattle kept moving. The creek curved away to the east, but the outlaws continued driving the rustled stock almost due north. John Henry judged the direction by the stars. The animals were bunched together, with the riders forming a line behind them.

Garrett rode along that line and called out, "Did we lose any men? Was anybody hit?"

No one answered that they were.

Purcell asked, "Did we down any of Montayne's men?"

"A couple," Garrett replied. "I couldn't tell how bad they were hurt. The others got away." He laughed. "This is going just like we planned it so far."

With Mallette tagging along beside him, John Henry moved closer to Garrett. "How far is it to this Packsaddle Gap?"

"We'll be there a little before dawn. That'll give us time to get in position to give Montayne a warm welcome."

"This fella Montayne, he's one of the big ranchers around here, right?"

"Yeah, that's right," Garrett said. "What about it?"

"And he was on the jury that convicted your brother?"

"He was. That's why he's got to die."

"What'll happen to his ranch after he's gone?"

"How the hell do I know?" Garrett said. "Somebody else will take it over, I guess."

Somebody like J.C. Carson of the Anvil, John Henry thought. That idea led to all sorts of interesting speculation.

He put it out of his mind for the moment, to concentrate on the matter at hand—preventing

Montayne and his men from being wiped out in an ambush.

Enough of the outlaws had experience working cattle that they were able to keep the rustled stock moving steadily through the night. Garrett knew where they were going, so he took point and led the way. John Henry and Mallette found themselves riding flank on the left side of the herd.

"Men drove cattle hundreds of miles this way?" Mallette said as if he found that hard to believe.

"They sure did," John Henry replied. "They did it for years, moving the herds from Texas, across Indian Territory, to the railheads up here in Kansas. Then the railroad built a line down to Fort Worth, so the herds don't have nearly as far to go."

John Henry couldn't say anything about it, of course, but in his job as a deputy U.S. marshal he'd had something to do with the successful completion of that rail line into Texas, and he was justly proud of his contribution.

The moon rose and cast its silvery glow over the landscape. It was bright enough for the pursuit to trail the stolen cows, and Garrett was counting on that to lure his quarry into the trap.

The moonlight was also bright enough to reveal two rounded hills that bulked on either side of the trail up ahead. John Henry pointed them out to Mallette. "That must be Packsaddle Gap. See the shape they make."

"I'll have to take your word for it, John. I wouldn't know a packsaddle if I saw it."

Garrett rode back along the herd's left flank and called, "Drive 'em on through the gap. Two men keep them moving once they're through, while the rest drop off and head up on those hills. Find good places to hunker down and wait for Montayne's bunch."

"Maybe we should be the ones to keep driving the cattle, John," Mallette suggested.

John Henry shook his head. "You can if you want to. I'm going to be where the action is." He had to take part in the ambush in order to fire a premature shot and warn Montayne of the danger. That was the only thing he'd been able to figure out.

"I guess I'll stick with you," Mallette said, although he didn't sound happy about it.

The gap was wide enough for the cattle to go through without having to bunch up even more. It didn't take long for them to clear it. John Henry and Mallette headed for the hill to the right.

The sound of hoofbeats coming up behind them made John Henry look around.

Purcell galloped up to join them, slowing his horse as he drew even with them. "I'll throw in with you boys."

"Glad to have you," John Henry replied, not meaning it at all. Purcell had acted suspicious about Gunderson's death, and it was possible he still didn't trust John Henry and wanted to keep an eye on him. Garrett might have even assigned him to do just that.

John Henry would just have to deal with the problem.

Purcell said, "This looks like a good spot," and reined in. The other two men followed suit. Several good-sized rocks were scattered along the slope. They would provide cover and a good field of fire across the gap below.

"Nick, take the horses on up to the top of the hill and hold them there," John Henry told the gambler.

"Wait a minute," Purcell said. "We're all supposed to take part in the ambush."

"There won't be an ambush if Montayne spots a bunch of horses up here," John Henry said. "He'll guess they belong to us and know we're waiting to bushwhack him."

Purcell thought it over and shrugged. "Go ahead with the horses, Mallette. But if you can find a place to tie them, do that and get back down here."

"Sure," Mallette said, but John Henry didn't expect him to return. He had suggested that Mallette hold the horses because he knew the man didn't really want to shoot at the J/M ranch hands. The horses were a convenient excuse for him not to have to. Mallette took the reins from John Henry and Purcell and started on up the slope with the three mounts.

"All right," Purcell said as he took his Winchester and settled down to kneel behind one of the slabs of rock. "Now we wait."

But not for long. The eastern sky was already

gray with the approach of dawn. By the time the sun was rising, Jed Montayne and his men ought to reach Packsaddle Gap.

When they did, the grass in the gap was liable to be red with more than the glare from the early morning light . . . unless John Henry could prevent it somehow.

Chapter Seventeen

In the morning haze, the sun was a sullen red orb a few inches above the eastern horizon when John Henry heard hoofbeats. The rumble from the rustled herd had faded as the cattle continued to drift north, pushed along by the two men who had stayed with them. The quiet allowed John Henry to hear the approach of a large group of riders.

Montayne might have brought along enough men that they would outnumber the bushwhackers. The element of surprise would counteract that advantage, and so would the fact that the outlaws held the high ground.

If John Henry could stop the pursuers from entering the gap and getting caught in a crossfire, it would change everything. His hands tightened on the rifle he held as he glanced over at Purcell.

"Here they come," Purcell said. A note of vicious anticipation had come into his voice. He was looking forward to the killing.

John Henry saw dust in the air as the riders approached the gap. The men on horseback came into view, galloping along at the base of that dust cloud.

"That damned Mallette never did come back," Purcell complained.

"I reckon he didn't find a good place to leave the horses."

Purcell snorted in disgust. "He's just yellow, that's all, like all gamblers. Doesn't want to risk catching a slug."

"Don't worry about him," John Henry said. "Let's just worry about doing our job."

"You're right." Purcell propped his elbows on the rock and nestled his cheek against the smooth wood of his rifle stock as he peered over the Winchester's barrel. "Garrett will start the ball when he's good an' ready. Until then, hold your fire."

"Sure," John Henry said. But holding his fire was the last thing he intended to do. The pursuers were already almost as close as he intended to let them get.

"What the hell!" he suddenly exclaimed. "What's that?"

"Where?" Purcell asked. "I don't see anything."

John Henry took several quick steps that brought him to the outlaw's side. He dropped down on one knee behind the rock and pointed. "Right there."

Purcell leaned over to peer in the direction John Henry was pointing. "What—"

John Henry drove the Winchester's butt against the side of Purcell's head in a short, swift stroke.

It was a hard blow, meant to put the outlaw down and keep him down.

Purcell slumped, his rifle slipping from his fingers to clatter against the rock. He toppled over loosely onto the ground.

John Henry glanced around. More of the outlaws were scattered along the slope, some of them less than fifty yards away, but no cries of alarm sounded from them. Chances were that all of them were concentrating on the approach of Montayne and his men and hadn't even noticed John Henry knocking out Purcell.

John Henry aimed his Winchester into the air and fired three times as fast as he could work the rifle's lever, the universal frontier signal for distress or danger.

The shots rang out loudly in the early morning air and echoed back from the hill on the other side of Packsaddle Gap where more of the bushwhackers were located. The riders down below couldn't fail to hear the shots.

As John Henry lowered the rifle he saw evidence of that. The men on horseback hauled back on their reins and brought the mounts to a halt outside the gap. He heard a faint shout, saw a man fling up an arm and point at the hillside.

Somewhere not too far off, Garrett shouted, "Saxon double-crossed us! Kill that son of a bitch!"

Well, the masquerade was over, John Henry thought as he pivoted and saw one of the outlaws aiming a rifle at him. John Henry's Winchester blasted first, the slug ripping through the man and kicking him backward.

Garrett continued to shout orders, but John Henry's actions had plunged the planned ambush into confused chaos. Nobody was shooting at him at the moment, so he turned and sprinted up the slope toward the spot where Mallette waited with the horses. That drew attention to him, and shots began to blast.

John Henry threw a glance over his shoulder and saw spurts of flame and puffs of smoke coming from the group of riders down on the plain. Montayne and his men were getting into the fight, peppering the slopes of both hills with lead.

With lunging strides, John Henry reached the top of the hill. He spotted Mallette standing there holding the reins of all three horses.

The gambler's eyes were wide with fear and confusion. "John!" he exclaimed. "What the hell's going on?"

"I've got to get out of here, Nick," John Henry told him. "Give me my horse."

At the same time, Simon Garrett, mounted again, charged up the slope toward them, smoke billowing from the muzzle of his revolver as he fired. "Stop him!" Garrett yelled. "Get him, Mallette!"

"John . . ." Mallette said uncertainly. He held the gathered reins in his left hand as his right drifted toward the butt of his holstered Colt.

John Henry didn't give Mallette time to make

up his mind. His right fist shot out and cracked against Mallette's jaw.

The punch slewed Mallette's head around and sent his hat flying. He let go of the reins as his knees unhinged and dropped him to the ground, out cold.

John Henry grabbed Iron Heart's reins and was in the saddle a second later, hauling the big gray around.

He meant to ride down the far side of the hill and swing back to the west, toward the Silver Skull Ranch. With most of the outlaws engaged in the battle with Montayne's men, he thought he could get to the spread before them and arrest Lottie Dalmas. While he was at the ranch he could free Deputy Baird as well. That would be a nice reversal of fortune.

There would still be the matter of hunting down Garrett and the rest of the gang, but with Lottie behind bars, John Henry didn't think they would continue their campaign of terror.

But it all hinged on getting away from where he was, and as a bullet whipped past his ear, he knew that might not be easy. A furious Simon Garrett was determined to stop him.

John Henry twisted in the saddle as Garrett barreled toward him. Might as well take care of this now, he thought grimly as he jerked the Winchester to his shoulder.

Before he could fire, somebody else yelled,

"Saxon!" and a figure lurched into view at the hill's crest. With a thread of blood trickling down the side of his face from a cut John Henry's rifle butt had opened up, Purcell thrust a revolver toward him. The gun in the outlaw's hand boomed.

John Henry felt the bullet's impact like the kick of a Missouri mule. It twisted him in the saddle and almost knocked him off Iron Heart's back. He had to drop his rifle and grab the saddle horn to stay mounted.

Pain flooded through him from the spot where the bullet had torn through his left side. He didn't know how bad the wound was, but for the moment, anyway, he wasn't in much of a shape to continue the fight.

He jabbed his boot heels into Iron Heart's flanks and sent the gray lunging down the far slope. More bullets whined around his head as Garrett kept trying to kill him.

Iron Heart responded with all the speed and guts that John Henry had come to expect, bounding down the hill with reckless abandon, seemingly out of control but really as sure-footed as ever.

John Henry clung to the saddle. It was all he could do.

Garrett howled curses and gave chase, but his yelling and shooting abruptly stopped.

Dimly aware of that, John Henry looked over his shoulder and saw that Garrett's horse had stumbled and fallen, throwing the outlaw. Garrett rolled over a couple times and came to a stop.

"Hope you broke your damn neck," John Henry muttered.

As Iron Heart reached the bottom of the hill, John Henry thought about trying to join up with Jed Montayne and his men since he was wounded. He discarded the idea when he realized that none of them would know who he was. If he came galloping up, they would probably take him for one of the outlaws and blast him out of the saddle before he had time to explain.

The best thing he could do was get away from there while he had the chance, he decided. Once he had put some distance between himself and the battle, he could pause and see how badly he was hit, maybe patch up the wound and push on to the Silver Skull.

If there was any way in hell to finish this job, he was going to do it.

Nobody else came after him as he raced across the plains. He tried to keep an eye on his back trail, but after a while that got to be too much effort in his weakened condition. He was in and out of consciousness as he rode.

After what seemed like hours but might have been only minutes, he started trying to rein in the big gray. John Henry was weak, though, and after being given his head and running for so long, Iron Heart didn't want to stop.

Gradually the horse slowed, and at last John Henry was able to bring him to a halt. Staying in the saddle, he looked around to make sure there was no pursuit.

He didn't see anything except an endless vista of rolling prairie and arching blue sky. He couldn't even see the hills that formed Packsaddle Gap, so he didn't know if he had been going the right direction or not.

First things first, he told himself. Carefully, hunched to the side against the pain, he climbed down from the horse's back.

He dropped the reins, knowing that Iron Heart wouldn't wander off. In fact, since his legs were weak and unsteady, he leaned against the gray for support as he pulled up his bloody shirt and explored the injury with his fingertips.

John Henry closed his eyes in relief as he realized that the bullet had gone in and out cleanly, and not very deep, at that. It hurt like blazes, and he had lost a chunk of meat and a good deal of blood.

But the wound wasn't going to kill him unless it festered. It needed medical attention, but he settled for taking a flask of whiskey from one of his saddlebags.

Some people made a joke out of carrying liquor "for medicinal purposes," but in John Henry's case it was true. He didn't drink other than the occasional beer.

He used his teeth to pull the stopper from the flask and poured whiskey into his cupped hand. He splashed it on the entrance and exit wounds, groaning and gritting his teeth against the liquor's fiery sting.

Better than nothing, he thought. He put the flask away and went to mount up again.

His strength deserted him, completely and unexpectedly. He felt himself reeling backward and tried to catch his balance, but it was lost.

So was everything else. He hit the ground, out cold.

Chapter Eighteen

Simon Garrett was still seething by the time he and the other members of the gang reached the Silver Skull late that morning.

Three of them—Currier, Hillman, and Palmer—came in draped facedown over their saddles, dead from wounds they had suffered in the battle. Several others were wounded, including Purcell, who had a nasty gash on his head where that traitor Saxon had clouted him with a rifle butt.

Every one of those deaths and injuries could be laid right at the feet of John Saxon.

Garrett muttered a curse every time he thought the man's name. No matter how Lottie felt about Saxon, Garrett had never trusted him, not one damned bit. That was why he had told Purcell to keep an eye on him.

Unfortunately, that precaution hadn't done any good. Saxon had still managed to betray the rest of them and ruin the carefully set-up ambush. Jed

Montayne had gotten away, and Garrett had lost three good men.

Saxon would pay for that . . . if he was still alive. Purcell had wounded Saxon as he was getting away. Part of Garrett hoped that Saxon was already lying on the prairie somewhere, dead from that bullet hole, but another part hoped that Saxon had survived being ventilated.

Garrett wanted to settle the score with him personally.

Lottie stepped out onto the porch to greet the men as they rode up to the ranch house. She wore mannish garb again, including her gun belt and the hidden bowie knife that dangled from the rawhide choker around her neck.

Her eyes narrowed as she looked over the group of riders. Her voice lashed out. "I don't see Montayne."

"He got away," Garrett said bluntly. "Saxon double-crossed us and fired some warning shots just as Montayne and the rest of the J/M bunch were about to ride right into our trap."

A sharply indrawn breath caused Lottie's breasts to lift dramatically under her shirt. Under other circumstances, Garrett would have enjoyed that view, but not at the moment.

"Saxon did that? You're sure?"

"Damn right I'm sure. He knocked out Dave Purcell before he did it, too."

"What about Mallette?"

Garrett jerked his head at some of his men, who moved their horses aside to reveal a dispirited Nick

Mallette sitting with slumped shoulders on his mount. An ugly purple bruise discolored the gambler's jaw.

"Looks like I was wrong about him," Garrett admitted. "He tried to stop Saxon and got walloped for his trouble."

Mallette lifted his head. "I didn't know what John was going to do, Miss Dalmas, I swear it. I still don't understand it. I don't know why he . . . what he thought he was—"

"That's enough," Lottie snapped. She looked at Garrett again. "So Saxon got away?"

"Yeah, but he was wounded. Purcell managed to wing him. I don't know how bad he was hurt."

"You didn't go after him?"

The tone of disapproval in Lottie's voice made Garrett flush with embarrassment and anger. "Montayne and his crew had us outnumbered almost two to one. It was all we could do to fight a running battle with them and get out of there. Like I already told you, we lost three men doing it."

Lottie didn't seem to care about that. "You didn't mount a search for Saxon?"

"By the time Montayne gave up the chase, Saxon could've been anywhere. But as soon as they get some fresh horses, some of the men are going back out to look for him."

"See that they do," Lottie said. "And then come inside." She turned and stalked into the house.

Garrett bit back the words of anger and frustration he wanted to shout after her. Wearily, he turned to the other men and called the names of three of them. "You gents get fresh horses and see if you can find out what happened to Saxon. You ought to be able to pick up his trail at Packsaddle Gap."

"It's a damned long ride all the way back there, Simon," one of the men said.

"And we've already been in the saddle for what seems like a week," another outlaw added.

Garrett bristled. He might not be able to let his temper get away from him where Lottie was concerned, but he wasn't going to have his orders questioned by the likes of these men. "I said go find Saxon, damn it," he growled as he fixed them with a cold, angry stare. His ungloved right hand wasn't far from the butt of his gun.

"I'll go," Nick Mallette said.

Garrett turned his head to glare at the gambler. "What did you say?"

"I said I'd go," Mallette repeated. He touched the bruise on his jaw. "I'd sort of like to ask John a few questions about what he did . . . assuming he's still alive, that is." Mallette's voice had a tone of hard, flat anger in it.

Garrett grunted. "Maybe I misjudged you, Slick."

"It's—" Mallette stopped short and didn't bother to finish correcting Garrett. He let out a little chuckle instead.

"All right, you can go, too. But if you find Saxon alive, I want him to stay that way until you get him back here. I want to hear him howl before he dies." Garrett waved a hand toward the barn. "The rest of you put up your horses, and tend to mine, too."

He swung down from the saddle and stepped up onto the porch, intending to follow Lottie into the house.

"What about Montayne?" one of the men asked. "Are we still going after him?"

"He still owes blood for what he did to Henry," Garrett answered harshly. "Damn right he's going to pay."

But first he needed to discuss the next move with Lottie, although he wasn't going to admit that in front of the men. It was bad enough that some of them already seemed to believe that Lottie was in charge. He wasn't going to confirm that assumption for them.

When he went in, she was standing stiffly beside the fireplace with a drink in her hand. She tossed it back. "You let me down, Simon."

Garrett couldn't keep his anger completely contained any longer. "It wasn't my idea to trust Saxon when we'd only known him for a few days," he shot back at her. "That was all your doing, Lottie."

"When a man's that fast on the draw, you've got to try to put him to good use."

"Well, he was either playing a game of his own all along . . . or else he's a damned lawman," Garrett said. "He was never what he was pretending to be, though, that's for sure."

She went over to a sideboard and picked up a bottle to splash more whiskey into her glass. She half turned and held up the bottle to ask him if he wanted any.

Garrett nodded. He took the glass that Lottie

handed him and downed the shot, letting the fiery liquor brace up his body and spirit, both of which had grown weary. "Carson won't be happy when he finds out that Montayne got away from us."

"I don't give a damn about Carson. *I'm* not happy that Montayne got away." Lottie sighed. "But at least nothing that happened in the past twelve hours points to us. If anything, Montayne will blame Carson for the rustling and the ambush, since they've been feuding with each other for years. So maybe Montayne won't be on his guard when we strike at him again."

"When will that be? Right away, so he won't be expecting it? That would keep Carson happy."

"I told you, I don't care about Carson. I've decided we're going to shake things up. We're going after the fruit at the very top of the tree."

Garrett frowned. "You mean . . . ?"

Lottie reached behind her neck, under the thick auburn hair, and drew the bowie knife from its hidden sheath. She ran her left thumb along the razor-sharp blade until a tiny drop of blood appeared, standing out redly against her tanned flesh.

She pressed that thumb against her lips and sucked on it for a second. "We're going after the arrogant man who passed that death sentence on Henry. We're going after Judge Ephraim Doolittle."

* * *

John Henry came to with Iron Heart nudging his shoulder. The big gray prodded his nose against the lawman until John Henry began to stir.

As he opened his eyes, he winced at the sunlight that seemed to stab into his brain like a knife.

Even that slight movement was enough to set up an annoying clamor inside his head. He did his best to ignore it as he lifted his head a little and looked around.

The sun was barely above the horizon, so he figured he hadn't been passed out for long. The ambush at Packsaddle Gap had taken place shortly after dawn.

Something struck him as being wrong. He frowned as he tried to puzzle out what it was. In his condition, thinking was hard.

The answer came to him with stunning force. The sun wasn't in the same place it had been earlier. It wasn't newly risen.

It was about to *set*.

He had been lying on the prairie, unconscious, all day.

A bitter curse welled up his throat. It was the white man half of him; Indians seldom cursed and didn't even have many words in their tongue for such things.

The opportunity to capture Lottie Dalmas was long gone. The battle at the gap had been over for hours, and he had no idea how it had turned out.

He knew he was lucky none of the outlaws had come along and found him, though. If they had, he wouldn't be alive, that was for damned sure. So in that respect, the pain in his side and his head was a good thing. It meant he was still on the right side of the great divide.

He got his hands underneath him and pushed himself into a sitting position. His head spun crazily for a few seconds, but soon began to settle down.

The pain from the bullet wound in his side was a dull, throbbing ache. At least it wasn't bad enough to keep him from moving, he told himself.

Iron Heart nosed his shoulder again.

"I know, I know. I need to get up and get out of here."

Where was he going to go? He frowned as he pondered that question.

Returning to the Silver Skull seemed out of the question. Injured like he was, he wouldn't stand any chance of getting in and out of there alive. More than likely at least some of the gang had survived the battle with the J/M and would have limped back there.

After the way he had double-crossed them, there was nothing the outlaws would like better than to get their hands on him. His death would make what had happened to Charles Houston and Lucas Winslow seem like a Sunday picnic.

His job was far from over, though. If he could make it back to Kiowa City, he could reveal his true identity to Sheriff Mike Rasmussen and get some help from the local lawman. Plus he could get the bullet holes in his side patched up properly, so they wouldn't fester and kill him. He couldn't finish his assignment from the grave.

After a few minutes of muddled thoughts brought him to the conclusion that he ought to head for Kiowa City, he reached out and caught hold of the stirrup that dangled near him. "Hold steady, Iron Heart."

The pain and effort of climbing to his feet brought more groans and curses from him, but finally he was upright again. He stood there for long minutes, resting and trying to catch his breath, before he was ready to attempt getting into the saddle.

The blazing sun was halfway down by the time John Henry was mounted. Using it to orient himself, he turned the gray southeast, knowing that direction ought to take him to the vicinity of Kiowa City.

If nothing else, eventually he would hit the railroad and could follow the tracks to the settlement. Assuming, of course, he was thinking straight enough to turn in the right direction.

With that thought putting a grim smile on his lips, John Henry nudged Iron Heart into motion.

The big gray's gait was the smoothest of any horse he had ever ridden, but even so, each step was enough to send a fresh throb of pain through John Henry's side.

He would just have to put up with it, he told himself. He sure couldn't walk back to Kiowa City. That would hurt even more.

The sun went down, but an arc of golden light

lingered in the western sky, which faded to a pale blue streaked by lines of thin clouds turned orange by the sun. It would have been beautiful, if he had been in more of a mood to appreciate it.

The view would have been more appealing, too, if it hadn't suddenly been marred by two figures on horseback coming over a rise to his left and galloping toward him. He heard their shouts, followed by the bark of guns as they charged.

Chapter Nineteen

The men were too far away for John Henry to recognize them. There were really only two possibilities when it came to their identities, though.

Either they were a pair of Jed Montayne's men who had taken him for one of the bushwhackers . . .

Or they were two of the outlaws who were looking for the man who had double-crossed them at Packsaddle Gap.

Either way, their goal would be to put a bullet in his hide.

John Henry pulled Iron Heart's head to the right, kicked the big gray into a run, and leaned forward in the saddle to make himself a smaller target. The range was pretty long for handguns, and the light was already uncertain. The odds of the gunmen being able to hit him were small, but it made sense to decrease those odds.

Iron Heart responded gallantly, as always, stretching out into a smooth, ground-eating stride that had man and horse flashing across the landscape.

The pursuers had a good angle on him, but John Henry was beginning to think that Iron Heart could outrun them.

Suddenly, two more riders appeared . . . in front of him.

John Henry groaned. The excitement of the chase had made him forget for a moment that he was wounded, but the pain in his side wouldn't be ignored for long.

On top of it, he had a fight on his hands. The two men in front of him forced him to turn more to his right, so that he was almost galloping back the way he had come from.

He needed to break through them somehow—not easy to do, the shape he was in. At least he still had his Colt. His Winchester had been lost when he dropped it back at Packsaddle Gap, after Purcell shot him.

He drew the revolver, but didn't waste bullets by shooting it. His pursuers would have to get closer, as they did steadily with one group turning him toward the other. The first two riders had cut in behind him and he was trapped.

If he was going to survive to finish his job, he would have to fight his way out.

John Henry turned the gray and made a dash in a different direction, thinking he could squirt between the two groups.

Each pair split up, completely surrounding him. He had to rein in to keep himself out of their gunsights.

As he brought Iron Heart to a halt, the four

pursuers slowed as well, coming to a stop about fifty yards from him, each at a different point of the compass. They holstered their handguns, and John Henry realized they hadn't really been trying to hit him.

They were just herding him, like he was a dumb animal. That knowledge was a bitter pill to swallow.

The men pulled rifles from their saddle sheaths, but only one raised the weapon to his shoulder. "Throw your gun down, Saxon!" he shouted.

That answered one question, anyway, John Henry thought. Montayne's men wouldn't have known the name he'd been using, so they were members of Garrett's gang.

In fact, one of them looked particularly familiar, even in the fading light.

"I said throw down your gun!" the spokesman yelled again. "If you don't, I'll shoot that horse right out from under you!"

Anger boiled up inside John Henry. He brandished the Colt and shouted back, "Come on! It's four against one! Aren't those odds good enough for you? Come on and fight!"

"We're not gonna kill you, Saxon, but we'll put you afoot and lasso you if we have to! You're going back to the Silver Skull! I reckon Garrett and the Flame have special plans for a no-good double-crosser like you!"

So that was it. They were supposed to take him back to be tortured to death. Well, that came as no surprise, knowing the terrible things that

Lottie Dalmas had done already in her quest for vengeance.

Beautiful or not, the Flame had a cruel, bloodthirsty streak inside her. Simon Garrett wasn't much better.

"Go to hell!" John Henry shouted. "You'll have to kill me to take me back there!"

The one who seemed in charge called to his men. "Move in slow. I'll shoot his horse, and one of you wing him. As long as he doesn't bleed to death on the way, I reckon Garrett and the Flame won't mind too much if he's shot up a little more."

They could do it, John Henry knew. They were in easy rifle range already, but still too far away for him to count on the accuracy of his Colt.

Besides, not even the best gunslick west of the Mississippi could shoot in four directions at once. They had him, and all he would accomplish by putting up a fight would be to get Iron Heart killed.

He couldn't do that to the big gray.

There was a slim chance, and John Henry took it. He lifted his voice again and said, "Don't do this, Nick. I helped you before. Remember, we're partners."

He had recognized the man to his right as Nick Mallette. The gambler had his Winchester leveled, and after what had happened back at Packsaddle Gap, he didn't have any more reason to trust John Henry than any of the other men did.

But the lawman appealed to him anyway. It was the only chance he had.

"Partners?" Mallette repeated bitterly. "Partners

don't punch each other in the jaw, John, and try to get each other killed."

"That was never my intention," John Henry said. "I give you my word on that." He was telling the truth. By knocking out Mallette, his hope was that Garrett and the other outlaws would be convinced the gambler hadn't had anything to do with John Henry's actions.

Evidently that was the way things had turned out, otherwise Garrett wouldn't have sent Mallette out to help chase him down.

"Sorry, John," Mallette said. "I can't trust you anymore. I'm starting to think I never could."

"Sure you can, Nick." John Henry knew it was time to play the lone card he had left. "I'm a deputy U.S. marshal. I work for Judge Isaac Parker in Fort Smith. He's a federal judge, and if there's anybody who can do something about that bogus murder charge hanging over your head, it's him."

John Henry kept his eyes on Mallette. He knew his admission was a risk. He was counting on the outlaws to not forget their orders from Garrett and start cutting loose at him.

The revelation that he was a star packer brought angry curses from the outlaws, but they didn't shoot.

John Henry's spirits rose slightly when he saw the barrel of Mallette's rifle sag a little.

"A federal lawman?" Mallette said. "You can't do anything about a murder charge, and neither can that judge of yours. That's a state crime."

"You think the law in Kansas City won't listen if Parker asks them to take another look at your case?

The judge wields more influence than any two-bit local politician. I give you my word on that, Nick. I'll do everything in my power to see that justice is done and your name is cleared."

The outlaw leader had had enough. "Shut your mouth, Saxon! You've spouted enough lies!" The rifle in his hands cracked wickedly as he fired.

John Henry moved as the outlaw spoke, his instincts telling him that he had run out of time. His boot heels jabbed into Iron Heart's flanks and sent the gray leaping to the side, as the outlaw squeezed the trigger. The slug whipped past them, barely missing.

To John Henry's amazement, he saw Mallette twist in the saddle and swing his Winchester around to trigger a shot at the man who had just fired.

Mallette's aim was good. The outlaw's rifle flew from his hands as the slug's impact jerked him halfway around in the saddle. Blood spurted from his bullet-shattered shoulder.

At the same time, John Henry charged toward the nearer of the other two men. The man fired, but he rushed his shot and the bullet whipped past John Henry's head.

A few leaping bounds from Iron Heart brought John Henry into handgun range. His Colt blasted at the same time his opponent levered the Winchester and fired again.

The deputy marshal's shot found its target first, ripping through the man's throat. The outlaw rocked back as blood fountained from the wound, then toppled from the saddle as his horse shied violently.

More guns were roaring. John Henry wheeled Iron Heart toward the third outlaw and saw the man trading shots with Mallette.

In the blink of an eye the man had gone from being one of those in charge to being outnumbered and caught in a crossfire. He tried to spur his way out of trouble, but John Henry's revolver bucked in his hand again and the outlaw sagged as the bullet tore into his side.

The next instant, Mallette's rifle cracked again, and the wounded outlaw pitched off his horse as the gambler's slug drilled him through the head.

Echoes of the gun thunder rolled away across the prairie. Two of the outlaws were down. The lead man Mallette had shot in the shoulder was still mounted. His right arm was useless, but he reached across his body with his left hand and clawed his gun from its holster. Flame spurted from its muzzle as he charged John Henry.

The lawman aimed and fired, and the man flew backward off his horse as John Henry's bullet drove into his chest with the impact of a giant fist.

When the echoes of those final shots faded away, a grim silence hung over the plains.

Taking fresh cartridges from the loops in his shell belt was painful, but John Henry reloaded the Colt before doing anything else. Then, still holding the revolver, he walked Iron Heart toward Nick Mallette.

The gambler's face was pale. He still had the

Winchester in his hands, but he held it at a slant across his chest instead of pointing it at John Henry. If he had told the truth about his life, he had never taken part in a gunfight that big before.

Mallette had been cool under fire, though, and his aim with the rifle had been deadly.

John Henry reined in a few yards away. "That was some good shooting, Nick."

Mallette let the rifle's barrel drift a little toward John Henry. "There's liable to be more, if you don't tell me the truth right now. They're all dead, so you don't have any reason to lie anymore. Are you really a federal marshal?"

"I am. My real name is John Henry Sixkiller."

"So I can keep on calling you John."

"Sure."

"And you really think your boss can help me?"

"I know he can. He can wire Kansas City and get your case reopened. Hell, if that doesn't do any good, I'll go there myself and make sure the truth comes out."

"That's assuming you get out of this mess alive."

"Yeah," John Henry said with a smile. "And right now, unless I get back to Kiowa City and get some proper medical attention, that's a mighty big assumption." A wave of weakness hit him and he clutched at the saddle horn with his free hand to steady himself.

"I'm not sure you can get there by yourself," Mallette said. "And if I go with you, Sheriff Rasmussen will throw me back in jail and turn me over to those deputies from Missouri."

"Maybe," John Henry said through teeth gritted against the pain. "Maybe not, when I tell him who I am . . . and that you're now a special deputy working for me."

Mallette's eyes widened. "You can do that?"

"Well . . . as far as the sheriff's concerned, I can."

Mallette took several Winchester rounds from his vest pocket and thumbed them through the rifle's loading gate. Then he slid the weapon back in its saddle boot. "I sure hope you're telling me the truth, John . . . because you've got yourself a special deputy."

John Henry grinned. "Consider yourself a lawman, for the time being."

"Never thought I'd see the day," Mallette muttered as he turned his horse and fell in alongside John Henry. They started southeast toward Kiowa City.

After a few minutes, the gambler said, "You *can* prove who you are to Sheriff Rasmussen, can't you?"

"We'd better hope so," John Henry said. "Otherwise we'll both wind up behind bars again, and I don't reckon he'll ever let us out!"

Chapter Twenty

As darkness fell, John Henry guided them by the stars that popped out on the ebony curtain hanging above them. He was in and out of full consciousness, though, so to a certain extent he relied on Mallette to keep them going in the right direction.

At some point, the gambler pointed to a clump of lights in the distance and asked, "Is that the settlement, John? Is that Kiowa City?"

"Got to be. Keep your eye on those lights, Nick, and head us straight toward 'em."

"All right. I'm still not sure this is what I should be doing, but I guess I've come too far to back out now. One thing is sure. If I'd stayed with Garrett and the Flame, I'd have been on the dodge from now on. Maybe with you, I've got a chance not to be a fugitive for the rest of my life."

The lights got steadily brighter as they drew closer. From a few hundred yards away, John

Henry could make out some of the buildings and knew they were in the right place.

"Hold on," he told Mallette. "We need to make it to the courthouse without anybody recognizing us. If they do, they might start shooting before we get a chance to talk to Rasmussen."

"How do you know he won't shoot us on sight himself?"

"I don't think an honest lawman would do that. He'll let us turn ourselves in and explain." John Henry paused a moment before he could go on. He felt weak and shaky as a newborn foal. "When we left town, you were wearing that gambler's suit. Keep your hat brim pulled down and there's a good chance nobody will pay any attention to you."

"Unless the man I stole this horse from sees it and recognizes it," Mallette said. "They hang horse thieves out here on the frontier, don't they?"

"You were already acting as a special deputy when you took that saddle mount. We'll see to it that the hombre gets his horse back, and maybe something for his trouble." John Henry chuckled. "The judge may not like seeing something like horse stealing on the expense account, but he'll understand."

"All right," Mallette said. "Hat brim down, ride slow and easy, head for the courthouse, and hope the sheriff is in his office. Is that about the size of it?"

"You've got the idea. Let's go."

They moved ahead again and a few minutes later entered the town on one of the side streets.

Most of the houses in the residential area were already dark, their occupants having turned in for the night.

It was a different story when they cut over to the main street and turned toward the courthouse in the town square. All the saloons were open, and some of the other businesses were, too.

John Henry tensed as they rode past the Paradise Saloon. If anybody was going to recognize them, it would probably be while they were traveling through that stretch.

The sounds of music and laughter drifted past the batwings, but they were strangely subdued. The people of Kiowa City hadn't forgotten what had happened to Charles Houston and Lucas Winslow. It was enough to cast a pall over the whole settlement.

A couple men came out of the saloon while John Henry and Mallette were riding past. John Henry held his breath, but the men just glanced at the two riders and then looked away, not taking any particular notice of them.

As they came closer to the courthouse, Mallette said quietly, "The lamps are burning in the sheriff's office. Somebody will be on duty, even if it isn't Rasmussen."

"As long as whoever it is doesn't get trigger-happy, we'll be all right."

"John . . . do you think the outlaws killed Carl Baird when they got back to the ranch?"

"Maybe not," John Henry said. "Their reasons

for keeping him alive are just as valid whether we're there or not."

"You, uh, you weren't going to kill him either of those other times, were you? That was just an act?"

"That's right. I had to convince everybody, even you, that I was John Saxon, outlaw and cold-blooded killer. Sorry I couldn't tell you the truth all along, Nick, but I figured other folks would be more likely to believe the act if you believed it, too."

Mallette sighed. "I hope you're not lying to me now. If you are really Saxon, I don't see any reason why you'd ride back here like this, though."

"I wouldn't. I'd be putting Kiowa City as far behind me as I could."

"That's what I thought." Mallette drew rein in front of the courthouse. "Well, here we are."

John Henry brought Iron Heart to a stop. "I'll need something out of my saddlebags. You think you can help me down?"

"Sure. You don't want to fall on your face after coming this far." Mallette swung down from the saddle, then helped John Henry to the ground.

John Henry leaned on Iron Heart while he opened one of the saddlebags and slid a hand inside. The pocket that contained his badge and identification papers was hidden so cunningly that somebody could turn those saddlebags inside out and not find it. He had it open in a matter of seconds.

He took out the badge, but left the leather folder containing his bona fides. He could always show them to the sheriff later if he needed to. "All right. Let's go."

He leaned on Mallette for support as they made their way across the courthouse lawn and up the steps to the entrance.

The night-duty deputy bolted to his feet as they stepped into the building. He drew his gun, pointed it at them, and yelled down the hall. "Sheriff! Sheriff, you better get out here!"

Mike Rasmussen appeared in the open door of his office, stopping short at the sight of John Henry and Mallette. His shock at seeing them kept him immobile only for a couple heartbeats. He yanked his Colt from its holster, stalked toward them, and bellowed, "Stand right there, damn you! Don't move!"

"We're not going anywhere, Sheriff," John Henry said with a weary smile. "I can't make any promises about standing, though. I've been shot, and I might fall down."

"Is that why you came back?" Rasmussen demanded. "Looking for help since you're hurt?"

"That . . . and to tell you the truth."

Mallette said, "You'd better listen to him, Sheriff. You might be surprised what he has to say."

"Oh, I'll listen, all right." Rasmussen's face was flushed with anger. "Once I've got the two of you locked up behind bars where you belong!"

"You might want to . . . think twice about that, Sheriff"—John Henry's strength was suddenly deserting him again—"after you've . . . taken a look at this." He held out his right hand and opened it.

The badge of a deputy United States marshal rested on his palm.

"My name is . . . John Henry Sixkiller. You can wire . . . Judge Parker in Fort Smith . . . if you don't—"

Those were all the words John Henry got out. The courthouse corridor spun madly around him for a second before a black shroud dropped down over him and blotted out everything.

". . . iron constitution," a man was saying as awareness seeped back into John Henry's brain. The voice faded in and out. "Most men . . . dead by now . . . that much blood."

"I think he's coming around," another man said. That voice was familiar, and after a second John Henry was thinking straight enough to realize that it belonged to Nick Mallette.

"Let me give him this," the first voice said. Somebody slipped a hand behind John Henry's head and lifted it slightly.

He felt something against his lips and opened them. Liquid fire flowed into his mouth and down his throat, making him gasp and open his eyes. The weatherbeaten face of a gray-haired, middle-aged man looked down at him.

"That was just a sip of whiskey, son," the man said. "A restorative. Perhaps I shouldn't have given it to you. If your name really is Sixkiller, you're probably an Indian, and redskins are notorious for not being able to handle liquor."

Even in his condition, that statement annoyed John Henry. He pushed it aside since there were more pressing matters. "Are you . . . a doctor?" he husked.

"That's right," the gray-haired man said as he straightened. "You're in my office. The sheriff brought you down here when he saw how badly you were wounded. I'm Dr. Joseph Harmon."

"Those . . . bullet holes . . ."

"Don't worry. I've cleaned and bandaged them. They look better than they have any right to, considering what you've been through. I believe they'll heal properly, and you'll be back on your feet in a few weeks."

John Henry closed his eyes for a moment. He wasn't going to waste time and energy arguing with the sawbones, but he knew he probably didn't have a couple weeks to lay around recuperating.

Besides, he wasn't going to need that long to get better. He knew his own abilities, knew from experience that he always bounced back from injuries faster than most men. As the doctor had said, he had an iron constitution.

John Henry opened his eyes again and looked around the room. He was lying on a table between a grim-faced Sheriff Rasmussen and Dr. Harmon. Nick Mallette sat in a ladderback chair against the wall to one side. The deputy from the courthouse stood in the doorway with a shotgun cradled under his arm.

John Henry summoned up a smile for the gambler. "Thanks for . . . getting me here, Nick."

Mallette held up his hands to display the steel cuffs locked around his wrists. "I sure hope you're playing straight with me this time, John."

"I am." John Henry looked at Rasmussen. "Sheriff, Nick's been helping me. He's a special deputy."

"He's a fugitive from Missouri is what he is," Rasmussen said harshly. "A wanted murderer. If you think I'm going to let him go on the word of some Texas gunslinger—"

"Deputy U.S. marshal," John Henry cut in. "You saw my badge."

"Which you could have taken off the body of a real marshal after you killed him."

"I have identification papers—"

"Same thing. They could be stolen."

John Henry took a deep breath and felt the pull of the bandages wrapped tightly around his torso. "Did you wire Judge Parker in Fort Smith?"

"I sent the wire," Rasmussen admitted grudgingly. "The judge probably won't get it until tomorrow morning, though, so I don't expect a reply until then at the earliest. The doc says you've got to stay here, but a deputy will be staying right with you, and there'll be another posted outside. As for Mallette, he's going back to his cell." Rasmussen's stern demeanor eased just slightly as he added, "He wanted to come along and make sure you were all right. Didn't figure it would hurt anything as long as he was cuffed and unarmed."

"I appreciate it, too, Sheriff," Mallette said. "Even though John here is the one who gave me this bruise on my jaw."

"I can explain that," John Henry said.

"In the morning," Dr. Harmon said. "You can explain everything in the morning. For now, Sheriff, I think you should take your prisoner—your *other* prisoner—and clear out. This man needs rest more than anything else right now."

"All right," Rasmussen said, "but Deputy Wheeler stays."

"As long as he doesn't get in my way, that's fine."

The sheriff motioned for Mallette to get up.

As he did so, the gambler said, "Hope I see you again, John."

"You will," John Henry promised. "You can count on it."

Harmon was right about him needing rest. His eyelids had gotten mighty heavy during the past few minutes. John Henry didn't know if the doctor had given him something to make him sleep or if exhaustion had just caught up to him at last. Either way, he knew he wasn't going to be able to stay awake much longer. He summoned up the strength to slightly lift a hand in farewell as Rasmussen ushered Mallette out of the room.

Then John Henry drifted off into oblivion again.

Chapter Twenty-one

Light woke John Henry. It was bright and warm and shining in his face, and when he forced his eyes open he saw that it was slanting in through the gap between a pair of curtains over the window.

A graceful figure moved between John Henry and the window and threw the curtains open wide. He winced as more sunlight flooded into the room. The figure turned toward him, and while it was in silhouette and he couldn't make out any details, the form was definitely female.

"Good morning." The woman's voice was just about as bright and cheery as the sunlight.

"Well, it's morning, anyway," John Henry said. To his ears, his voice sounded rusty as an old hinge. "And I'm alive, so that's better than I expected. Is this . . ." His voice trailed off as he searched his memory for the name of the doctor he vaguely recalled from the night before.

"You're in a bedroom in Dr. Harmon's house, if that's what you're trying to ask," the woman said as she moved around the bed. "He keeps his patients here. It's the closest thing Kiowa City has to a hospital."

"Yeah, Doc Harmon," John Henry said. The image of a middle-aged man with thick gray hair swam into his mind. "I remember him now. Likes to talk about redskins."

"Well, I wouldn't know about that. But he's a good doctor. I help him out some as a sort of unofficial nurse, you might say. I'm Clarissa Doolittle."

The name made John Henry take a better look at her. She was young, no more than twenty-two or so, with dark, thick, glossy hair and wholesomely pretty in a blue dress with white, lacy trim around the neck and sleeves.

At first, he'd thought she might be Judge Ephraim Doolittle's wife, but she was too young for that unless the judge was a randy old goat who had robbed the cradle. That was possible, of course, but he figured it was more likely she was Doolittle's daughter.

"The judge is your father?"

"You mean Uncle Ephraim? He might as well be my father, I suppose. He and Aunt Mildred took me in and raised me after my folks died of a fever. My father was Uncle Ephraim's younger brother."

Well, that clarified that, John Henry thought.

However, other questions still remained, so he asked one of them. "It was just last night the sheriff brought me here to the doc's house, wasn't it? I got to worrying that I might have been out for more than one night."

"Set your mind at ease, Marshal Sixkiller," Clarissa said. "It was just last night. You haven't lost any days."

It took a second for everything she'd said to soak in on John Henry's brain. Then his eyebrows rose in surprise. "You called me Marshal Sixkiller."

"Well, that's your name, isn't it?"

"Yeah, but the last I recall, the subject was still open for debate as far as everybody else in town was concerned."

"Not anymore. Sheriff Rasmussen got a telegram from Judge Parker in Fort Smith early this morning." Clarissa smiled. "Evidently it was worded in a rather blistering fashion. But it confirmed that Judge Parker sent a deputy United States marshal named John Henry Sixkiller here to Kiowa City, and it described you to a T, from what I heard."

That was a relief. Now he wouldn't have to worry about being locked up again, John Henry thought.

"The sheriff asked Dr. Harmon to send word to him whenever you woke up," Clarissa added. "He wants to talk to you. I think it can wait, though, until after you've had some breakfast. Are you hungry?"

"Ravenous." John Henry realized that he really was. "And what I'd really like more than anything else right now is a cup of coffee."

"I think we can do something about that," Clarissa said with a smile. "Wait right here."

John Henry returned the smile. "It's not like I'm liable to run off anywhere."

Clarissa was back a little while later with a tray containing a cup of steaming Arbuckle's and a plate piled high with hotcakes and bacon. She helped him sit up, propping pillows behind him in the bed. "Do you need help feeding yourself?"

"I don't think so, but we'll find out."

The coffee was hot, black, and strong, just the way he liked it, and when he drank some he felt better immediately. As he ate and washed down the food with sips of the potent brew, he felt strength flowing back into him.

He thanked Clarissa, then asked, "Has the doctor checked those bullet holes in my side this morning?"

"Yes, and he said they looked like they were healing cleanly. No sign of infection yet."

"Good. I'll be up and around before you know it."

"After losing so much blood?" she asked with a frown. "Dr. Harmon said you should rest in bed for at least two weeks."

"No offense meant to the doc, but he doesn't know me. I'll heal better on my feet."

"You'll have to work that out with him. Should I send word to the sheriff now?"

"That's a good idea," John Henry agreed. "I'll be finished with breakfast by the time he gets here."

In fact, he was just draining the last of the coffee from the cup when Sheriff Rasmussen came in, trailed by Dr. Harmon.

"I don't want you wearing out my patient, Sheriff," the doctor warned.

"I'm not gonna wear him out, but he's damned sure going to answer some questions." Rasmussen took off his hat when he spotted Clarissa Doolittle sitting in the corner. "Pardon my language, Miss Doolittle."

"That's all right, Sheriff. Uncle Ephraim can get rather salty in his language when he's worked up about something, too."

She stood up. "I'll be outside if you need me, Doctor." With a smile for John Henry, she left the room.

"Just take it easy on him, that's all I ask, Sheriff," Harmon told Rasmussen. Then he followed Clarissa out of the room.

Rasmussun got the chair Clarissa had been sitting in, dragged it closer to the bed and sat down. "I heard back from your boss."

"That's what Miss Doolittle told me. You're convinced now that I'm who I say I am?"

"I don't reckon I have any choice but be convinced. Your story checks out, Marshal." Rasmussen glowered darkly. "I just wish you'd told me who you were before I threw you in jail."

"Well, if I'd done that, it wouldn't have helped me get on the inside of the gang that's going after blood vengeance for Henry Garrett, would it?"

Rasmussen leaned forward, obviously interested. "That's what those killings were really all about, just like I suspected?"

"That's what they're all about," John Henry confirmed.

He spent the next half hour explaining everything that had happened since his arrival in Kiowa City a week earlier, starting with the fatal gunfight with Jimmy Deverill.

"Deverill slapped leather because he recognized me as a marshal from Indian Territory. I arrested him a year ago for running whiskey to the Nations. Running into him here was a lucky break for me. I planned to start some sort of ruckus that would land me in jail, so I could break out later and pretend to be on the run. Killing Deverill achieved the same result, and at the same time it got rid of a lowdown skunk who needed killing."

"So you figured all along on establishing yourself as an outlaw and working your way into the gang?"

"Yep," John Henry said. "Having Nick Mallette being locked up at the same time was another break for me. He knew where we needed to go."

He told Rasmussen about the Silver Skull Ranch, Lottie Dalmas, and her relationships with both Henry and Simon Garrett. The story continued through the rustling of the J/M cattle, the ambush planned for Jed Montayne and his men, and how John Henry had ruined that ambush and gotten wounded in the process.

The sheriff's suspicious frown eased as he took a cigar from his vest pocket and offered it to the deputy marshal. John Henry shook his head, so

Rasmussen stuck the cheroot between his own lips and clamped his teeth on it, leaving it unlit.

"I've heard rumors about some sort of outlaw haven around here," he said around the cigar, "but I've never been able to track it down. Now that I know where it is, I'll be able to get up a posse and do something about it."

"You try to hit the place head-on with a posse and you'll just get some good men killed," John Henry cautioned. "It may take the army to root Garrett and his bunch out of there. It'll take some planning, at the very least."

"I didn't figure on going off half-cocked," Rasmussen growled. "But I'm not gonna let them get away with what they've done, either. You said Carl Baird's their prisoner, and I'll be damned if I'm going to abandon him."

"I can't guarantee that Baird's still alive. But if he is, I agree with you. We've got to get him out of there. Besides, Judge Parker sent me here to stop their campaign of terror and bring them to justice, and that's what I intend to do."

"Doc Harmon says you'll be laid up in bed for the next few weeks."

"Doc Harmon is wrong," John Henry said confidently.

"All right, there's something else I'm curious about. Nick Mallette. He's not really a special deputy, is he?"

"Well . . . I suppose that depends on how you want to look at it."

"When he helped you break out of jail, when he

escaped from custody himself, he didn't know that you were a federal lawman, right?"

"I figured it would be better if he didn't know. He couldn't accidentally give away anything that way."

Rasmussen chewed on the cheroot for a moment. "Then he's really just a wanted murderer who broke out of jail and ought to be sent back to Missouri to hang."

"I think he was railroaded into that murder conviction, Sheriff. Somebody accused him of cheating at cards and drew on him first. Mallette was just defending himself."

"That's what he told you, but you don't have one damned bit of proof that it's true."

"No, I don't," John Henry admitted. "But I've been around a lot of cold-blooded killers, and Nick doesn't strike me as being one of them. I believe his story."

"A jury in Kansas City didn't."

"The man he shot was the brother of a local politician with a considerable amount of influence," John Henry pointed out. "As officers of the law, we'd like to believe that doesn't make any difference, but you and I both know that in reality it sometimes does, Sheriff. Not only that, but Nick talked Garrett and the Flame into sparing Deputy Baird's life and keeping him there as a prisoner instead of killing him. Nick risked his own life to help me when those outlaws tried to capture me yesterday, and then he gave up his freedom to bring me back here so I wouldn't die from that bullet wound. Those don't sound like things a murderer would do, either."

Rasmussen spread his hands. "Well, what do you want me to do? I can't just turn him loose on your say-so!"

"No," John Henry agreed reluctantly. "You can't."

"And I've got deputies from Missouri sitting over in the hotel who want to take him back with them. Their papers are all legal and in order. I can't very well refuse to turn him over to them."

John Henry thought about it for a moment. "You can if you tell them that he's being held here as a witness in a federal investigation at the special request of Judge Isaac C. Parker, pending the conclusion of said investigation."

"Will Parker go along with that?"

"He will if I ask him to," John Henry said, hoping he was right about that. "And when you get right down to brass tacks, it's not far from the truth. Mallette was there when Lottie Dalmas and Simon Garrett were talking about getting revenge for Henry Garrett. He can testify about those things and about how they tried to bushwhack Jed Montayne and his men."

John Henry considered telling the sheriff about the suspicions he'd had regarding the connection between J.C. Carson and the attempt on Montayne's life, but he decided that theory was too vague so far. Even if it turned out to be true, it didn't really change things as far as the most pressing problem went, which was bringing Lottie, Garrett, and the other outlaws to justice.

If Carson actually was mixed up in it, he could be dealt with later.

"All right," Rasmussen said after chewing on his cigar a little more. "I'll keep Mallette locked up for now, and your pet judge can see about trying to get his case reopened. That suit you?"

John Henry winced a little, but not from the pain of his wound. "That suits me just fine, Sheriff, but I've got one other favor to ask of you."

"What's that?"

"Don't ever refer to Judge Parker as my pet judge where it could get back to him. If it did, I might wind up being thrown in his jail in the basement of the federal courthouse in Fort Smith!"

Chapter Twenty-two

Despite John Henry's confident statements about recovering faster than Dr. Harmon expected, the shock of being shot and the amount of blood he had lost couldn't be shrugged off. For the next couple days he was too weak to get out of bed for more than a few minutes at a time, and he kept going to sleep.

That gave his body the chance to regain some of its strength. By the third day he felt well enough to sit up in a rocking chair most of the day.

When Harmon changed the dressings and checked the wounds that night, he frowned. "I don't understand it. The way these wounds are healing, you look like more than a week has passed since you were shot, instead of only a few days."

"Must be because I was raised by redskins, Doc. Heap big spirit medicine."

"I meant no offense by what I said the other day, Marshal. I just worried that you might not be able to handle the liquor."

"It's all right, Doc. I've been called a half-breed and worse plenty of times in my life, and it hasn't killed me yet. You might not know this, but some Indians will give a fella just as much grief for being half white as some whites will give him for being half Indian."

"No, I didn't know that," Harmon admitted. "I don't know what's causing you to heal so quickly, either, but it's astounding. If you want to call it spirit medicine I suppose that's as good a description as any."

"I reckon that means I'll be able to get on about my business pretty soon."

The medico frowned. "I didn't say that. I think you'd be wise to continue recuperating for at least another week before you attempt anything more strenuous than, say, walking to the table for meals."

"We'll see." John Henry's tone made it clear that his recovery would proceed on his timetable, not the doctor's. "There's something else I've been meaning to ask you. Have you said anything to anybody about me being here?"

"I'm not in the habit of discussing my patients with anyone, Marshal," Harmon replied rather tartly.

"I'd appreciate a straight answer to my question, Doctor. Does anyone besides Sheriff Rasmussen and Miss Doolittle know I'm here?"

"Well . . . I believe the sheriff has shared the situation with Judge Doolittle. And the deputy who helped him bring you here probably knows who you are, too. Other than that, I really couldn't say.

But I can assure that *I* haven't gone around town talking about you."

"That's good. Let's keep it that way."

John Henry hadn't forgotten how Lottie had talked about using Mallette as a spy later on, when the gang had finished avenging Henry Garrett and set out to clean up all the loot in this part of Kansas. It was possible that Lottie already had spies in Kiowa City, too, and John Henry didn't want the news that he was still alive getting back to her and Garrett.

It was possible he might take them by surprise one of these days, and he wanted to keep that option open.

Clarissa Doolittle spent quite a bit of time at Dr. Harmon's house, helping out, and John Henry enjoyed her company. He didn't have any romantic interest in her—there was a Cherokee girl back in Indian Territory with whom he had a sort of understanding—but it was natural for any man to be pleased to have a pretty girl nursing him back to health.

The day after John Henry had had his talk with Harmon about spirit medicine, Clarissa brought her uncle to the doctor's house to introduce him to the lawman.

Judge Ephraim Doolittle was a rotund man with a round face and white hair parted in the middle of his head. The steely gleam in his pale blue eyes told John Henry the judge might not be quite as mild-mannered as he appeared.

"I'm pleased to meet you, Marshal," he said as

he shook hands with John Henry. "Pleased as well that my old friend Isaac Parker took my worries seriously enough to send a man to look into them. According to Sheriff Rasmussen, you chose a rather, ah, unorthodox method of doing so."

"It got me on the trail of the varmints who killed Charles Houston and Lucas Winslow, Your Honor," John Henry said. "And I was able to keep them from torturing and killing Jed Montayne."

"Yes, I know. That was excellent work, and I intend to let Judge Parker know as much. But we're left with the fact that Simon Garrett and his paramour Miss Dalmas are still out there plotting against me and the surviving members of the jury that convicted Henry Garrett. The sheriff tells me that they're holding Deputy Baird prisoner as well."

Clarissa had left John Henry and her uncle alone in the room, or else John Henry might not have mentioned what he said next.

"They may have killed the deputy by now, Judge. I'd say it's about a fifty-fifty chance either way."

"I know," Doolittle said with a grim look on his face. "If they've harmed him, that's something else they'll have to answer for. What I want to know is what you intend to do now. I think you should summon a whole posse of deputy marshals to clean out that devil's sanctuary."

"It may come to that, Your Honor."

"If there's anything I can do to help, you have only to ask, young man."

"Thank you, sir."

Doolittle smiled. "On a more positive note, I

hear that my niece is helping Dr. Harmon take care of you."

"Yes, sir, she is," John Henry said, "and she's doing a fine job of it, too."

"I'm glad to hear it. Clarissa is like a daughter to me."

"She speaks mighty highly of you as well."

The judge shook hands again and then left.

Clarissa came into the room and asked John Henry, "Did the two of you have a good visit?"

"We did. Your uncle strikes me as a good man, the sort of judge we need more of out here in the West." John Henry was wearing a bathrobe over the bandages around his torso and the bottom half of his long underwear. He hadn't seen his boots or his gunbelt since he woke up in the doctor's house, and he had a hankering for both. "You wouldn't happen to know where my clothes are, would you?"

"Your shirt had too much blood on it to be saved—not to mention the bullet holes, but I suppose those could have been mended. I'm afraid the doctor threw it out and it was burned."

John Henry sighed. "I've got a couple spare shirts in my saddlebags. I reckon my gear is stored somewhere?"

"Yes. Your saddlebags and the other clothes you were wearing are here. They're in that wardrobe."

John Henry stood up and went over to the piece of furniture she indicated. He had thought about looking in there before but hadn't gotten around to it. He opened it and felt better at the sight of his coiled gunbelt and the holstered Colt attached to it. "The sheriff told me my horse is being taken care of, down at the livery stable."

"Yes, of course." Clarissa frowned slightly. "You sound like you're thinking about getting dressed and going somewhere, Marshal Sixkiller. The condition you're in, I don't think that would be a very good idea."

"I'm not going anywhere. Not just yet." He drew in a deep breath and was pleased when it didn't hurt the wounds in his side too much. "But soon. Mighty soon."

Kiowa City slumbered peacefully again that night. A faint breeze stirred the leaves of the cottonwoods that grew along Kiowa Creek, just north of the settlement.

That breeze didn't carry the sound of hoofbeats to the town, because the men who slipped through the darkness had left their horses a good distance away and approached the settlement on foot.

Simon Garrett had half a dozen of his best men with him. He would have liked to bring the whole gang, charge down Main Street, and rain down fire, death, and destruction on Kiowa City. If it had been completely up to him, that sort of open warfare would have been the tactic he chose to avenge his brother.

That wouldn't satisfy Lottie's thirst for vengeance, though. She wanted her enemies to suffer, not just die.

So she had hatched the plan to kill the members

of the jury one by one, then Sheriff Rasmussen, and finally Judge Ephraim Doolittle. She had struck an alliance with J.C. Carson, who at one time had been an outlaw himself, well acquainted with Harley Dalmas, Lottie's father. Things had been going along fairly well until Carson had rushed them into going after Montayne.

That failure had done something to Lottie, Garrett knew. Her patience had disappeared, and her orderly, well-planned campaign of terror had been abandoned. The citizens of Kiowa City would still know terror, but it would no longer be dragged out.

Garrett held up a hand and signaled silently for his companions to halt. They were still in the shadows of the trees along the creek, so the chances of anyone spotting them were pretty slim.

So late at night, nobody was out and about much in the settlement, anyway, except the men who were drinking in the saloons. They wouldn't have any reason to look for danger lurking in the trees beside the creek.

Garrett motioned for the men to gather around him and pointed to a whitewashed, two-story house about a hundred yards away. "That's the judge's place," he whispered.

"Looks like they've gone to bed," one of the men said, keeping his voice equally quiet. "I don't see any lights burnin'."

Another man asked, "You reckon they've got any guards posted?"

"I don't know, but if they do, it'll be too bad for

them," Garrett said. "Be ready to move when the ball opens up."

Instead of attacking with everybody at his disposal, Garrett had split his force. Eight more members of the gang were waiting on horseback a few hundred yards from town. They would create a diversion while he and his companions sprinted toward the judge's house and forced their way inside. It was just a matter of waiting for the right moment. . . .

Garrett stiffened as he heard the sudden drumming of hoofbeats. That would be the other group launching their raid, right on time.

"Get ready!" he said in a low, urgent tone.

None of the outlaws carried rifles. Any gun work they needed to do would be close up. They drew their revolvers and gripped the weapons tightly as they waited for their leader's signal.

Shots blasted from downtown as voices were raised in strident howls. Even from where he was, Garrett could see the muzzle flashes that lit up the street with their glare.

"Go!" he told his men, and he broke into a run to lead them as they raced toward the Doolittle home.

The shooting continued from the area around the square. Garrett didn't care how much damage his men did there; their only purpose was to draw the attention of any guards around the judge's house.

Sure enough, he spotted a couple men running along the sides of the house, heading away from the back of the place where they had been posted. More than likely, their orders had been to stay put no matter what happened, but it was hard to ask excitable townies to do that. Once a commotion started, they had to go see what it was all about.

Garrett headed for the rear door of the house. He was just about to kick it open when a man with a rifle appeared at the corner and yelled, "Hey!"

Before the guard could raise the weapon, Garrett shot him. The bullet spun the man around and dropped him facedown on the ground.

Garrett turned his attention back to the door, lifting his foot and driving his boot heel against the wood just above the knob. The door tore free of the splintered jamb and flew open. He went in fast, alert for more guards. The other outlaws were right behind him.

He had never been in the house and didn't know the layout, but it seemed likely the bedrooms would be on the second floor. He headed for the front of the house, knowing he would find a staircase along the way.

Light suddenly spilled down from above. Somebody up there had lit a lamp, but that just helped Garrett locate the stairs. As he rounded the landing and looked up, he saw a bulky figure appear at the top of the stairs. In the light coming along the hallway, Garrett recognized the man as Judge Doolittle.

"Get out of my house!" the judge roared. He pointed a shotgun down the stairs and tripped both triggers.

Garrett was already diving to the side as the double-barreled weapon boomed deafeningly. The charge missed him, but the man right behind him wasn't so lucky. The buckshot tore into him, shredding flesh and throwing the outlaw backward.

Garrett could have killed Doolittle then. The judge had emptied the shotgun and would have to reload before he could fire again.

But Doolittle dying that night wasn't part of Lottie's plan. Garrett bounded up the stairs toward the judge.

Doolittle realized that he'd made a mistake by firing both barrels at once. He flung the shotgun at Garrett and turned to run.

Garrett ducked the flying Greener and charged after Doolittle. His gun rose and fell, crashing down on the back of the judge's head and sending him sprawling to the floor. His long white nightshirt billowed around him as he fell.

A woman screamed somewhere nearby.

Garrett snapped, "Get her!" at his men and paused to kneel beside Doolittle and check the judge. He was alive, but out cold.

The men rushed past Garrett. He called after them, "Find the girl, too!" He knew the Doolittles had taken in their niece and raised her like their own daughter. He'd had plenty of time in prison to study up on the men he hated.

A couple men dragged a middle-aged woman in nightclothes toward Garrett as he stood up. She was too terrified to put up a struggle.

That wasn't the case with Doolittle's niece. She

was fighting like a wildcat as two more outlaws forced her from her bedroom into the hallway. Her dark hair was disheveled, and her nightgown was twisted around what appeared to be a nicely shaped body.

At the moment, Garrett didn't care about that. He stepped closer and swung his left fist in a short, sharp blow that cracked against the young woman's jaw and jerked her head to the side. She sagged in her captors' grip, stunned by the punch.

"One of you can carry her. It's going to take two to lift the judge."

They moved quickly, knowing that the raid in the other part of town might not draw everybody away from the house. Somebody could have heard the shots, especially the blast of Doolittle's shotgun.

By the time they had gotten the three prisoners downstairs, the two men who had been in charge of the horses had brought the mounts to the back door of the house. They had brought an extra horse for the judge. His senseless form was thrown over the saddle and lashed down. Each of the women would ride double with one of the outlaws.

Garrett heard shouts of alarm not far off as they all mounted up. He shouted, "Let's go!" and raked his horse's flanks with his spurs. The animal leaped forward and broke into a run. The rest of the men were close behind him as he splashed across Kiowa Creek.

Within moments the settlement fell into the distance behind them. The group that had provided the diversion would be withdrawing, too, and they would all rendezvous several miles from town and head for the Silver Skull.

The first part of Lottie's plan had been completed successfully, Garrett thought.

And he took pleasure from the fact that the night was no longer quiet and peaceful in Kiowa City.

Chapter Twenty-three

John Henry was sound asleep when the shooting broke out, but his hazardous profession had trained his instincts to wake him at the first sign of trouble, even when he was deep in slumber. As usual, he went from sleeping to completely awake and alert in the blink of an eye.

He sat up in bed, feeling the bandages tug at him, but the wounds in his side didn't twinge at all. That was a good sign. He swung his legs out of bed and got to his feet. Still no real pain.

A couple steps took him to the wardrobe. He had left the holstered Colt in there, thinking that he probably wouldn't need it in town since so few people knew he was there and knew who he really was.

That might have been a mistake, he thought as he opened the wardrobe door and reached inside to close his hand around the revolver's smooth walnut grips. They felt good against his palm.

"Must be getting careless in your old age, John Henry," he said aloud.

He swung toward the window. The doctor's house had only one story, so he probably wouldn't be able to see much, but he swept the curtain aside anyway and peered out into the darkness. The hour was probably approaching midnight.

With all that shooting going on, more than likely most citizens were awake now. John Henry looked toward the square and saw the reflection of muzzle flashes splitting the night. It sounded like a small-scale war going on.

His first thought was that Simon Garrett and the rest of the gang had attacked the settlement. That was certainly possible, although it seemed a little straightforward for the devious Lottie Dalmas.

John Henry turned his head and frowned as he heard a faint, heavy boom. That sounded like a shotgun going off, he thought, but it didn't come from the same area where the rest of the gunplay was taking place.

Something else was going on.

With a grimace, he turned away from the window and went back to the wardrobe. He holstered the Colt and picked up his denim trousers, which lay neatly folded on the same shelf as his gun belt and hat.

Once he had stepped into the trousers and fastened them, he buckled on the gun belt. He moved swiftly and efficiently, not rushing but not wasting any time, either.

His boots were in the bottom of the wardrobe. It took him only a moment to pull them on.

As he turned toward the bedroom door, it swung open. John Henry put his hand on the butt of his gun again, but it was just Dr. Harmon standing there holding a lamp.

"I was afraid this is how I would find you," the doctor said. "You heard all that shooting, and you just can't stand it, can you, Marshal?"

"Trouble's my job. And that sounds like plenty of trouble."

"It's several blocks away. If you try to walk that far, you'll probably collapse. If you collapse, you might break those wounds open again."

"I think you underestimate me, Doc. You said yourself I was healing up faster than anybody you ever saw."

"But you're still far from recovered," Harmon argued. "Besides, listen to that."

John Henry listened, and a frown creased his forehead as he realized that the shooting was a lot more sporadic. It sounded like it was getting farther away, too.

The raiders, whoever they were, were retreating from Kiowa City.

"It's over," Harmon said, "or at least it will be by the time you could get there. So you might as well get back in bed—"

"Sorry Doc." John Henry took a step toward him, forcing the medico to step aside. "Whether it's over or not, I need to find out what happened."

"I can't very well tackle you and force you to

stop," Harmon said angrily. "But I want to make it clear that you're acting against medical advice."

John Henry nodded. "Duly noted. You won't be held responsible." He went to the front door and opened it. The shooting had stopped completely, but in the distance he heard the swift rataplan of fading hoofbeats. The attackers had lit a shuck, he was sure of that.

He was walking to the gate in the fence around the doctor's front yard when he spotted someone running toward him. It was too dark to see who the man was, so John Henry slid his Colt from leather and raised it. "Hold it!" he called. "Who's there?" He took a quick step to the side, just in case somebody aimed a shot at the sound of his voice.

The running man stopped short and exclaimed, "Sixkiller! Is that you?"

"Yeah," John Henry said, recognizing Mike Rasmussen's voice. "What's going on, Sheriff?"

"Some men charged into town and shot up a few businesses. Broke some windows and wounded half a dozen men, a couple of them pretty bad, from the looks of it. I was on my way to fetch Doc Harmon."

"I heard you, Sheriff." Harmon stepped out of his house carrying his black medical bag. His nightshirt was stuffed into a pair of trousers. He hurried past John Henry. "I'll go see to the wounded. Where should I start?"

"The Paradise," Rasmussen answered. "Several men were hit when they came running out and tried to put up a fight."

Harmon jerked his head in a nod and trotted toward the square.

"I was coming to check on you, too," Rasmussen went on to John Henry. "From what I was told, those rangy outlaws made a lot of noise and caused a lot of commotion, but they didn't seem to care how many people they shot or how much damage they did."

"A diversion," John Henry said. The same thought had occurred to him as soon as he heard that shotgun go off a few blocks away from downtown.

"Yeah, I thought maybe somebody else was after you."

"Not very many people know I'm here, or even still alive." Alarm bells went off in John Henry's brain. "But Garrett would know that he could find Judge Doolittle here in town. Where does he live?"

A curse ripped out of the sheriff's mouth. "Not far from here." He wheeled around to break into a run.

John Henry followed at a more deliberate pace, although every instinct in his body wanted him to dash after Rasmussen. As much as he hated to admit it, he knew that Dr. Harmon was right. He wasn't completely recovered and had to be careful not to cause himself a setback.

Having to take it slow was frustrating. He had lost sight of Rasmussen and didn't know where the sheriff had gone. He didn't know which house belonged to Judge Doolittle, either.

He was about to call Rasmussen's name when

the local lawman beat him to it, shouting, "Sixkiller! Over here!"

John Henry spotted Rasmussen standing in front of a large, two-story, whitewashed frame house. Just the sort of place where a judge would live, John Henry thought.

"Is this the Doolittle place, Sheriff?" he asked as he came up to Rasmussen.

"Yeah," Rasmussen replied in a bleak, flinty voice. "I left two deputies here to stand guard, just in case. One of them is lying dead behind the house, drilled through the heart."

John Henry went cold inside, and the feeling had nothing to do with his gunshot wound. "What about the judge and his family?"

"Gone. And there's a puddle of blood on the floor at the foot of the stairs."

John Henry sighed. "But there are no bodies in the house?"

"No. Whoever got in there took the judge and his wife and niece with them."

"You know it had to be Garrett. His gang is big enough to split it into two forces. One bunch came rampaging into town to draw everybody's attention while the others came here and grabbed the judge and his family."

"You're bound to be right," Rasmussen said with a nod. "Nobody else would do such a thing. I hope all that blood in there doesn't mean one of them was killed."

"I'll bet it came from one of the outlaws. Lottie would want Doolittle and the women to be taken alive, so she can make the judge suffer. I reckon making him watch while Mrs. Doolittle and Clarissa are tortured would be worse for him than being killed."

"A hell of a lot worse," Rasmussen rumbled. "You really think the woman would do something like that?"

"I know she would," John Henry replied without hesitation. "She gave orders the men were not to kill me. She wanted me brought back alive so she could use the bowie knife on me, more than likely. And she hates Doolittle a lot more than she hates me."

Wearily, Rasmussen scrubbed a hand over his face. He sighed. "They'll keep the prisoners alive for a while, then. We can go after them."

"It won't do any good. You can't get to the Silver Skull with a posse. The place is too well defended." John Henry paused to think. "But I may know a way—"

"Sheriff! Sheriff Rasmussen!" The shout came from a man who was running toward them.

Both lawmen swung around, guns at the ready.

"Hold on!" Rasmussen snapped a second later. "That's one of my deputies, Vince Fremont."

The man hurried up to them and stopped, panting a little. "Sheriff, somebody's comin'. We heard a horse gallopin' toward town."

"Well, for God's sake, let's go see who it is," Rasmussen said irritably. Even though the violence had broken out less than half an hour earlier, it already seemed like it had been a long, hard night.

Once again, John Henry had to lag behind as the sheriff and Deputy Fremont ran back toward the square. He halfway expected to hear more shots, but there were only excited shouts.

By the time he reached the square, Fremont and another deputy were helping a rider from the back of a lathered horse. It was an awkward process, and enough light came from the windows of nearby buildings for John Henry to see why. The rider's wrists were tied together behind his back.

A hood made from a flour sack was over his head, completely concealing his features. Something about the man's stocky build struck John Henry as familiar. He wasn't really surprised when Rasmussen jerked the hood off and revealed the pale face of Deputy Carl Baird.

The deputy was alive. Nick Mallette would be glad to hear that, John Henry thought.

Baird looked like he had been through the wringer. His face was swollen and bruised and streaked with dried blood from the beatings he had endured at the hands of the outlaws. In addition to the hood that had covered his head, he had a gag in his mouth, tied in place with a bandanna.

"Help him sit down, damn it," Rasmussen ordered. "Cut him loose and get that gag out of his mouth."

The deputies eased Baird to a sitting position on the steps leading up to the porch of the hardware store. One of them produced a clasp knife and used it to cut the rope around Baird's wrists. When the rope came free, Baird's shoulders sagged forward and he groaned softly. His muscles probably hurt like blazes.

Fremont untied the knot in the bandanna and threw it aside, then pried the wad of cloth from between Baird's jaws.

Rasmussen knelt in front of Baird. "Are you all right, Carl? Did Garrett turn you loose and send you here like this?"

John Henry knew that had to be what had happened. And he was sure that Garrett wouldn't have done such a thing without a good reason, more than likely because Lottie Dalmas had ordered him to. He sensed Lottie's hand in this.

Baird didn't reply to the sheriff's questions. He groaned again and made a choked, incoherent sound.

"What's wrong, Carl?" Rasmussen went on. "Why don't you answer me?"

"I don't think he can, Sheriff," John Henry said as a chilling realization came to him.

Rasmussen glanced at him and snapped, "What the hell are you talking about?"

"Check Deputy Baird's mouth," John Henry suggested. "I think there's a good chance you'll find that they've cut out his tongue."

Chapter Twenty-four

A horrified Rasmussen sent one of the deputies to find Dr. Harmon, and when the physician got there he quickly confirmed the gruesome diagnosis. "It actually looks like someone did a fairly skillful job of removing the tongue. Whoever did this has a deft touch with a blade."

"Lottie Dalmas." John Henry had no doubt about that.

Harmon rested a hand on Baird's shoulder. "I really need to get this man back to my office. I'd like to perform a more extensive examination and take steps to see that he has a successful recovery."

"A man doesn't recover from losing his tongue!" Rasmussen burst out. Obviously, he was barely able to contain the fury he felt over his deputy's mutilation. "He'll never be able to talk again!"

"No, but he'll be able to do everything else if he lives, and that's what I want to make certain of," Harmon said.

The sheriff grimaced and nodded. "Of course, Doc. Sorry I almost lost my temper. I just can't believe that anybody would do such a thing. Those damned people!"

He squeezed Baird's other shoulder. "We'll get 'em, Carl. I promise they'll pay for this and everything else they've done. You've got my word on that."

Rasmussen lifted his hand, but Baird reached up to take hold of his sleeve. He made noises again, with a note of urgency this time.

"What is it?" Rasmussen asked.

Baird reached inside his vest pocket with trembling fingers and drew out a folded piece of paper. He held it out to Rasmussen.

The sheriff looked at the paper almost like it was a coiled rattlesnake, ready to strike. "They sent this with you? It's a message for us?"

Baird nodded mutely.

Rasmussen took the paper. "Do you know what it says?"

Baird shook his head.

"We'll see about it," Rasmussen told him. "Right now, you go on with Doc Harmon and don't worry about anything except getting better. We'll take care of those damned outlaws."

Baird gave John Henry a walleyed look.

"Don't worry about him, either," Rasmussen said. "Turns out he's on our side after all."

"And I'm sorry about walloping you in the head,

Deputy," John Henry said. "I tried not to put too big a dent in your skull."

Baird rolled his eyes.

"Help him down to the doctor's house," Rasmussen ordered Fremont. "Sixkiller, you come with me."

"The doc already read me the riot act about how I'm supposed to be resting."

"Well, it's a little late for that, ain't it?"

Even under the grim circumstances, John Henry had to smile a little.

The two lawmen walked up the block to the town square and the courthouse. They went up the steps and down the hall to the sheriff's office, where Rasmussen nodded John Henry into the leather armchair and sank wearily into the chair behind his desk.

He dropped the folded piece of paper on the desk in front of him and glared at it. "There's a part of me doesn't want to open that and read it because I know whatever it has to say, it won't be anything good."

"I'm sure you're right about that, Sheriff, but as loco and poison mean as Lottie Dalmas is, I don't think she does much of anything without a reason. One that makes sense to her, anyway."

"I know, I know." Rasmussen picked up the paper. Slowly, he unfolded it, squinted at the words printed on it, and cleared his throat.

He began to read. "'We have Judge Doolittle and his wife and niece. They have been sentenced to death, and this sentence will be carried out at sunrise two mornings from now unless you bring the following men to me before then. Alvin Newton. Caleb Chandler. Jed Montayne. Fred Barnes—"

Rasmussen stopped reading and looked up at John Henry. "These are all the men who served on that jury. The ones who are still alive, anyway."

"She's decided not to take her time about it," John Henry said. "She wants to wipe out everybody at once and avenge Henry Garrett that way."

"She's crazy!"

"Nobody's going to argue with you about that, Sheriff. What else does the note say?"

Rasmussen looked at the paper again. "She claims they'll let Mildred Doolittle and Clarissa go if those other men are turned over to her. There are directions to her place, where they're supposed to be brought." He cleared his throat again. "And there's an eleventh man she wants turned over along with them. Me."

"You arrested Henry Garrett."

Rasmussen let the paper fall on the desk. "Yeah, but it's like he said the morning they hanged him. Me catching him was just pure dumb luck on my part. His horse stepped in a hole and went down. Otherwise he would've got away from me."

The two of them were quiet for a moment. Then John Henry said, "Obviously, Miss Dalmas plans to kill all of you, including the judge."

"You reckon she'd keep her word and let the two women go?"

"I think it's impossible to predict what she'll do. But she wants to hurt Doolittle as much as she can, so I think it's a pretty good bet she intends to kill Clarissa and Mrs. Doolittle, too."

"If there's even a chance she'll let them go, we've got to take it. I'll get in touch with all these fellas—"

"And do what? Ask them to turn themselves over to a crazy woman and a bunch of outlaws so they can be murdered?"

Rasmussen's fist came down hard on the desk. "By God, we have to do something!"

"We'll do something, and I've got an idea where we should start."

"Where's that?"

"Let's go downstairs."

Nick Mallette was awake, sitting on the bunk in his cell with his elbows resting on his thighs and his hands clasped together in front of him as he leaned forward. John Henry saw him in the faint light from the lamp at the top of the stairs and thought the gambler looked almost like he was expecting something.

Mallette lifted his head at the sound of their footsteps as they came down the stairs and approached the cell. He came to his feet and moved over to grip the bars as he recognized his visitors. "What's happened, John? I heard a bunch of shooting."

"That was Garrett and his bunch paying a call

on the town. They kidnapped Judge Doolittle and his wife and niece."

"Damn it! Is there no limit to what they'll do?"

"Doesn't seem like it," John Henry drawled. "They also cut out Carl Baird's tongue and sent him into town with a message saying they'll kill the judge and his family unless the rest of those jury members are turned over to them, along with the sheriff here."

"Carl . . ." Mallette said in a hollow voice. "They cut out . . . Good Lord!"

"They'll pay for it," Rasmussen said heavily. "That won't give Carl the ability to speak again, but they'll pay for it."

Mallette looked at John Henry again. "How are you doing, John? I haven't seen you since we got back to town."

"I'm all right. Doc says I'm healing up faster than I've got any right to. That's good, because I've got a plan for dealing with Lottie and Garrett and the rest of them."

Rasmussen frowned. "You haven't told me anything about a plan."

"That's because Nick here has a part in it," John Henry said with a nod toward the prisoner. "I figured it made sense to tell both of you at the same time."

Rasmussen and Mallette looked surprised.

The sheriff said, "You'd better not have any ideas about turning this killer loose again. I can't do that, not with those Missouri deputies still in town."

"What some Missouri deputies don't know won't hurt 'em. Nick can get back into that ranch house without getting killed, and we're going to need an inside man."

"Wait a minute," Mallette said. "What do you mean they won't kill me?"

"They don't know you're anything but what you seemed to be, a convicted murderer on the run. They're convinced that you and I weren't working together."

"That's because we weren't. You lied to me about who you really are, remember?"

"That's true," John Henry admitted. "And I feel a mite bad about it, Nick, I really do."

Mallette looked like he didn't know whether to believe John Henry or not. Finally he sighed. "All right, go on. What's this plan of yours?"

Rasmussen opened his mouth to say something, but he clamped it shut before any words came out. He gave John Henry a curt nod, indicating that he should continue.

"There's no way you can take a posse up that trail without most of you getting massacred, Sheriff. There's a deep ravine on the other side of the ranch, and you can't get horses across there. But I'm pretty sure that ravine is also a back door that leads right into the place."

For the next few minutes, he told them about how Sven Gunderson had attacked him while he was patrolling the rim and both of them had wound up at the bottom of the ravine, Gunderson fatally.

When John Henry mentioned the cave, Rasmussen snorted. "There aren't any caves in Kansas. At least not any that I ever heard about."

"Well, you're wrong about that, Sheriff. I've been in this one. I'm convinced that it connects up with the ranch house. If it didn't, somebody wouldn't have gone to the trouble of hacking those handholds into the opposite wall of the ravine in that particular spot. It's an escape route."

Rasmussen rubbed his jaw and frowned in thought. After a moment, he said, "Suppose you're right. Are you saying we can take men through that cave and get the drop on those damn outlaws at the ranch?"

"I don't see why not."

"You said they patrol the rim night and day."

"That's true, but if we can get a force into the ravine several miles away, they can hike down to the cave during the night without being seen. They'll just have to be mighty quiet."

Rasmussen wasn't convinced. "Maybe. Where does Mallette come in?"

"I was sort of wondering that, too," the gambler said.

"Nick, you'll go back to the ranch tomorrow. Tell Lottie and Garrett that I killed the three men who were with you, but I was wounded again and you spent the past few days trying to hunt me down. You finally found me, but I had already died from my wounds and the scavengers had been at me. That'll explain why you didn't bring my body back with you."

Mallette shook his head. "They're not going to believe that."

"They will when you give them my badge and identification papers. That'll explain why I double-crossed them when they tried to ambush Montayne."

Mallette narrowed his eyes and cocked his head to the side. "I've been a gambler for a long time, John. That sounds to me like I'll be playing mighty long odds."

John Henry nodded. "I won't lie to you. It'll be dangerous. But I believe you can do it, Nick. I have faith in you."

Rasmussen frowned again. "I haven't agreed to let him out yet. If I do, I'll have to slip him out so nobody knows about it, especially those deputies from Kansas City."

"You can handle that, Sheriff," John Henry told him. "Nick, if we can get you into the house, you can find the prisoners and make sure they stay safe when all hell breaks loose. And if you can find where the tunnel comes out and get them there so we can take them back to safety before the shooting starts, so much the better."

Mallette grunted. "You don't ask for much, do you?"

"Just what needs to be done."

The gambler had another question. "And who's going to lead this rescue party? You keep talking like you're going to do it, but you can't. You're injured."

Rasmussen agreed. "That's right. Ain't no way Doc Harmon is gonna agree to let you go traipsing across the prairie, crawling through caves, and shooting it out with a bunch of outlaws and a crazy woman."

"I don't plan on asking the doc's permission," John Henry said. "I've got to go along, since I'm the only one who knows where that cave is. I'll just bandage up these bullet holes nice and tight. . . ."

Rasmussen just sighed and shook his head "I'm starting to wonder if the two of us are really the crazy ones, Sixkiller."

"Make it three," Mallette said. "I'm in."

Chapter Twenty-five

By the time they got back to the ranch, the two female prisoners had finally stopped screaming and crying, although not before their carrying on had gotten on Simon Garrett's nerves quite a bit. Lottie had given orders for them not to be gagged unless it was absolutely necessary.

She'd wanted them to be able to give in to their terror and wail about it.

Finally, Mrs. Doolittle and her niece had fallen silent except for the occasional whimper.

That wasn't true of the judge. Once Ephraim Doolittle had regained consciousness, he had cursed and threatened and yelled questions at his captors and hadn't stopped even though he was belly-down over a saddle. Garrett wasn't sure where he got the breath for it.

The outlaws reined to a halt in front of the ranch house. Yellow lamplight shone in the windows, despite the late hour. Lottie didn't come out to greet them, though. Garrett knew she would be waiting inside.

He swung down from the saddle, stepped over to the horse carrying Doolittle, and took hold of the judge's wildly askew white hair. He used the grip to lift Doolittle's head, which was dangling over the side of the horse.

"Shut up that bellyaching," Garrett warned. "It would have been all right with me to put a bullet through your brain, mister, so you'd be wise not to tempt me."

"You'll never get away with this," Doolittle blustered for what seemed like the hundredth time since they had ridden away from Kiowa City.

"Whether we do is none of your concern. You'll be dead either way." Garrett let go of Doolittle's hair.

The judge's head dropped. He moaned, probably sick to his stomach from riding draped over a horse for so long.

Garrett motioned to a couple of his men and ordered, "Get him down from there."

When all three prisoners were on their feet and huddled together, Garrett drew his gun and motioned for them to go up the steps. "Let's go. Somebody's waiting to meet you."

The judge looked like he wanted to argue, but quickly realized the futility of it. He was still pretty unsteady on his feet. "Don't worry, my dears. It'll be all right."

He put one arm around his wife's shoulders and the other around his niece and drew them against him protectively . . . although what he thought he could do with nearly twenty hardened killers surrounding them, Garrett didn't know.

With guns prodding them, the prisoners trudged to the steps and went up them.

Lottie was waiting inside by the fireplace, as Garrett had expected. She wore her gun and bowie knife and looked fierce. She was a warrior through and through, and Garrett felt a surge of desire go through him.

It wasn't the time or place for such, and it was probably the last thing on Lottie's mind. She glared at the prisoners. "Judge Doolittle, do you know who I am?"

The judge drew himself up to his full height, which wasn't all that impressive, and squared his shoulders as he glared right back. "No, madam, I do not, but if you have any influence over these scoundrels you should advise them to let us go right now."

Lottie walked closer to them. "My name is Lottie Dalmas, Judge. Some people call me the Flame, but what I really am right now is the angel of death." Moving almost too fast to be seen, she whipped the knife from its sheath at the back of her neck and held the blade to Doolittle's throat. "Your death."

The judge's wife and niece screamed, but Doolittle stood there stolidly. "Kill me if you wish, but spare these two innocents."

Lottie stepped back, taking the knife away from his throat, and laughed. "You sound like a character from a bad melodrama, Judge. But I suppose I do at times, as well. The hatred I feel makes me get carried away." She slid the bowie back in its sheath. "You're here because you sentenced Henry Garrett to death."

"Garrett sentenced himself to death when he chose to be an outlaw and a killer. All I did was carry out the inevitable result of that choice."

Lottie ignored that and told Garrett, "Take the women away from him."

Garrett nodded to his men, and even though the judge tried to hang on to his wife and niece, they were pulled from his grip. Mrs. Doolittle didn't struggle, but the younger woman did. She was no match for the outlaws holding her arms.

Clarissa, that was her name, Garrett recalled.

Lottie stepped over to her, lifted a hand, and cupped Clarissa's chin. She moved the young woman's head from side to side. "You're pretty. My men are going to enjoy getting to know you better."

"Leave her alone!" Doolittle raged. "By God—"

Lottie jerked the gun from the holster on her hip and brought it up in a flashing move that slammed the barrel against the judge's head above his left ear. The blow staggered him. His wife and niece both screamed. Blood welled from the cut opened up by the gunsight, startlingly crimson against his white hair.

"There's no God on the Silver Skull," Lottie said. "Only me."

"The devil herself!" Doolittle gasped.

Garrett figured she might shoot the judge, but Lottie controlled herself with a visible effort and pouched the iron. "Take them and put them in the smokehouse for now. No one touches the women." Lottie paused and smiled. "Let them think about what's going to happen to them later on."

Both women were sobbing as they were dragged out. Doolittle cursed and raved. Lottie watched with a faint smile curving her lips.

When she and Garrett were alone in the room, she asked, "Did we lose any men?"

"Not one. Nobody was even wounded."

"Good," she said with a nod. "What about Deputy Baird?"

"We did what you said."

Garrett felt a faint stirring of revulsion as he recalled the procedure, but he had long since learned to ignore such reactions. There was no point in getting upset about carrying out Lottie's orders.

"They got the message in town?"

"I'm pretty sure they did, but I can't guarantee that. Baird's horse carried him all the way into town. I watched to make sure. And he knew he was supposed to give that note to Rasmussen. I think we can count on the fact that they got the word."

"The question now is what will they do about it."

"They'll give in," Garrett said. "You know they won't risk those women."

"I wish I could be as certain. Those men are cowards. They couldn't kill Henry themselves, so they had the law do it for them." Lottie shook her head.

"But it doesn't really matter. Sooner or later they'll all die."

Garrett didn't share her confidence. This play had changed the game. The law now knew where to find them. Garrett had argued against that and tried to persuade Lottie to make the trade—the women for the other jury members and Rasmussen— somewhere away from the ranch. In her arrogance, she had been insistent, and as usual, she had gotten her way.

As far as Garrett could see, everything was now riding on this one throw of the dice.

He rubbed his crippled left hand. One way or another, in less than thirty-six hours it would all come to a head. They would live and have their revenge . . . or they would die.

Either way, Simon Garrett was ready. All he asked was the smell of powder smoke and the feel of a gun bucking in his good hand as he took vengeance on his enemies.

Several of the men who'd been injured in the outlaws' raid on Kiowa City had fairly serious wounds, but Dr. Harmon expected all of them to survive. He was going to be busy tending to them for the rest of the night.

John Henry figured the doctor could use the extra room for patients, so he went back to Harmon's house and gathered up the remainder of his gear.

"What do you think you're doing?" Harmon

asked when he saw John Henry fully dressed again, with the pair of saddlebags slung over his shoulder.

"Figured I'd get a room at the hotel," John Henry explained. "One of those fellas who was shot probably needs the bed more than I do."

"You were shot, too, let me remind you."

"Yeah, but that was a while ago. I'm better now."

Harmon shook his head and blew out an exasperated sigh. "All right, go on. It's not like I could stop you anyway, is it?"

"No, Doc, I reckon you couldn't," John Henry said with a smile.

By the time he settled down in a hotel bed to catch a few more hours of sleep, he had to admit that he was pretty tired and that his side had started aching. But it was nothing he couldn't stand, and he assumed that by the time it was all over, he would be a lot more tired and stood a good chance of hurting a lot worse.

He had never been one to have problems haunt his dreams, so he slept well. When he woke up the next morning he got dressed and went downstairs for a good breakfast in the hotel dining room.

As he ate, he thought about how Clarissa Doolittle had brought him breakfast the first day he woke up at Doc Harmon's house. That memory brought a troubled frown to his face.

He was enjoying a hearty breakfast in Kiowa City while she was being held prisoner at the Silver Skull Ranch, certainly terrified and possibly suffering all sorts of degradation and humiliation. Her aunt was in the same perilous position. If he could have gone after them the night before and spared them any ordeal, he would have done so without hesitation.

He was a practical man, though, and knew that his only real chance of saving the women, and Judge Doolittle, too, was the plan he had hatched in the courthouse basement with Sheriff Rasmussen and Nick Mallette. And that certainly wasn't a sure thing.

It was even possible that Lottie had already killed the judge, although John Henry considered that unlikely. She would want to draw things out as long as she could in order to inflict the maximum suffering on those she hated.

Also, keeping all three prisoners alive might be necessary for her to achieve her goal of having the other jury members delivered to her.

After John Henry finished his coffee, he walked to the doctor's house where Harmon greeted him with a weary, harried look. "Did you get any sleep, Doc?"

Harmon snorted disgustedly. "I'm accustomed to not sleeping. A doctor who's on call twenty-four hours a day gets used to it. But it doesn't help matters that I've lost my nurse to a . . . a madwoman."

"I'm sorry, Doc. I'll do my best to get her back for you. In the meantime . . . you think you could check these dressings and bandage me up real tight, so if I have to move around a lot there'll be less chance of those bullet holes starting to bleed again?"

"Madness," Harmon muttered. "Sheer madness.

But of course, I'll do as you ask. Come into the examining room. . . ."

A short time later, after Harmon had checked the wounds and reluctantly admitted that John Henry's activities of the night before didn't seem to have done him any harm, John Henry walked into Sheriff Rasmussen's office and found it crowded with men he didn't know.

One of them looked vaguely familiar. The man was dressed mostly in black and had a rugged face, lined and tanned to the color of old saddle leather from years of exposure to the sun. Crisp white hair stuck out from under his black Stetson.

After a moment John Henry realized where he had seen the man before. He had gotten only a brief glimpse of the white-haired man, and that had been from a distance. He had been leading the crew from the J/M as they approached Packsaddle Gap, so he had to be Jed Montayne.

Rasmussen caught sight of John Henry through the crowd. "Marshal, I'm glad you're here. You can explain your plan to these men. I sent for them this morning, and they're all anxious to meet you."

Ten pairs of eyes swung to stare at John Henry with varying degrees of hostility and confusion.

He knew without having to ask who they were. He was looking at the surviving members of the jury that had convicted Henry Garrett.

The men Lottie Dalmas and Simon Garrett had sworn to kill.

Chapter Twenty-six

"You're all grown men, and you all know what happened last night," John Henry began. "I'm not going to pull any punches with you. Judge Doolittle and his wife and niece have been kidnapped by the same bunch that murdered Charles Houston and Lucas Winslow. They're threatening to kill the women unless all of you turn yourselves over to the gang."

A burst of angry muttering came from the men, dominated by Jed Montayne's exclamation of "That's loco, mister!"

"I agree," John Henry said calmly. "The whole thing is as loco as it can be, because the woman who's behind it is mad with hate and the need for revenge. Her name is Lottie Dalmas."

That just drew puzzled frowns from the men crowded into the sheriff's office.

"She was Henry Garrett's lover," John Henry went on. "She runs a stopover for outlaws on an old abandoned ranch northwest of here. The

Garrett gang operated out of the place when Henry Garrett was leading it, and even before that when his older brother Simon was in charge, before Simon got sent to prison."

One of the men turned to Rasmussen and demanded, "Did you know about this . . . this so-called outlaw ranch, Sheriff?"

"I'd heard rumors about such a place, but I didn't know where it was," Rasmussen replied honestly. "Now I do."

"So you can take a posse out there, wipe out those owlhoots, and rescue the judge and his family."

John Henry held up his hands. "It's not that simple. There's not a good way into the place. If Sheriff Rasmussen tried a direct attack with a posse, they'd just wind up being slaughtered."

"You're not sayin' you want us to give up and surrender to that woman, are you?" Montayne growled.

"That's exactly what I'm telling you," John Henry said.

That caused another hubbub that lasted several moments until Montayne's voice overrode the others.

"Just who the hell are you, again?" he asked John Henry.

"My name is Sixkiller. I'm a deputy United States marshal out of Fort Smith. I work for Judge Isaac Parker."

"Well, hell. If you're a federal lawman, just call in the army! No bunch of two-bit desperadoes would be able to keep them out."

"Probably not," John Henry admitted. "Although

it might take artillery to blast the gang out of there. And that wouldn't help Judge Doolittle and the two ladies. In fact, it would pretty much guarantee they would die long, slow, agonizing deaths."

"What should we do, then?" another man asked. "If we give this woman, this Lottie Dalmas, what she wants, how can we be sure she'll keep her word and release the women?"

John Henry shook his head. "We can't. In fact, I think there's a pretty good chance she would kill them anyway. That's why we have to try something else. We have to make her think she's going to get what she wants by pretending to turn you men over to her."

"How in blazes are you gonna do that?" Montayne asked.

"She wants you there by sunrise tomorrow morning. You'll be there, unarmed—at least as far as those outlaws can tell—ready to ride up the trail to their stronghold. But while they've got all their attention focused on you, I'm going to be leading a posse in the back way."

He explained about the cave that opened into the ravine and his belief that it functioned as an escape route leading to the Silver Skull ranch house.

Montayne's lined face got even more creases in it as he frowned. "You said you didn't follow the cave all the way to the house. You don't know that it goes through."

John Henry took a deep breath. "For a fact, I don't. But it's the only thing that makes any sense.

I know air was moving through it from the direction of the ranch house."

The cattleman snorted. "That don't mean a damned thing. Could be just a little hole somewhere that lets the air come through."

"You're right, that's possible. But when you don't have a chance any other way, you take whatever is left."

"You don't even know the women are still alive."

"That's true, too. But until we know otherwise, we have to proceed as if they are."

Rasmussen stepped in. "Marshal Sixkiller is right. Luck will have to be with us for his plan to work, but it's the only chance Mrs. Doolittle and Clarissa have." The sheriff was standing behind his desk. He leaned forward and rested his hands on it as he continued. "But I'll be damned if I'm going to force any man to put his life on the line like we're asking you to. You're gonna have to agree with it, or as far as I'm concerned, we don't go ahead."

More muttering came from the former jury members as they grouped together and talked it over. Most of them were townsmen, unaccustomed to danger. If there was a natural leader among them, it was Jed Montayne.

"There's one other thing you should know, Mr. Montayne," John Henry said to the rancher. "It was Simon Garrett and his men who rustled your stock the other night and then tried to ambush you at Packsaddle Gap. That was part of Lottie Dalmas's plan to have her revenge on you, too." He didn't say anything about the connection he suspected existed between Lottie and J.C. Carson.

"It's thanks to me that you and your men didn't ride into that trap," John Henry went on. "I'm the one who fired those warning shots. I risked my life doing that."

"Are you tryin' to make me feel guilty?" Montayne asked with a frown.

"No, sir, just trying to make you see that I wouldn't be asking you and these other men to risk your lives if I didn't think there was a good chance we can pull this off. I don't want any of the rest of you to die . . . but I don't want the judge and his ladies tortured and killed, either."

Montayne glared at him for a moment longer, then jerked his head in an abrupt nod. "All right. Tell us the rest of the plan."

Just as John Henry hoped, the other men nodded and muttered agreement. He had won them over by getting Montayne to go along with him. "Later today the ten of you, along with Sheriff Rasmussen, will ride out to the Silver Skull. That's the old ranch where the outlaws are. You'll time it so that you'll get there in the late afternoon, not long before dark. Garrett and the Flame will have men watching from the rim of the bluff, and they're bound to see you. Make camp a half mile or so away from the bottom of the trail. Build a big fire if you want, and move around enough so the watchers will know you're still there."

"What if they start taking potshots at us from the rim?" Montayne asked.

"They won't. That's not part of Lottie's plan."

"You sound mighty sure of that, but you're not the one bettin' your life on it."

"Stop when you're a little farther away then," John Henry said. "As long as they know you're there, that's all that matters. We want them paying more attention to what's going on in front of them, rather than behind them."

Rasmussen asked, "We wait for the morning before we break camp and go on in?"

"That's right. The longer this lasts, the better Lottie will like it, so we'll give her what she wants . . . and that'll give me and the men with me all night to get into position."

"Let's say you're right about the cave," Montayne said. "Don't you reckon it's likely this Dalmas woman will have the door at the other end locked, or at least guarded?"

"More than likely," John Henry agreed. "But I've got a plan to deal with that, too." He didn't explain that he was counting on Nick Mallette to handle that problem. It would be Nick's job to make sure John Henry and the men he led through the cave could get into the house.

"Once we're there, if it's possible we'll free the prisoners and some of the men will take them back out through the cave. The rest of us will hit the outlaws from behind. When we do that, when you hear all hell break loose up on the bluff, that's when you charge up the trail and we catch Garrett and his gang between us."

"And wipe 'em out," Montayne growled.

"Well, since I'm a duly appointed officer of the law, I sort of have to give them a chance to surrender." John Henry shrugged. "But for all practical purposes, yeah, that's when we wipe 'em out."

Montayne pointed a finger. "I like that part of it. But there are a hell of a lot of things that can go wrong with that plan."

"Yes, there are," John Henry said. "We'll just have to hope that enough of them go right. If they do, we'll be able to bring those men to justice and make sure they don't murder anybody else." He looked around the group. "Is everybody still in?"

One by one, the men nodded or voiced their resolve. They might not be professional fighting men, but they were willing to stand up and do what was right.

John Henry left Sheriff Rasmussen to go over a few more details with them while he headed downstairs to the cell block. Nick Mallette was still the only prisoner. He stood up and came to the bars as John Henry walked down the aisle between the cells.

"Well?" Mallette asked with a look of nervous anticipation on his face. "Did they agree to do it?"

"They did. I don't think they were too fond of the idea, but they went along with it."

Mallette smiled. "I don't know whether to be happy about that . . . or be disappointed."

"You've got a chance to help save those women, and to do yourself some good at the same time. I think you should be happy."

"And all I have to do is put my life in the hands

of two dozen bloodthirsty outlaws and a crazy woman."

"Well . . . try not to look at it like that," John Henry suggested with a smile.

They talked awhile, going over the plan and the story Mallette would tell when he showed up again at the Silver Skull.

"There's probably a trapdoor or something like that somewhere in the house," John Henry said. "It'll open into a shaft that leads down to a tunnel, and that tunnel will connect with the cave I found. Did you hear any of the gang gossiping about anything like that while we were there?"

Mallette shook his head. "No, I don't recall that at all. Maybe it just didn't come up."

"Maybe . . . but I think it's more likely that Lottie never told any of them about it except maybe Simon Garrett. And it's possible he may not even know. So I doubt that she has a guard posted on the door. But it's pretty likely she'll have it bolted on the inside. It'll be up to you to find it and unbolt it so we can get in."

Mallette wiped a hand over his face and shook his head. "If she catches me snooping around the house, she's liable to have me killed. That's her domain. All the outlaws except Garrett stay in the old bunkhouse."

"I know. But when the sun comes up in the morning and those jury members start riding toward the trail, Lottie's going to want to be there to see it. The rest of the bunch will probably be with her. That'll be your chance to slip away, get to the house, and find the trapdoor. If you can free the prisoners, so much the better, but at the very least you've got to find the door and get it open for us."

"That's going to be cutting it mighty close."

"I know." John Henry's face was grim. "We don't have any other choice."

"In other words, the plan works or everybody dies."

John Henry grimaced. "Well, yeah, but I sort of wish you hadn't put it quite like that."

"At least there's one good thing about it." The gambler let out a hollow laugh. "I don't have anything to lose in this game."

"And everything to win."

Chapter Twenty-seven

Simon Garrett was sitting in a chair on the porch of the ranch house, a stub of a cigar smoldering between his lips and his right foot propped on the railing, when he saw the rider galloping toward him from the direction of the rim.

The rider's apparent urgency prompted Garrett to stand up. He threw his cigar away and put his hand on the butt of his gun. "Lottie!" he called through the open door. The temperature had been rising steadily ever since the sun had come up several hours earlier.

Lottie came out onto the porch. "What is it?"

"One of the rim guards." Garrett nodded toward the rider. "Coming fast like that, it looks like he's got something to tell us."

The outlaw drew rein in front of the house and nodded to Garrett and the Flame. "We spotted a fella on horseback comin' out on the flats, boss."

"Someone from Kiowa City?" Garrett asked tensely.

"No, not exactly. We put the spyglass on him.

You won't believe this, but it's that gambler, Mallette."

Garrett stiffened in surprise. "Mallette?" he repeated. "I didn't figure we'd ever see him again."

When Mallette and the three men who had gone out to search for Saxon hadn't come back, Garrett had sent more men to look for them. They had found the bodies of the three outlaws, but no sign of Mallette. The welter of hoofprints around the corpses hadn't told them anything.

Garrett hadn't known what to think about that. Even though he had never fully trusted Mallette, it seemed highly unlikely the gambler could have double-crossed his companions and gunned them all down. Not without losing his own life in the process, anyway.

A more reasonable explanation was that Saxon had bushwhacked the bunch and killed the three outlaws. Mallette might have turned tail and run. If that was the case, he would probably keep running for a long time and try to put the whole affair far behind him.

Garrett trusted the men he had guarding the rim. If they said Mallette was approaching, then he believed them. "If he comes up the trail, bring him on in," he ordered.

"You don't want us to shoot him?" the guard asked.

"Not until I've had a chance to talk to him, anyway."

The man nodded, wheeled his horse, and rode

back toward the big rock formation that gave the place its name.

Garrett looked over at Lottie. "That suit you?"

"Yes. I want to hear what Mallette has to say, too." She went back in the house, but Garrett waited on the porch.

A short time later, three riders came from the direction of the trail. Nick Mallette was in the center, flanked by two guards.

The gambler didn't seem nervous. In fact, he appeared to be calm and icy-nerved. As the men came to a halt, Mallette smiled faintly and lifted a hand in greeting. "Howdy, boss. I'll bet you never expected to see me again."

Garrett frowned. That was what he had been about to say to Mallette, but the gambler had jumped the gun on him and gotten it in first.

"Where the hell have you been?" Garrett snapped. "I sent you and those other men to look for that damn double-crosser Saxon."

"And we found him. Or rather, he found us. He jumped us. I reckon he was pretty desperate to take on four-to-one odds. But he was wounded, you know, so I guess he figured he didn't have much chance of getting away unless he did something bold."

"But he did get away, didn't he?"

"As a matter of fact . . . no, he didn't. And I have proof. More than that, I now know who he really was."

Lottie had come out on the porch in time to

hear most of the conversation. She told the gambler, "Come inside. I want to hear this."

Mallette didn't wait for Garrett's okay. He swung down from the saddle and handed his reins to one of the guards.

Garrett made an impatient gesture and told the guard, "Take care of his horse."

The three of them went into the house. Lottie asked, "Would you like a drink, Nick?"

"It's a little early in the day," Mallette said with a shrug, "but I suppose it's already afternoon somewhere. Sure, Miss Dalmas. Thank you."

Lottie poured him a shot of whiskey and handed the glass to him. Mallette tossed back the drink.

"Now, what's this about Saxon?" she asked.

"Like I said, he ambushed us. Knocked one of the men out of the saddle with his first shot. But the rest of us fought back." Mallette touched a finger to a little mark on his cheek. "That's how close I came to dying. One of his bullets did this. But I was lucky. He downed the other two men. We got more lead into him, though, and he took off."

"And you went after him?" Lottie guessed.

"That's right. Maybe I should have stayed to tend to the others, but I could tell they were done for." Mallette shrugged again. "And in the heat of battle, especially since Saxon had pretended to be my friend and then tried to kill me, I wanted to catch up to him and give him what he had coming to him. So I . . . what's the expression? I lit a shuck after him."

"That was three days ago," Garrett said. "Where have you been since then?"

"I just told you. Trailing Saxon."

Garrett sneered. "No offense, Mallette, but that just doesn't seem like something you'd do."

"Hey, it surprised me, too. But I guess I've changed some since I've been around here. And like I said, I had a score to settle with Saxon."

He paused, and Lottie urged him to go on.

"It took me until late yesterday to catch up to him," Mallette said. "I don't mind admitting that I'm not the best tracker in the world. I lost the trail a few times, but I always found it again. And when I did find him, a long way north of here—"

"Let me guess," Garrett said. "You shot it out with him and killed him."

His tone made it clear that he was going to have a hard time believing that.

"No," Mallette said quietly with a shake of his head. "I didn't have to do that. He was already dead. He was wounded at Packsaddle Gap and then winged again later on when he bushwhacked us. I guess he finally lost enough blood that it killed him. I found his body in a little dry wash."

The gambler grimaced as if he were remembering something distasteful. "The, uh, coyotes and buzzards had already been at him. There wasn't much left, but enough that I knew it was him. John Saxon . . . except that's not who he really was."

"What do you mean?" Lottie asked.

Mallette reached in his vest pocket and took out a couple things. "I found these on him." He held out his right hand. A deputy United States marshal's badge rested on the palm.

In his other hand was a small leather folder. "There are identification papers in here. His real name was John Henry Sixkiller."

"A federal marshal!" Garrett said. "And we let him waltz right in here."

"He was pretty shrewd about it," Mallette said. "From what I heard back in Kiowa City, he really did gun down that Deverill fellow . . . probably because Deverill recognized him as a lawman, if I had to guess. He certainly fooled me, or I never would have helped him escape from jail. I think that's what he wanted all along, to pretend to be an outlaw so you would take him in."

"Why would he be after us?" Garrett asked.

Lottie answered that question. "Because somebody in Kiowa City, either Rasmussen or that damned judge, figured out that we were after them for what they did to Henry and sent for help. A federal lawman could get involved because of those train holdups where you robbed the express car and stole the mailbags."

"Damn it!" Garrett said. "I never planned on getting Uncle Sam after us."

"Don't worry about it," Lottie told him. "It's all right. Saxon . . . I mean, Sixkiller . . . is dead and won't bother us anymore. By the time the federals can send in anyone else, we'll have our revenge."

"You believe Mallette's story?"

"I don't have any reason not to."

"Thanks," Mallette said dryly.

"Besides," Lottie went on, "he's got that badge. How else could he have gotten it if he didn't take it off Saxon's body?"

"I don't know," Garrett said. "Maybe *he's* really the deputy marshal."

That brought a genuine-sounding laugh from Mallette.

Lottie smiled. "No offense, Nick, but you don't strike me as the sort to be a lawman."

"None taken," he told her. "And I'm not, you can count on that."

"All right, all right," Garrett said in a surly tone. "So maybe you're not really a lawman."

"No maybe about it."

"That still doesn't mean I'm prepared to trust you all the way."

"If I've been lying to you, would I even come back here?" Mallette argued. "What reason would I have for doing that? If I didn't feel some loyalty to you and the rest of the bunch, I would have just kept going."

That was exactly what Garrett had thought earlier, so he couldn't really argue with what Mallette said. And Lottie obviously believed the gambler, so maybe there really wasn't any point in continuing to be suspicious.

"All right," Garrett said again. "Let me see that badge."

Mallette handed it over. Garrett studied it, turning it over and over in his fingers. It certainly looked authentic. Despite what he'd said earlier, he knew it was ridiculous to suspect Mallette of being a deputy U.S. marshal.

That left the gambler's explanation of where he had gotten the badge as the only one that made any sense.

Garrett tossed the badge back to Mallette, who plucked it deftly out of the air. "You'll probably want to keep that as a souvenir, I reckon. Since you're the only one left from the bunch that went after Saxon, I suppose you deserve it."

"Thanks, boss." Mallette slid the badge and the leather folder back in his vest pocket. "So what are we doing now? The fellas on guard out at the rim seemed a little jumpy, like maybe something's going to happen."

"We're going to have our revenge on those men who are responsible for Henry's death," Lottie said. "That's what's going to happen. Do you still want to be part of that, Nick?"

"Sure. I've been on my own long enough. I like having partners."

"All right. Sometime between now and tomorrow morning, the rest of those jury members and Sheriff Rasmussen are going to show up here and surrender to us."

A surprised frown creased Mallette's forehead. "Why in the world would they do that?"

"Because we have hostages locked up in the smokehouse. Judge Ephraim Doolittle and his wife and niece are our guests for the moment."

Mallette let out a low whistle of admiration.

"You've been busy while I was gone, haven't you? You plan to wipe them all out at the same time?"

"That's right," Garrett said. "And when we're done with that, we'll start the job of taking over this part of the state. It won't be easy. We'll have plenty of lawmen and maybe even the army to deal with. Could be a lot of blood spilled before it's all over. You still want to throw in with us, Mallette?"

The gambler took a deep breath and nodded. "You can count on me."

"We had better be able to," Lottie told him. "Otherwise some of the blood that gets spilled will be yours."

Chapter Twenty-eight

With the help of Sheriff Rasmussen and Jed Montayne, John Henry put together a force of twenty men to take with him through the cave. Most of the volunteers were J/M cowhands. Because of his ongoing trouble with J.C. Carson's Anvil spread, Montayne kept a pretty salty crew working for him, so John Henry was confident they would be gun-handy fighting men.

A few townsmen were also in the bunch, including one leathery old-timer in buckskins who had a black patch over his left eye. He was a former army scout and buffalo hunter named Ezra Jenkins.

The old frontiersman informed John Henry, "Lost this here eye o' mine when a Pawnee buck carved it out with a knife, back in '66, 'fore I opened him up from gizzard to gullet with my own bowie. Hope that don't rub you the wrong way, you bein' part redskin and all."

John Henry was glad to have the old Indian fighter coming along. He knew he could count on

Ezra to have cool nerves under fire. "That's fine, Mr. Jenkins. When two men are trying to kill each other, skin color doesn't matter anymore. All that counts is survival."

"You're sure right about that, youngster."

John Henry gathered his men together at the courthouse and went over the plan with them, answering any questions they might have. "If any of you are bothered by being in tight, enclosed places, we'd all be better off if you'd speak up now and stay behind. I don't know what we're going to find in that cave, but it may not be easy to get through it."

No one said anything, so John Henry assumed they were all willing to venture in there. He hoped none of them would panic once they were inside the cave. Sometimes a man didn't know he couldn't stand being closed in until it actually happened.

They waited until nightfall to saddle up and set out for the Silver Skull. John Henry intended to lead them in a wide circle to the north, so they ought to strike that ravine a good long way from the ranch. It would have been nice if he'd had a day or two to reconnoiter, but there just wasn't time for that.

Before the rescue party left town, Dr. Harmon checked John Henry's wounds and rebandaged them one last time, pulling the bandages as tight as possible so the wounds would be less likely to break open again.

"I still think you're insane for doing this,"

Harmon said. "Any normal man would still be resting in bed."

"There'll be time for that when this is all over," John Henry told the doctor. "Once the judge and his ladies are back home safely and those outlaws have been dealt with."

"You're assuming you'll live to see that."

"I always assume I'll make it through whatever I'm doing, Doc. Otherwise what's the point of living?"

Harmon didn't have an answer for that other than a shrug and a nod.

Night had fallen. As the men rode out of town, John Henry thought about Nick Mallette. The gambler had ridden out of Kiowa City earlier that day after being smuggled out the back door of the courthouse by Sheriff Rasmussen. The sheriff had sent one of his deputies to keep an eye on the two lawmen from Kansas City, who had been sitting around the hotel for the past few days enjoying their *per diem*. As long as they were drawing their expense money, they weren't going to be in any hurry to head back to Missouri.

They might not take kindly to it, though, if they found out that the local law was releasing the convicted murderer they had been sent to fetch. They could raise quite a stink over that if they wanted to.

When John Henry had handed over his badge and bona fides to Mallette he had said, "Now you know, Nick, no matter how fond I may be of you personally, if you take off for the tall and uncut instead of going to the Silver Skull like you're supposed to, I'll feel duty-bound to track you down and drag you back to that gallows in Kansas City myself."

"Don't worry, John," Mallette had told him. "I don't want to spend the rest of my life looking over my shoulder for you or any other lawman. I figure you'll keep your word and help me with that murder conviction if I live through this, and if I don't . . . well, I won't have to worry about being hanged, will I?"

"That's true."

"Never thought I'd say it, but if it has to be one way or the other, I think I'd rather go out fighting. You're a bad influence, John Henry Sixkiller."

"Not the first time I've been told that."

John Henry smiled faintly, remembering the conversation. He had confidence in Mallette. He had been fooled a time or two in the past, but overall he thought he was a pretty good judge of character. Mallette had the right stuff inside him. The gambler just hadn't been aware of it.

When they were several miles out of town, Ezra Jenkins, the old frontiersman, edged his horse up alongside John Henry's. "You know where it is you're goin', youngster?"

"I know the direction I'm going. And I'm pretty good at steering by the stars. I think we'll hit that ravine sooner or later."

"O'Hara's Draw."

"I beg your pardon?" John Henry said with a frown.

"O'Hara's Draw," Ezra repeated. "That's the name o' that big gully, or ravine, as you call it. It got the name because years ago, back in the days when there weren't any white men in these parts 'cept for buffalo hunters, one of 'em got the bright idea of stampedin' a herd of those shaggy varmints into the gully. He figured the fall would kill 'em, and then all he'd have to do was come along and skin the hides off 'em. That was all well and good, I suppose, but ol' O'Hara, he didn't take into account just how many buffler there was in that herd he stampeded. They fell into the gully, all right, but they kept fallin' in on top of the ones that was already dead, and they piled up and piled up until the whole dang gully was full to the top with dead buffler! There weren't no way to get to the ones on the bottom, so all they could do was sit there and rot.

"After a while the stink from O'Hara's Draw was so bad you could smell it from ten miles away. Wouldn't nobody come through this part of the country because of it. So the fella who started the ranch where we're headed was able to move in without nobody competin' with him for range-land. He had it all to hisself. But he still couldn't make a go of it, and even after years passed and all the buffler had rotted away to bones and all the bones had done been carried away, when the wind was right on a hot day the smell that carried to the ranch was still bad enough it'd make your toes curl."

John Henry wondered how much, if any, of that story was true, but all he said was, "I've been in that ravine. I didn't smell anything."

"Well, that was years and years ago. The stink's gone now. But I seen it with my own eye, buffler bones piled so high you could walk across that draw on 'em. A man don't never forget somethin' like that."

"I imagine not. So you're saying you know how to find this O'Hara's Draw?"

"Darn right I do. Most folks back in Kiowa City think I'm just a crazy ol' coot who's full o' stories. But I been to see the elephant, youngster, and the only reason I ain't still out there hellin' around in the wild lonesome is that my rheumatiz got so bad I can't stay in the saddle more than eight, nine hours at a time. An hombre gets that soft, he needs to find hisself a rockin' chair somewheres. So that's what I done. But I can take you right to that gully, if you'll let me, and I can still fight, too."

"I don't doubt it for a second, Ezra. Lead the way."

The old-timer nodded and then moved his horse out in front. His head was held high.

John Henry trusted that Ezra was telling the truth, but at the same time he was going to keep an eye on the stars and make sure they were headed in the right direction. If Ezra began to veer off, John Henry would correct him as gently as possible.

As it turned out, John Henry didn't have to

worry about that. Ezra led the group straight as a string several more miles to the north, then cut almost due west.

"We'll hit the gully about five miles northwest of that big rock that looks like a skull," he told John Henry. "I knowed it was there—I've seen it many a time—and I knowed that old ranch was up on the bluff behind it, but I ain't been that way in years and didn't know outlaws had moved in and tooken over. It's a good place for a hideout. Hard to get into and out of."

"Have you ever heard anything about an escape tunnel?" John Henry asked.

"No, but it don't surprise me. The Injuns was pretty bad around these parts for a long time. Folks who was smart always had theirselves a bolt hole."

"I think that's what that cave is, only it was probably the law Lottie's father wanted to be able to get away from if he needed to, not Indians."

The stars continued to wheel through the sky overhead as time passed. John Henry estimated that it was close to midnight, and he was glad he had allowed the entire night for him and his men to get into position. They might need it.

His side ached a little from the long ride, but he was confident the wounds wouldn't cause him any real trouble. He was more worried about not being able to know for sure what was going on at the ranch.

Had Mallette been able to convince Lottie and Garrett to believe his story?

Had Rasmussen and the members of the jury

showed up like they were supposed to and drawn the attention of the outlaws?

Were the three prisoners still alive, and had Mallette been able to find out where they were being held? That was maybe the most important question of all.

No, John Henry amended to himself. When the time came, would Mallette be able to find the hidden entrance into the ranch house and open it? That was the most important question. The success of the rest of the plan depended upon it.

If Mallette failed, a lot of innocent people would die when the sun came up.

Sheriff Mike Rasmussen tried not to give in to his nerves. His impulse was to stalk back and forth across the camp, but he wasn't going to do it even though Marshal Sixkiller had said to move around a lot and keep the outlaws' attention focused on the group of men. Rasmussen wanted to appear cool and calm, even though he was far from it on the inside.

He knew he had a reputation as a plodding, unimaginative lawman. A lot of the citizens of Kiowa City even thought he was dumb. Rasmussen didn't believe that was true, but he knew he wasn't anything like the daring adventurer Sixkiller seemed to be. He was willing to settle for being persistent, dogged in his determination to do what needed to be done.

To that end, he had led the group of ten men

miles from town, under the watchful eyes of a gang of owlhoots who wanted them dead. Late that afternoon, they had reached the flats in front of the escarpment where the big, skull-like rock was located. It was still light enough for the outlaws to see them as they made camp.

Rasmussen had a hunch the outlaws had studied them through field glasses or telescopes. Because of that, none of the men wore holstered guns, and the saddle scabbards where Winchesters and other rifles usually rode were empty. They didn't have any saddlebags where weapons could be carried, either.

Each man had a pair of .32 caliber revolvers stuck down in their boots, however. The guns had been provided by the owner of the general store, Charles Houston's former partner. The little Smith & Wessons packed five-shot cylinders, so each man had ten rounds loaded and another ten rounds in extra cartridges. If that wasn't enough to put up a good fight against the outlaws . . . well, then, they'd have bigger problems to worry about.

Jed Montayne came over to the sheriff with the usual glare on his craggy face. "I still say I could've taken my whole crew and fought our way up that trail."

"Even if you did, you'd lose at least half your men," Rasmussen said. "You probably would've caught a few slugs yourself, Jed, because I imagine you'd have been right there in the front."

"Damn right I would have. I don't ask my riders to do anything I won't do."

"If the marshal's plan works, we'll all have a lot better chance of coming through this alive."

Montayne snorted. "Sixkiller may be a deputy marshal, but he's half Indian, too. I ain't real fond of puttin' my life in the hands of such as that."

"You seem to forget that your life has already been in Sixkiller's hands . . . when he got himself shot warning you about that ambush in Packsaddle Gap."

Montayne had the decency to mutter something and look down at the ground. When he looked up again, he said, "All I know is that if the marshal's high-and-mighty plan don't work, we're all liable to die in the morning. I don't plan to sleep much tonight, but if I did, I'd sleep better knowin' that he was right about that damned cave or tunnel or whatever you want to call it."

Rasmussen nodded. "I've got to admit, Jed, I wouldn't mind knowing about that myself."

Chapter Twenty-nine

Ezra Jenkins was true to his word. The rescue party reached the ravine, or O'Hara's Draw, as the old frontiersman called it, not long after midnight.

"We'll leave our horses here," John Henry told the men as they dismounted. He pointed to one of them. "You'll be responsible for keeping up with the horses and driving them down toward the Silver Skull when it gets close to dawn."

The man was one of Montayne's riders. He protested, "Why pick me for that job? I want to get in on the fight, damn it!"

"Because I need a man who can handle that many saddle mounts," John Henry said. "Anyway, the fight may not be over by the time you get there."

"Hope not," the puncher muttered. "I was at Packsaddle Gap when those damn owlhoots tried to bushwhack us. I got a score to settle with them."

"We all do," John Henry said, thinking of the bullet holes in his side.

The next step was finding a way down into the ravine. That took some time, but Ezra finally located a place where the wall was rugged enough to climb down. John Henry had warned the men before they left Kiowa City to fashion slings for their rifles, so they could carry the weapons while they were making the descent into the ravine.

Once they were all down except for the man who'd been left with the horses, John Henry told them quietly, "The closer we get to the ranch, the more we'll have to worry about not making any noise the guards up on the rim might hear, so we might as well get in the habit of being quiet now. We're going to move fast, but don't make any more racket than you have to."

The men muttered in understanding. With Ezra beside him, John Henry started south along the bottom of the ravine. The other men followed.

They were able to move fairly fast most of the time. The ravine was wide enough that they didn't have to travel single file, and the bottom of it was level. Enough moonlight and starlight penetrated into the ravine for them to see where they were going.

Here and there the bottom was partially choked with brush that had piled up during flash floods, and that slowed them down some as they worked their way though the obstacles. Overall, though, John Henry was pleased with the progress they were making.

No one said anything, and they were careful not to let their rifle barrels bang against rocks. After a while, John Henry held up his hand in a signal for the others to halt. As they did so, he listened intently.

The faint sound of voices drifted to his ears, followed by hoofbeats. He knew those noises came from the guards patrolling the rim. That meant his party ought to be getting close to the cave mouth. He waved them ahead.

A few minutes later, he spotted the dark maw of the cave, a deeper patch of ebony against the shadowy bulk of the ravine wall. He pointed it out to Ezra, who passed the word along to the other men, communicating with them by gestures.

John Henry reached out and let his hands explore the opening, making sure it was the same one he had found a few days earlier. Confident that it was, he moved slowly into the cave.

He had taken only a couple of steps before pitch blackness surrounded him. The darkness completely swallowed what little light filtered in from the opening.

Tension gripped his nerves, but he forced himself to ignore the atavistic fear of the dark and continued deeper underground, guiding himself with his outstretched left hand trailing against the wall of the cave.

When he felt like he had gone far enough that a light wouldn't be noticed from the rim, he stopped and lit a match. Even the tiny flame seemed glaringly bright in that stygian gloom.

He turned to look back along the narrow passage. "Is everybody here? Sound off back there."

One by one, the men did so. By the time everyone was accounted for, the match had burned down nearly to John Henry's fingers. He lit another one from it, then reached under his shirt for the first of several torches he had fashioned back in Kiowa City before they left. He lit the torch and held it above his head. The light revealed the cave twisting off into the distance ahead of them.

And once again, the flame at the end of the torch leaned far enough to the side to confirm that fresh air was moving through the cave, just as it had been the first time he was there.

"Everybody doing all right?" he asked. "Anybody need to turn back?"

No one spoke up.

After a moment, Ezra said, "Reckon we're all good to keep movin', youngster."

John Henry smiled. He resumed the underground trek.

After a few hundred more yards, the cave narrowed. The rock walls on both sides squeezed in on John Henry's shoulders. He had to turn sideways to get through.

He heard men muttering behind him. Even if a man wasn't particularly scared by tight places, the feeling of being so completely enclosed by thousands of tons of dirt and rock would begin to get on a fellow's nerves after a while. It was certainly getting on John Henry's nerves.

The fading light as the torch burned down didn't help matters. He lit the second one from what was left of the first. The brighter illumination made him feel a little better.

So did the fact that after another hundred yards or so, the passage widened out again until it was a good ten feet from side to side. He breathed easier after that, and felt certain the men with him did, too.

A few minutes later, however, he stopped so short that Ezra Jenkins bumped into him from behind.

"Somethin' wrong?" the old frontiersman asked.

John Henry peered at the hole in the cave floor in front of him. It ran from one side of the passage to the other and was at least eight feet wide. A man might be able to jump it if he had a good running start, but that wasn't possible under the current circumstances.

Ezra stepped up beside John Henry and cursed. "How deep you reckon it is?"

"Let's find out." John Henry took a coin from his pocket and tossed it into the hole. Seconds counted off in his head. After what seemed like a long, long time, he heard a faint splash as the coin struck water somewhere far below them.

"If a man fell in there, he'd never get back out," Ezra said.

John Henry held out the torch so that its light fell on the passage on the far side of the hole. Propped against the wall was a long, wide plank. "There's the way across. Somebody put that board there to use as a bridge. But since they planned on using this as an escape route from the ranch, it's on that side, not this one."

"It doesn't do us any good over there," one man said.

Another added, "We can't get to it."

John Henry thought for a moment, then said, "Maybe we can bring it to us. I need some belts. Take 'em off and pass 'em up here."

He handed the torch to Ezra as he took the belts the men provided and knotted them together into a crude rope. When it was long enough to reach across the hole, he passed one end of it through the trigger guard of his Colt and tied it as securely as he could. The weight of the gun at the end of the makeshift lariat would help.

He got as close to the edge as he could without toppling in. "All right. A couple of you fellas grab hold of my shirt so you can pull me back if you have to."

He swung the revolver back and forth a few times to build up some momentum, then slung it across the chasm toward the top of the plank. He hoped to hook the revolver around the board and jerk it toward them so that it would fall across the opening in the cave floor.

That cast failed . . . and so did the next and the next and the one after that. John Henry felt frustration building inside him. He paused and took out his watch to check the time.

Almost three hours had passed since they had left their horses and entered the ravine. In another hour and a half the sky in the east would begin to grow bright with the approach of the new day.

"You're gonna have to snag that board dead

solid perfect," Ezra warned. "If you don't, it'll just fall in the hole and be gone."

"I know," John Henry said. "It's the only chance we've got, though."

More important, it was the only chance the judge, Mrs. Doolittle, and Clarissa had. John Henry kept that thought foremost in his mind as he got ready to make another try.

Time seemed to race by with maddening speed. He had to force himself not to rush his throws.

He had been at it for so long that he almost didn't notice in time when the Colt's handle hooked around the plank.

John Henry's instincts kicked in, galvanizing his muscles. He jerked on the strung-together belts. The gun remained caught on the plank and dragged it toward them.

Suddenly it was toppling toward the hole.

It was going to fall short, John Henry realized in a moment of near-panic. He yelled, "Hang on to me!" and lunged forward above the chasm, reaching out with his free hand, straining to get every inch from the desperate grab.

The men behind him planted their feet and shouted for others to grab hold of them. John Henry swayed out over the emptiness. The board fell toward his outstretched fingers . . .

And he caught the end of it, barely able to maintain the grip as it tried to slip away from him. He managed to pull the plank an inch or so toward him and carefully shifted his grip. When he thought he had the board secure, he said through gritted teeth, "Pull me back!"

His boot heels were planted at the very edge of the brink. Using them as leverage, the men who had hold of John Henry's shirt lifted him. He dragged the board closer, took a step back as the men maintained their hold on him, and lowered the end until it rested on the floor on their side of the chasm. He took a deep breath and wiped away the beads of sweat that had sprung out on his forehead.

"That was a mighty near thing," Ezra said.

"Yeah, but we've got a way across now." John Henry took his gun loose from the belts and holstered it. He gave the belts back to the men they belonged to and continued. "We'll go across one at a time. That plank looks pretty sturdy, but we won't take any chances with it. I hope everybody has good balance. It would probably be a good idea not to look down while you're crossing."

"I don't intend to," one of the punchers said with such heartfelt fervor that it drew chuckles from some of the other men.

John Henry positioned the plank so that it was centered. "I'll go over first."

"Be careful." The old frontiersman lifted the torch higher so that it would cast more light where John Henry would be walking.

Keeping his attention on making it to the other side, he shut out everything else. He took a deep breath, waited until his racing heartbeat had calmed some, then walked across the plank in a steady pace, never rushing but never slowing down.

Turning to face the others, he said, "Just like that. Nothing to it."

"Yeah," one of the men said bitterly. "Simple as long as you don't miss a step."

"I don't intend to." Ezra crossed the bridge in several easy, long-legged strides.

The other men all made it across, although a few of them swayed dangerously as they did so. The last man asked John Henry, "What do we do with the board?"

"We probably won't be coming back this way—"

"I sure as hell hope not," a man said under his breath.

John Henry ignored that and went on. "But we'll leave it where it is, anyway, just in case we do. We might be in a hurry."

They pressed on, with John Henry taking the torch back and soon lighting the third and final one he had brought. They had to be getting close to the ranch house, he told himself.

A short time later, Ezra said, "Look at the walls."

"I noticed that, too," John Henry said. "Somebody has worked them and widened them. This is more of a tunnel than a cave now."

"We must be nearly there."

"That's what I hope."

A few minutes later, they came to a blank wall with a ladder propped against it. A shaft led up toward the surface.

John Henry lifted the torch and saw a trapdoor about ten feet above their heads, just as he expected. He handed the torch to Ezra. "I'll check it out."

"Careful," the old-timer cautioned. "You don't want to open that and climb out into a roomful of owlhoots."

"I'm just going to see if it'll budge. I don't plan to open it all the way yet."

John Henry's heart slugged in his chest as he climbed the ladder. When he was high enough, he reached above him and rested a hand against the bottom of the trapdoor. He pushed gently.

Nothing. The door didn't move.

He pushed harder. The trapdoor still didn't budge, and he could tell by the way it felt that it was bolted somehow on the other side.

He had expected that, too, but he felt a twinge of disappointment, anyway. It would have made things easier if he and his companions could have gotten into the house without any help from inside.

Now they would have to wait for Nick Mallette to carry out his part of the plan and let them in.

And hope that nothing had happened to the gambler.

Chapter Thirty

Nick Mallette leaned forward and asked tensely, "What are they doing now?"

Simon Garrett lowered the field glasses through which he had been peering. "Looks like they're getting ready to break camp." He turned to Mallette as the two men stood in the shadow of the massive, skull-shaped rock formation. "As soon as they start riding toward us, you go back to the house and let Lottie know. She'll want to be here to watch this."

Mallette nodded and tried to keep his face impassive. He didn't want his expression to reveal that Garrett was playing right into his hands. He had wondered how he was going to get back to the ranch house to locate the opening to the escape tunnel, and now Garrett had given him that opportunity. Mallette wasn't going to waste it.

It had been a long night, waiting for the morning and the inevitable dangers it would bring. All his life, Nick Mallette had taken the easy way out whenever he could, running away from conflict if at all possible, but now he was running right into it, figuratively speaking.

He had told John Henry Sixkiller the truth. If he didn't come through this alive, at least he would have gone out trying to do something worthwhile for once in his life. That might not be enough to redeem him for all the bad things he had done, but it was the only chance in his grasp.

All along the rim of the bluff, members of the gang were posted. They would cover the men from Kiowa City as they approached.

Out on the flat, at the camp where they had spent the night, men were saddling their horses and getting ready to mount up. To the east, the first edge of the sun touched the horizon.

"I don't like this," Garrett said suddenly. "I just don't believe they'd give themselves up this easily. Nobody throws away his own life for somebody else."

"You've risked your life more than once to avenge your brother," Mallette pointed out. "If you could have traded places with him on the gallows—"

"Don't ask me that," Garrett broke in sharply. "By God, don't ask me." He drew in a deep breath. "I don't know. I just don't know. This was my gang. Lottie was my woman. Henry took them over. I don't hold it against him. It doesn't make me want to avenge him any less. But . . ." His voice drifted off. "Oh, the hell with it. Here they come."

Eleven riders started slowly toward the base of the trail leading up the escarpment.

"Go tell Lottie," Garrett rasped.

Mallette turned to his horse. Quickly, he swung up into the saddle and prodded the animal into a run toward the ranch house.

Lottie was waiting on the porch. As Mallette reined in, he called to her, "They're coming!"

"I knew they would." She stepped down and went over to the horse that was tied, waiting for her. With a lithe grace, she mounted.

"I'll be back out there in a few minutes," Mallette told her. "I left my rifle in the bunkhouse."

She all but ignored him, as he had figured she would. She was too anxious to see the impending drama with her own eyes. As she leaned forward in the saddle, she headed for the rim at a gallop.

Since Lottie wasn't even looking back, Mallette didn't bother continuing with his ruse. He just dismounted and ran into the ranch house.

The building wasn't that big. There couldn't be too many places where a trapdoor could be hidden. But as he hurried from room to room without finding what he was looking for, a sense of desperation began to grow inside him. His pulse hammered inside his head. Lottie might be too caught up in her lust for revenge to be thinking straight, but Garrett might start to wonder why he hadn't come back from the house with her.

The entrance wasn't there, he thought. Sixkiller had been so sure it would be. Maybe in one of the other buildings?

Not in the bunkhouse; he had spent enough time there to know that. And not in the smoke-house, either. The judge and the two women were locked in there. Lottie wouldn't put prisoners where there was a way out.

The barn, maybe? Mallette discarded that idea. The cave was an escape route. If the ranch was under attack, the defenders would retreat to the house. That was where the escape route needed to be, for when it became obvious they couldn't hold the place.

So it had to be somewhere in the house, he thought as he stood in the doorway of Lottie's bed-room, staring at her bed.

Even as the thought formed in his mind, he leaped forward to put it into action and shoved the bed aside.

The door was there, fastened with a simple bolt.

Mallette was reaching for it when a man's voice came from behind him. "I knew I was right not to trust you."

He whirled, clawing for the gun on his hip, but he was too late. Simon Garrett stood in the door-way, Colt in hand. The revolver blasted deafen-ingly.

Mallette felt lead tear into him, knocking him backward. Pain filled his entire being—except for the tiny part of his brain screaming at him to fight back. His gun had cleared leather just as he was hit. Somehow, he found the strength to jerk it up and pull the trigger.

Garrett fell back out of the doorway, blood spurting from his neck.

Mallette rolled onto his side and peered toward the door. He couldn't see Garrett anymore, but he didn't know if it was because the outlaw was gone or because his vision was failing him. His strength was deserting him, that was for sure. The gun slipped from his fingers and thudded against the floorboards.

A sense of urgency warred with the pain washing through him and forced him to push with his feet, twisting him around toward the trapdoor. A fresh burst of agony made him press his hand against his chest where Garrett's bullet had struck him.

After a moment, the pain subsided slightly. Mallette moved his hand and reached for the bolt. His fingers were coated with bright, slick blood, making them slippery as he fumbled with the bolt. He couldn't seem to find the strength to draw it back, and he knew his life was slipping swiftly away from him. . . .

John Henry stiffened as he heard the shots close above him, on the other side of the trapdoor. He wanted to call out, to see if Mallette was up there, but he didn't dare. He couldn't risk revealing that somebody was down in the escape tunnel.

There were only two shots, one following hard on the heels of the other. Then nothing except a faint scrabbling sound. John Henry took off his hat and lifted himself on the ladder so he could turn his head and press his ear against the door.

He heard a faint, raspy sound that he identified as labored breathing.

Then a metallic *chink!*

That was a bolt being drawn back, he realized as excitement made his pulse leap. He put his shoulder against the door and shoved upward.

The trapdoor flew up and back, open at last. John Henry scrambled out and drew his gun as soon as his feet hit the floor of what looked like a bedroom.

Nick Mallette lay curled on the floor beside the trapdoor, the front of his shirt soaked with blood. The gambler's face was pale as a sheet of blank paper.

"Nick!" John Henry exclaimed.

Mallette's eyelids fluttered open. A weary smile tugged at the corners of his mouth. "John . . ." he whispered.

As John Henry dropped to a knee beside Mallette, he called down into the shaft. "Ezra! You and the rest of the men get up here!"

As the men poured out of the trapdoor one after another, John Henry turned back to Mallette. He wanted to check on the gambler's wound and try to help him, but there wasn't time. "Where are the prisoners?"

"Sm-smokehouse," Mallette gasped. "I couldn't . . . get to them. But they're . . . all right."

"We'll take care of them." John Henry's voice

was gentle as he added, "You did good, Nick. Really good."

"Not . . . so good. Garrett . . . was here . . . I think he . . . got away."

John Henry's jaw tightened. If Mallette was right about that, Garrett would warn the rest of the gang. The rescue party had probably lost the element of surprise. That meant it would be a tougher fight, but nothing could be done about it.

John Henry leaned forward. "We'll be back for you, Nick. Hang on."

"A little . . . late for that," Mallette said with a hollow laugh. "At least they won't . . . hang me . . ." His head fell back.

John Henry came to his feet and turned to the others. "There's a good chance the outlaws will know we're coming, but we've still got them between two forces. Let's go."

Gripping their rifles, the rescue party ran out of the house. John Henry was in the lead. As he leaped down the steps, a bullet whipped past his head and smacked into a porch post behind him. More shots roared from the riders racing toward the house from the rim.

"Spread out and take cover!" John Henry shouted to his companions. He spotted the smokehouse. The building where the prisoners were being held was sturdy, with thick walls that would probably stop a bullet.

That was good, because plenty of them were already flying through the air, buzzing around like deadly hornets.

John Henry knelt at the corner of the porch and opened fire with his Colt as the outlaws swept up to the ranch house. One man flew out of the saddle as a pair of slugs bored through him. The deputy marshal pivoted and fired again, but just as he squeezed the trigger a bullet struck the porch railing near him and chewed splinters that stung his face as they flew through the air. It spoiled his aim.

One of the riders charged toward him, gun blazing. John Henry peered past the horse's head and recognized the man in the saddle. Purcell had wounded him back at Packsaddle Gap, and the outlaw was bent on finishing the job.

John Henry's Colt roared and bucked against his palm as he squeezed off another round. Purcell's face dissolved into a crimson smear as the bullet smashed into it. He flung his arms out to the side and went backward out of the saddle, landing in the limp sprawl of death.

All around the ranch, men were fighting and dying. Ezra Jenkins was locked in hand-to-hand combat with one of the outlaws. The old frontiersman planted a razor-sharp bowie knife in his opponent's belly and ripped to the side with the blade, spilling the outlaw's guts from the hideous wound. Ezra shoved the dying man away, then looked at John Henry and grinned. "Not bad for an old man with the rheumatiz!" he shouted, then plunged back into battle with the bloody knife in his hand.

"Saxon!" somebody bellowed nearby.

John Henry twisted and saw Simon Garrett

standing on the porch stiff-legged. Blood was splashed over his shirt from a wound in the side of his neck. Mallette had winged him during their exchange of shots.

Garrett should have stayed to make sure the gambler was dead, John Henry thought. Either Garrett had been convinced that Mallette was done for or had wanted to get back to his men and warn them before he passed out from losing so much blood.

Either way, he hadn't prevented the rescue party from reaching the ranch, and that was all that mattered.

The balance of power was about to shift. The men from Kiowa City were galloping in with a thunder of hoofbeats. The revolvers they wielded cracked and spouted fire as they slammed into the surviving outlaws. The area between the house and the bunkhouse was utter chaos filled with men, horses, dust, powder smoke, and death.

John Henry saw all that in the blink of an eye, and threw himself forward. He hit the ground as the gun in Simon Garrett's hand boomed. Thrusting his weapon in front of him, he squeezed the trigger.

The slug drove into Garrett's chest and knocked him back a step. Garrett swayed, but stayed on his feet. His arm sagged. With a visible effort, he struggled to raise it and get off another shot, but before the revolver came level, blood welled from his open mouth. His eyes widened and he pitched forward on his face.

John Henry surged to his feet, thumbing fresh cartridges into the Colt as he ran toward Garrett. The man's gloved, crippled left hand was making twitching motions, inscribing meaningless patterns in the dust. His body spasmed, then lay still.

John Henry hooked a toe under Garrett's shoulder and rolled the outlaw onto his back. Garrett's eyes stared sightlessly into the dawn sky.

He was as dead as his brother.

"You hurt, youngster?" Ezra asked as he came limping up to John Henry.

The shooting had stopped, John Henry realized as he turned to the old frontiersman. The battle was over.

And since the only men he saw still on their feet were members of the rescue party and the men from Kiowa City, he knew that they had won. All the outlaws were down, either dead or wounded.

"I'm fine," he told Ezra. "Where's the sheriff?"

"Right here," Mike Rasmussen said as he walked up with a still-smoking Smith & Wesson in his hand. "What about the prisoners?"

"They're in the smokehouse," John Henry said. "They should be all right."

Rasmussen nodded. "I'll go see about getting them out of there."

As the sheriff hurried off, John Henry walked around with his gun held ready as he examined the bodies of the outlaws.

"What are you lookin' for?" Ezra asked him.

"Not what. Who." John Henry's face was bleak. "I'm looking for Lottie Dalmas. Did you see her during the fighting? A red-haired woman, dressed like a man?"

"I don't recollect it," Ezra said. "But if she's just one woman, what does it matter?"

John Henry didn't answer that, but his expression grew more grim as he searched for Lottie's body without finding it. As much as he hated to think about it, as long as the Flame of the Prairie was still alive, the battle might not be over.

Chapter Thirty-one

Other than the cut on his head where he had been pistol-whipped, Judge Ephraim Doolittle was all right, and his wife and niece, although terrified, were unharmed. When they came out of the smokehouse, Clarissa threw her arms around John Henry and gave him a grateful hug.

Then she stepped back. "Oh, my. Did I hurt you, Marshal Sixkiller? I was so glad to see you that I forgot you'd been wounded!"

"I'm fine," John Henry assured her. "Those bullet holes ache a mite, but the sheriff checked the dressings and said it doesn't look like they started bleeding again."

"Maybe now that this is all over, you can actually rest for a while," Clarissa said with a smile.

John Henry didn't mention his concern that Lottie Dalmas had disappeared.

He had figured there would probably be wounded to transport back to Kiowa City, so he'd had a couple wagons follow Rasmussen and the jury members the day before. They had stopped a couple of miles away, out of sight. John Henry sent a rider to bring them in, and while that was going on the wounded were carried down the trail on stretchers.

Three members of the rescue party had been killed in the fighting. Their bodies would be taken back to town so they could be laid to rest properly.

Only two of the outlaws had survived. The corpses of the others would be hauled out to the ravine and dumped in. Their ghosts could join those of all the buffalo Ezra had talked about. Some might say it was a callous thing to do, but John Henry had little sympathy for those who deliberately chose a life of evil and lawlessness.

With all the details that had to be taken care of, it was early afternoon by the time everyone got back to Kiowa City. The wounded were left at Dr. Harmon's house. The prisoners were taken to the courthouse and locked up in the basement jail.

The arrival of the rescue party created quite a stir in the settlement. The streets were thronged with people wanting to congratulate the rescuers and get a look at the freed prisoners. An air of festivity and celebration filled the town. People didn't have to worry any longer about being murdered in their beds.

As far as John Henry was concerned, it would be enough of a celebration to crawl into bed and sleep for about eighteen hours straight. It seemed like ages since he had closed his eyes.

When he left the courthouse with Rasmussen,

people crowded around him, wanting to shake his hand or slap him on the back. John Henry tolerated it as well as he could, putting a weary smile on his face and accepting the accolades with what he hoped was grace.

They were only about halfway to the hotel, on the boardwalk across the street from the Paradise Saloon, when John Henry paused to look at a man who had just pushed the batwings aside and stepped out of the saloon. "Who's that over there? The hombre who just came out of the Paradise?"

"You mean J.C. Carson?" Rasmussen said. "That's him, and the fella right behind him is his ramrod, Dell Bartlett."

John Henry had seen the cattleman's hawk-like face only once before, but there was no mistaking it. The barrel-chested, heavy-featured man who followed Carson out of the saloon was familiar, too. John Henry had no doubt where he had seen both of them before.

That was all the justification he needed to wrap up another loose end. "Back me up, Sheriff. I've got a couple arrests to make."

"What the hell are you—"

John Henry had already stepped down from the boardwalk and started making his way across the crowded street. He wished there weren't so many people around, because he had a hunch there might be gunplay when he confronted Carson and Bartlett.

J.C. Carson had been leading that group of riders he'd seen leaving the Silver Skull a week earlier, before the rustling raid on Montayne's J/M spread. Bartlett had been with the rancher. John Henry was convinced that Carson was tied in somehow with Lottie and Garrett, using them to get rid of Montayne, and he intended to get to the bottom of it.

But before he could reach them, a woman screamed and a commotion broke out in the street. People began scurrying to get to cover. Rasmussen exclaimed, "What in blazes—!"

"Carson!" a woman shouted. "There he is! There's Sixkiller! Shoot him!"

John Henry reached for his Colt as he twisted toward the sound. As the frightened crowd cleared, he saw Lottie stalking along the boardwalk toward the saloon, gun in one hand, bowie knife in the other.

"Kill him now, Carson!" she screamed at the rancher. "Or I'll tell everybody who you really are!"

"You loco bitch!" Carson cried. He jerked his pistol from the holster on his hip and fired.

But not at John Henry. His shot crashed into Lottie and rocked her back on her heels.

John Henry broke into a run. "Carson, drop that gun!"

Dell Bartlett stepped past his boss and slapped leather. His gun boomed, sending a slug screaming past John Henry's head.

With so many innocent bystanders around, John Henry knew there was no time to waste. His gun blasted twice. Both slugs punched into Bartlett's chest and flung him backward. He hit the saloon's big front window and crashed through it, sending glass flying everywhere.

Lottie's gun barked, the shot staggering Carson. He fired again and struck Lottie a second time. The shot spun her off her feet and sent her toppling from the boardwalk into the street.

John Henry yelled, "Carson, I said drop it!"

The cattleman whirled toward John Henry. His hawk-like face was contorted with hate. He had seen his world collapse in a matter of seconds, with no warning, and he was in no mood to surrender. Flame spouted from the muzzle of his gun as he fired at the lawman.

Coolly, John Henry squeezed off another round. It took Carson in the belly and doubled him over. He dropped his gun and collapsed on the boardwalk.

A stunned Sheriff Rasmussen demanded, "What the hell just happened here?"

"Justice," John Henry said. "Check on Carson and Bartlett, but be careful. They were working with Lottie and Garrett."

Keeping his gun leveled and ready, the deputy marshal approached Lottie. She lay curled on her side as blood welled from the wounds in her body and was soaked up by the thirsty dust of the street.

John Henry kicked away the gun and knife she had dropped, then knelt beside her. "Lottie. Lottie, can you hear me?"

Her eyelids were fluttering. Her breathing was quick, ragged, harsh. She turned her head enough to gaze toward him with an unfocused stare. "S-Sixkiller?" she whispered.

"That's right. Carson's either dead or soon will be. He was working with you, wasn't he?"

"We both wanted . . . Montayne dead . . . It made sense . . . for Carson to pay us . . . for doing his dirty work."

John Henry glanced up. A number of townspeople were close by, and even though they were shocked and stunned by the sudden outburst of violence, he could tell by the surprise on their faces that they had heard and understood her words.

That tied everything up with a neat little bow, as far as Carson was concerned.

"You got away from the ranch and followed us here, didn't you?" John Henry said to Lottie. "You wanted one more shot at me, and when you saw Carson you decided to use him like he tried to use you."

"He . . . used me . . . all right," Lottie said, grimacing. "He used to . . . ride the owlhoot . . . came to the Silver Skull . . . when my father was still alive . . . Carson took a fancy to me . . . My pa . . . never knew . . ."

John Henry's mouth was a grim line. This affair was even more tangled than he had known.

But it was finally over. He could tell that Lottie was only moments from death, and with her would die the twisted lust for vengeance that had plunged Kiowa City into a reign of terror.

Amazingly, there was a smile on her face. She

husked, "Looks like . . . the Flame of the Prairie . . . is about to go out." She laughed, a hollow, breathless sound. "I always had . . . a taste for melodrama . . ."

She stiffened as the last of her life escaped from her in a throat-rattling sigh. The staring eyes began to glaze over.

Rasmussen stood over Lottie's dead body. "Carson and Bartlett are both dead. You reckon you could explain all this to me, Marshal?"

John Henry got to his feet. "I can try."

A week had passed since the battle at the Silver Skull and the ensuing shootout on Kiowa City's Main Street. In that time the wounds in John Henry's side had healed enough that they didn't have to be bandaged anymore. He was probably in good enough shape that he could head back to Fort Smith anytime and find out what job Judge Parker had for him next.

But he wanted to check on one of Dr. Harmon's patients first.

He stepped into one of the bedrooms in the doctor's house and took off his hat, nodding politely to Clarissa Doolittle, who was back at her job as a part-time nurse.

She had been feeding the patient some soup, but she set the bowl aside and smiled at John Henry. "Hello, Marshal. I told Nick I thought you'd probably be by to see him today."

"And here I am," John Henry said, returning her smile. "How are you feeling, Nick?"

"Good enough I wouldn't mind getting up a poker game," Nick Mallette said from where he was propped up in the bed. "You want to sit in, John?"

"I'm not sure you're ready for that much excitement just yet. Doc said you were going to have to take it easy for a couple months until that chest wound heals."

"Yeah, he told you to take it easy, too, but you went adventuring anyway, didn't you?"

"Didn't have much choice in the matter," John Henry drawled. "If I hadn't, you might not have had such a pretty nurse to look after you."

Clarissa blushed. She reached over, rested a hand on Nick's hand, and squeezed.

Over the past week, John Henry had seen something growing between the two of them, and he was glad. He'd been happy to discover that Mallette had just passed out, there in the ranch house, and then they had gotten him to Kiowa City in time for Dr. Harmon to save his life.

"Thought you might be interested in the telegram I got this morning," John Henry went on as he reached in his pocket to pull out a yellow telegraph flimsy. "It's from my boss, Judge Parker. He says that the authorities in Kansas City have located enough witnesses who'll swear you shot that fella in self-defense that there's no doubt your conviction will be overturned. You'll be able to live as a free man and go back there if you want to."

"That's great news, all right." Mallette was still holding Clarissa's hand. "But I'm thinking I might just stay here in Kiowa City. It seems like it'd be a nice place to settle down."

"You reckon a tinhorn gambler could ever do that?" John Henry asked.

"He could," Mallette said as he looked at Clarissa, "if the stakes in the game he was playing were high enough."

John Henry laughed and said his farewells to the two of them. He had already told Sheriff Rasmussen and Judge Doolittle good-bye. After shaking hands with Mallette and getting a hug and a kiss on the cheek from Clarissa, he went to the livery stable to pick up Iron Heart. The big gray was already saddled and ready to hit the trail.

John Henry was ready, too. Somewhere out there laws were being broken and the lives of innocent folks were in danger. If there was one thing for sure on the frontier, he thought as he rode away from Kiowa City, it was that the job of a star packer would never be finished.

John Henry Sixkiller wouldn't have it any other way.

Turn the page for an exciting preview

WILLIAM W. JOHNSTONE & J. A. JOHNSTONE,
USA TODAY and *NEW YORK TIMES*
BESTSELLING AUTHORS,
PRESENT THE FIRST
IN A NEW WESTERN SERIES

FLINTLOCK

He is brave, tough as leather, takes no prisoners,
and has left behind a trail of deadly enemies—
outlaws he's hunted down or killed with the cold
heart of a man used to violence. A feared bounty
hunter and the scourge of bad men everywhere,
Flintlock carries an ancient Hawken muzzle-loader,
handed down to him from the mountain man
who raised him. He stands as the towering hero
of a new Johnstone saga.

BLOOD QUEST

Busted out of prison by an outlaw friend,
Flintlock joins a hunt for a fortune—
a golden bell hanging in a remote monastery.
Between the smoldering ruin of his former
jail cell and a treasure in the Arizona mountains
there will be blood at a U.S. Army fort, a horrifying
brush with Apache warriors, and a dozen wild
adventures with the schemers, shootists, madmen,
and lost women who find their way to Flintlock's
side. From a vicious, superstitious half-breed to
the great Geronimo himself, Flintlock meets
the frontier's most murderous hardcases—
many who he must find a way to kill . . .

FLINTLOCK
by William W. Johnstone
with J. A. Johnstone

Coming in October 2013
Wherever Pinnacle Books are sold

Chapter One

"I'm gonna hang you tomorrow at sunup, Sam Flintlock, an' I can't guarantee to break your damned neck on account of how I never hung anybody afore," the sheriff said. "I'll try, lay to that, but you see how it is with me."

"The hammering stopped about an hour ago, so I figured my time was near," Flintlock said.

"A real nice gallows, you'll like it," Sheriff Dave Cobb said. "An' I'll make sure it's hung with red, white, and blue bunting so you can go out in style. You'll draw a crowd, Sam. If'n that makes you feel better."

"This pissant town railroaded me into a noose, Cobb. You know it and I know it," Flintlock said.

"Damnit, boy, you done kilt Smilin' Dan Sedly and just about everybody in this valley was kissin' kin o' his. Ol' Dan was a well-liked man."

"He was wanted by the law for bank robbery and murder," Flintlock said.

"Not in this town he wasn't," Cobb said.

The sheriff was a middle-aged man and inclined to be jolly by times. He was big in the belly and a black, spade-shaped beard spread over the lapels of a broadcloth suit coat that looked to be half as old as he was.

"No hard feelings, huh, Sam?" he said. "I mean about the hangin' an' all. Like I told you, I'll do my best. I've been reading a book about how to set the noose an' sich an' I reckon I'll get it right."

"I got no beef against you, Cobb," Flintlock said. "You're the town lawman and you've got a job to do."

"How old are you, young feller?" the lawman said.

"Forty. I guess."

"Still too young to die." Cobb sighed. "Ah well, tell you what, I'll bring you something nice for your last meal tonight. How about steak and eggs? You like steak and eggs?"

"I don't much care, Sheriff, but there's one thing you can do for me."

"Just ask fer it. I'm a giving, generous man. Dave Cobb by name, Dave Cobb by nature, I always say."

"Let me have my grandpappy's old Hawken rifle," Flintlock said. "It will be a comfort to me."

Doubt showed in Cobb's face. "Now, I don't know about that. That's agin all the rules."

"Hell, Cobb, the Hawken hasn't been shot in thirty, forty years," Flintlock said. "I ain't much likely to use it to bust out of jail."

"You're a strange one, Sam Flintlock," the lawman

said. "Why did you carry that old gun around anyhow?"

"Call me sentimental, Cobb. It was left to me as a legacy, like."

"See, my problem is, Sam, you could use that old long gun as a club. Bash my brains out when I wasn't lookin'."

"Not that rifle, I won't. Your head is too thick, Sheriff. I might damage the stock."

Cobb thought for a while, his shaggy black eyebrows beetling. Finally he smiled and said, "All right, I'll bring it to you. But I see you making any fancy moves with that old Hawken, I'll shoot your legs off so you can still live long enough to be hung. You catch my drift?"

"You have my word, Sheriff, I won't give you any trouble."

Cobb nodded. "Well, you're a personable enough feller, even though you ain't so well set up an' all, so I'll take you at your word."

"I appreciate it," Flintlock said. "See, I'm named for that Hawken."

"Your real name Hawken, like?"

"No. My grandpappy named me for a flintlock rifle, seeing as how I never knew my pa's name."

"Hell, why didn't he give you his own name, that grandpa of yourn?"

"He said every man should have his father's name. He told me he'd call me Flintlock after the Hawken until I found my ma and she told me who my pa was and what he was called."

"You ever find her?"

"No. I never did, but I'm still on the hunt for her. Or at least I was."

"Your grandpa was a mountain man?"

"Yeah, he was with Bridger an' Hugh Glass an' them, at least for a spell. Then he helped survey the Platte and the Sweetwater with Kit Carson and Fremont."

"Strange, restless breed they were, mountain men."

"You could say that."

"I'll bring you the Hawken, but mind what I told you, about shootin' off a part of yourself."

"I ain't likely to forget," Flintlock said.

Chapter Two

"Pssst . . ."

Sam Flintlock sat up on his cot, his mind cobwebbed by sleep.

"Pssst . . ."

What was that? Rats in the corners again?

"Hell, look up here, stupid."

Flintlock rose to his feet. There was a small barred window high on the wall of his cell where a bearded face looked down at him.

"I see you're prospering, Sammy," the man said, grinning. "Settin' all nice and cozy in the town hoosegow."

Flintlock scowled. "Come to watch me hang, Abe?"

"Nah, I was just passin' through when I saw the gallows," Abe Roper said. "I asked who was gettin' hung and they said a feller with a big bird tattooed on his throat that goes by the name of Sam Flintlock. I knew it had to be you. There ain't another ranny in the West with a big bird an' that handle."

"Here to gloat, Abe?" Flintlock said. "Gettin' even for old times?"

"Hell, no, I got nothing agin you, Sam. You got me two years in Yuma but you treated me fair and square. An' you gave my old lady money the whole time I was inside. Now why did you do a dumb thing like that?"

"You had growing young 'uns. Them kids had to be fed and clothed."

"Yeah, but why the hell did you do it?"

"I just told you."

"I got no liking for bounty hunters, Sammy, but you was a true-blue white man, taking care of my family like that." Roper was silent for a moment, then said, "Sally and the kids passed about three years ago from the cholera."

"I'm sorry to hear that," Flintlock said. "I can close my eyes and still see their faces."

"It was a hurtful thing, Sam, and me being away on the scout at the time."

"You gonna stick around for the hanging, Abe?" Flintlock said.

"Hell, no, and neither are you."

"What do you mean?"

"I mean there's a barrel of gunpowder against this wall and it's due to go up in"—Roper looked down briefly—"oh, I'd say less than half a minute."

The man waved a quick hand. "Hell, I got to light a shuck."

Flintlock stood rooted to the spot for a moment. Then he yelled a startled curse at Roper, grabbed the rifle off his cot, and pulled the mattress on top of him.

A couple of seconds later the Mason City jail blew up with such force its shingle roof soared into the air and landed intact twenty yards away on top of the brand-new gallows. The jail roof and the gallows collapsed in a cloud of dust and killed Sheriff Cobb's pregnant sow that had been wallowing in the mud under the platform.

A shattering shower of adobe and splintered wood rained down on Flintlock and acrid dust filled his lungs. He threw the mattress aside and staggered to his feet, just as Abe Roper kicked aside debris and stepped through the hole in the jailhouse wall.

"Sam, get the hell out of there," Roper said. "I got your hoss outside."

Flintlock grabbed the Hawken, none the worse for wear, and stumbled outside.

As Roper swung into the saddle, Chinese Charlie Fong, grinning as always, tossed Flintlock the reins of a paint.

"Good to see you again, Sammy," Fong said.

"Feeling's mutual, Charlie," Flintlock said.

He mounted quickly and ate Roper's dust as he followed the outlaw out of town at a canter.

Roper turned in the saddle. "Crackerjack bang, Sammy, huh? Have you ever seen the like?"

"Son of a gun, you could've killed me," Flintlock said.

"So what? Who the hell would miss ya?" Roper said.

"Somebody's gonna miss this paint pony I'm riding," Flintlock said.

"Hell, yeah, it's the sheriff's hoss," Roper grinned. "Better than the ten-dollar mustang you rode in on, Sam."

"Damn you, Abe, Cobb's gonna hang me, then hang me all over again for hoss theft," Flintlock said.

"Well, he'll have to catch you first," Roper said, kicking his mount into a gallop.

After an hour of riding through the southern foothills of the Chuska Mountains, the massive rampart of red sandstone buttes and peaks that runs north all the way to the Utah border, Roper drew rein and he and Flintlock waited until Charlie Fong caught up.

"Where are we headed, Abe?" Flintlock said. "I hope you've got a good hideout all picked out."

He and Roper were holed up in a stand of mixed juniper and piñon. A nearby high meadow was thick with yellow bells and wild strawberry, and the waning afternoon air smelled sweet of pine and wildflowers.

"We're headed for Fort Defiance, up in the old Navajo country. It's been abandoned for years but the army's moved back, temporary-like, until ol' Geronimo is either penned up or dead."

Flintlock scratched at a bug bite under his buckskin shirt and said, "Is that wise, me riding into an army fort when I'm on the scout?"

"There ain't no fightin' sodjers there, Sammy, just cooks an' quartermasters an' the like," Roper said. "All the cavalry is out, lookin' fer Geronimo an' them."

"We gonna stay in an army barracks?" Flintlock said. "Say it ain't so."

"Nah, me an' Charlie got us a cabin near the officers' quarters, a cozy enough berth if you're not a complainin' man."

Roper peered hard at Flintlock's rugged, unshaven face and then his throat. "Damnit, Sam, I never did get used to looking at that big bird, even when we rode together."

"I was raised rough," Flintlock said. "You know that."

"Old Barnabas do that to you?" Roper said, passing the makings.

"He wanted it done, but when I was twelve he got an Assiniboine woman to do the tattooing. As I recollect, it hurt considerable."

"What the hell is it? Some kind of eagle?"

Flintlock built his cigarette and Roper gave him a match. "It's a thunderbird." He thumbed the match into flame and lit his cigarette. "Barnabas wanted a black and red thunderbird, on account of how the Indians reckon it's a sacred bird."

"He wanted it that big? Hell, it pretty much covers your neck and down into your chest."

"Barnabas said folks would remember me because of the bird. He told me that a man folks don't remember is of no account."

"He was a hard old man, was Barnabas, him and

them other mountain men he hung with. A tough, mean bunch as ever was."

"They taught me," Flintlock said. "Each one of them taught me something."

"Like what, for instance?"

"They taught me about whores and whiskey and how to tell the good ones from the bad. They taught me how to stalk a man and how to kill him. And they taught me to never answer a bunch of damned fool questions."

Roper laughed. "Sounds like old Barnabas and his pals all right."

"One more thing, Abe. You saved my life today, and they taught me to never forget a thing like that."

Roper, smiling, watched a hawk in flight against the dark blue sky, then again directed his attention to Flintlock.

"You ever heard of the Golden Bell of Santa Elena, Sam?" he said.

"Can't say as I have."

"You will. And after I tell you about it, I'll ask you to repay the favor you owe me."

Chapter Three

"Are you sure you saw deer out here, Captain Shaw? It might have been a shadow among the trees."

"Look at the tracks in the wash, Major. Deer have passed this way and not long ago."

"I see tracks all right," Major Philip Ashton said. He looked around him. "But I'm damned if I see any deer."

"Sir, may I suggest we move further up the wash as far as the foothills," Captain Owen Shaw said. "Going on dusk the deer will move out of the timber."

Ashton, a small, compact man with a florid face, an affable disposition, and a taste for bonded whiskey, nodded. "As good a suggestion as any, Captain. We'll wait until dark and if we don't see a deer we'll leave it for another day."

"As you say, sir," Shaw said.

He watched the major walk ahead of him. Like himself, Ashton wore civilian clothes but he carried a regulation Model 1873 Trapdoor Springfield rifle. Shaw was armed with a .44-40 Winchester because he wanted nothing to go wrong on this venture, no awkward questions to be answered later.

Major Ashton, who had never held a combat command, carried his rifle at the slant, as though advancing on an entrenched enemy and not a herd of nonexistent mule deer.

Shaw was thirty years old that spring. He'd served in a frontier cavalry regiment, but he'd been banished to Fort Defiance as a commissary officer after a passionate, though reckless, affair with the young wife of a farrier sergeant.

Shaw wasn't at all troubled by his exile. It was safer to dole out biscuit and salt beef than do battle with Sioux and Cheyenne warriors.

Of course, the Apaches were a problem, but since the Navajo attacked the fort in 1858 and 1860 and both times were badly mauled, it seemed that the wily Geronimo was giving the place a wide berth.

That last suited Captain Shaw perfectly. He had big plans and they sure as hell didn't involve Apaches.

The wash, dry now that the spring melt was over, made a sharp cut to the north and the two officers followed it through a grove of stunted juniper and willow onto a rocky plateau bordered by thick stands of pine.

In the distance the fading day painted the Chuska peaks with wedges of deep lilac shadow and out among the foothills coyotes yipped. The jade sky was streaked with banners of scarlet and gold, the streaming colors of the advancing night.

Major Ashton walked onto the plateau, his attention directed at the pines. His rifle at the ready, he stopped and scanned the trees with his field glasses.

Without turning his head, he said, "Nothing moving yet, Captain."

Shaw made no answer.

"You have a buck spotted?" the major whispered.

Again, he got no reply.

Ashton turned.

Shaw's rifle was pointed right at his chest.

"What in blazes are you doing, Captain Shaw?" Ashton said, his face alarmed.

"Killing you, Major."

Owen Shaw fired.

The soft-nosed .44-40 round tore into the major's chest and plowed through his lungs. Even as the echoing report of the Winchester racketed around the plateau, Ashton fell to his hands and knees and coughed up a bouquet of glistening red blossoms.

Shaw smiled and shot Ashton again, this time in the head. The major fell on his side, and all the life that remained in him fled.

Moving quickly, Shaw stood over Ashton and fired half a dozen shots into the air, the spent cartridge cases falling on and around the major's body. He then pulled a Smith & Wesson .32 from the pocket of his tweed hunting jacket, placed the muzzle against his left thigh, and pulled the trigger.

A red-hot poker of pain burned across Shaw's leg, but when he looked down at the wound he was pleased. It was only a flesh wound but it was bleeding nicely, enough to make him look a hero when he rode into Fort Defiance.

Limping slightly, Shaw retraced his steps along the dry wash to the place where he and Ashton had tethered their horses. He looked behind him and to his joy saw that he'd left a blood trail. Good! There was always the possibility that a cavalry patrol had returned to the fort and their Pima scouts could be bad news. The blood would help his cover-up.

He gathered up the reins of the major's horse and swung into the saddle. There was no real need to hurry but he forced his horse into a canter, Ashton's mount dragging on him.

It was an officer's duty to recover the body of a slain comrade, but Ashton had been of little account and not well liked. When Shaw told of the Apache ambush and his desperate battle to save the wounded major, that little detail would be overlooked.

And his own bloody wound spoke loud of gallantry and devotion to duty.

Lamps were already lit when Captain Owen Shaw rode into Fort Defiance, a sprawling complex of buildings, some of them ruins, grouped around a dusty parade ground.

He staged his entrance well.

Not for him to enter at a gallop and hysterically warn of Apaches, rather he slumped in the saddle and kept his horse to a walk . . . the wounded warrior's noble return.

He was glad that just as he rode past the sutler's store, big, laughing Sergeant Patrick Tone stepped outside, a bottle of whiskey tucked under his arm.

"Sergeant," Shaw said, making sure he sounded exhausted and sore hurt, "sound officer's call. Direct the gentlemen to the commandant's office."

"Where is Major Ashton, sir?" Tone said, his Irish brogue heavy on his tongue. Like many soldiers in the Indian-fighting army, he'd been born and bred in the Emerald Isle and was far from the rainy green hills of his native land.

"He's dead. Apaches. Now carry out my order."

Tone shifted the bottle from his right to his left underarm and snapped off a salute. Then he stepped quickly toward the enlisted men's barracks, roaring for the bugler.

Shaw dismounted outside the administration building, a single-story adobe structure, its timber porch hung with several large clay ollas that held drinking water. The ollas' constant evaporation supposedly helped keep the interior offices cool, a claim the soldiers vehemently denied.

After leaning against his horse for a few moments, the action of an exhausted man, Shaw limped up the three steps to the porch, drops of blood from his leg starring the rough pine.

He stopped, swaying slightly, when he saw a woman bustling toward him across the parade ground, her swirling skirts lifting veils of yellow dust.

Shaw smiled inwardly. This was getting better and better. Here comes the distraught widow.

Maude Ashton, the major's wife, was a plump, motherly woman with a sweet, heart-shaped face that normally wore a smile. But now she looked concerned, as though she feared to hear news she already knew would be bad.

Maude mounted the steps and one look at the expression on Shaw's face and the blood on his leg told her all she needed to know. She asked the question anyway. "Captain Shaw, where is my husband?"

As the stirring notes of officer's call rang around him, Shaw made an act of battling back a sob. "Oh, Maude . . ."

He couldn't go on.

The captain opened his arms wide, tears staining his cheeks, and Maude Ashton ran between them. Shaw clasped her tightly and whispered, "Philip is dead."

Maude had been a soldier's wife long enough to know that the day might come when she'd have to face those three words. Now she repeated them. "Philip is dead . . ."

"Apaches," Shaw said. He steadied himself and managed, "They jumped us out by Rock Wash, and Major Ashton fell in the first volley."

Maude took a step back. Her pretty face, unstained by tears, was stony. "And Philip is still out there?"

Boots thudded onto the porch and Shaw decided to wait until his two officers were present before he answered Maude's irritating question.

First Lieutenant Frank Hedley was in his early fifties, missing the left arm he'd lost at Gettysburg as a brevet brigadier general of artillery. He was a private, withdrawn man, too fond of the bottle to be deemed fit for further promotion. He'd spent the past fifteen years in the same regular army rank. This had made him bitter and his drinking and irascible manner worsened day by day.

Standing next to him was Second Lieutenant Miles Howard, an earnest nineteen-year-old fresh out of West Point. His application for a transfer to the hard-riding 5th Cavalry had recently been approved on the recommendation of the Point's superintendent, the gallant Colonel Wesley Merritt, the regiment's former commander.

Howard had a romantic view of the frontier war, his imagination aflame with flying banners, bugle calls and thundering charges with the saber. He'd never fought Apaches.

"Where is the major?" Hedley said.

"He's dead," Shaw said. "We got hit by Apaches at Rock Wash and Major Ashton fell."

Hedley turned and saw the dead officer's horse. "Where is he?"

Shaw shook his head and then stared directly and sincerely at Maude. "I had to leave him. The Apaches wanted his body but I stood over him and drove them away. But I was sore wounded and could not muster the strength to lift the gallant major onto his horse."

Lieutenant Howard, more perceptive and more sympathetic than Hedley, watched blood drops from Shaw's leg tick onto the timber.

"Sir, you need the post surgeon," he said.

"Later, Lieutenant. Right now I want you and Mr. Hedley in the commandant's office," Shaw said, grimacing, a badly wounded soldier determined to be brave.

GREAT BOOKS, GREAT SAVINGS!

When You Visit Our Website:
www.kensingtonbooks.com
You Can Save Money Off The Retail Price
Of Any Book You Purchase!

- All Your Favorite Kensington Authors
- New Releases & Timeless Classics
- Overnight Shipping Available
- eBooks Available For Many Titles
- All Major Credit Cards Accepted

Visit Us Today To Start Saving!
www.kensingtonbooks.com

All Orders Are Subject To Availability.
Shipping and Handling Charges Apply.
Offers and Prices Subject To Change Without Notice.

THE EAGLES SERIES BY
WILLIAM W. JOHNSTONE

Available Wherever Books Are Sold!

Visit our website at **www.kensingtonbooks.com**